"Clever holiday humor and off... of this tender, relatable roman... and heartfelt truths."

—Nicole Dees... ...d–winning author

"Sarah Monzon has crafted a story with humor, the wonder of Christmas, the joy of gathering with friends and family, and a swoon-worthy romance. The added light she shines for mental health is much needed and provides an #OwnVoices experience."

—Toni Shiloh, Christy Award–winning author

"Sarah Monzon delivers a cute Christmas romance filled with deeper undertones of being seen, overcoming our fears, and discovering how love makes us brave. Christmas magic is in the air for the most timid of romantics, but all Mackenzie needs to do is hold to her faith, believe in her skills, and trust that the most unlikely romance might end up being the perfect Christmas match."

—Pepper Basham, award-winning author
of *Authentically, Izzy*

"Sarah Monzon's *All's Fair in Love and Christmas* is not just another sweet or funny Christmas romance. It has heart and depth, handling social anxiety and other topics, like dementia and raising your sibling's children, with care and kindness. It's funny, at times heart-wrenching, and written with truly great lines and faith woven throughout. If you're looking for a heartwarming, happy read that doesn't gloss over the hard parts of the holidays but instead offers hope, this is the perfect choice!"

—Emma St. Clair, *USA Today* bestselling author
of *Royally Rearranged*

"Sarah Monzon has long been one of my favorites, and *All's Fair in Love and Christmas* only deepened my love. Few authors can make me laugh, cry, and swoon as reliably as Sarah can. Inspirational rom-com readers are going to love this one."

—Bethany Turner, bestselling author of *The Do-Over*

"*All's Fair in Love and Christmas* wasn't only fun, but it made me squeak with emotion at the end. If you want all the holiday feels, this is the book for you."

—Angela Ruth Strong, author of *Husband Auditions*

ALL'S FAIR IN LOVE AND CHRISTMAS

ALL'S FAIR IN LOVE AND CHRISTMAS

SARAH MONZON

BETHANYHOUSE
a division of Baker Publishing Group
Minneapolis, Minnesota

© 2023 by Sarah Monzon

Published by Bethany House Publishers
Minneapolis, Minnesota
www.bethanyhouse.com

Bethany House Publishers is a division of
Baker Publishing Group, Grand Rapids, Michigan

Printed in the United States of America

                    Library of Congress Cataloging-in-Publication Data
Names: Monzon, Sarah, author.
Title: All's fair in love and Christmas / Sarah Monzon.
Other titles: All is fair in love and Christmas
Description: Minneapolis, Minnesota : Bethany House Publishers, a division of Baker
    Publishing Group, [2023]
Identifiers: LCCN 2023002700 | ISBN 9780764242052 (trade paper) | ISBN
    9780764242601 (casebound) | ISBN 9781493444052 (ebook)
Subjects: LCGFT: Christian fiction. | Romance fiction. | Christmas fiction. | Novels.
Classification: LCC PS3613.O5496 A79 2023 | DDC 813/.6—dc23/eng/20230320
LC record available at https://lccn.loc.gov/2023002700

Scripture quotations are from THE HOLY BIBLE, NEW INTERNATIONAL VERSION®, NIV® Copyright © 1973, 1978, 1984, 2011 by Biblica, Inc.® Used by permission. All rights reserved worldwide.

Cover design and illustration by Mary Ann Smith

Author is represented by the Rachel McMillan Agency.

Baker Publishing Group publications use paper produced from sustainable forestry practices and post-consumer waste whenever possible.

23   24   25   26   27   28   29   7   6   5   4   3   2   1

FOR JOSÉ,

whose favorite pastime when we met was to see
how many shades of red you could turn my cheeks.
All these years later, you still make me blush.
I love you.

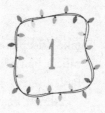

M y boss is so generous. She gave me three whole days to *look forward to* our meeting this morning. Isn't that just the sweetest, most considerate employer of all time? In my *anticipation,* I've spent the last seventy-two hours having no less than a dozen one-on-ones with her in my mind. After all, she never said what the meeting was in regard to, only that she wanted to talk to me about something important on Friday morning.

My mental scripts have ranged from approaching her office like a recalcitrant student about to be reprimanded by a stern principal (which isn't really fair, as Sofiya Bondaruk is more like Glinda the Good Witch in *The Wizard of Oz* than Ed Rooney from *Ferris Bueller's Day Off*) to the even more improbable scenario my housemate, coworker, and best friend, Keri, speculated— the promotion that always seems to take place around the holidays.

In the cases of extremes, the answer usually lies somewhere in the middle. I just haven't been able to figure out what that middle is, and it's spiking my anxiety.

The clock on my computer screen ticks off another minute. I

take a deep breath and stand, my momentum pushing my rolling office chair a little too far out behind me. It crashes into the long table used as a second row of communal desks.

I flinch, heat blooming in my cheeks as if an invisible spotlight burns down on me. I duck my head so I don't have to see my coworkers staring over their MacBooks. If Kryptonite is Superman's weakness, then being on the receiving end of the attention of others is mine. Even now, pinpricks of uncomfortable awareness press into my skin, as if Lincoln, Frank, and Rosa's gazes were needles that could actually pierce flesh.

Quietly, and as unobtrusively as I can, I push the chair back where it belongs and straighten my maroon sweater dress. Like it or not, it's time to face my boss and get this meeting over with.

The tips of my brown leather ankle boots bob in and out of my view of the polished concrete floor as I make my way from the industrial-sized main working space to Sofiya's office. I look up in the nick of time to avoid colliding with a pair of broad shoulders encased in a perfectly ironed button-up dress shirt. Even before the man with impeccable taste turns and looks down at me with brown eyes that have a ring of amber around the pupil, I know who the shoulders belong to.

Jeremy Fletcher.

Up close and personal.

A queer feeling twists low in my gut.

Usually, my glimpses of Jeremy are furtive. Quick, secretive snatches no one sees that I tuck away to be pulled out in private. We've worked together for almost two years. Which means I've been pathetically pining over this elite specimen of a man for nearly as long. The same amount of time that he's barely been aware of my existence.

We've talked before, of course. If you count me barely squeaking out a *thank you* after he's opened the door for me as satisfactory interactions. But while I've hardly said more than two words to Jeremy in as many years, I've had innumerable conversations with him in my head. In those instances, I've always been impossibly witty, undeniably charming, and not the least bit tongue-tied.

So basically, my complete opposite in real life.

Jeremy tilts his head toward Sofiya's closed door. His layered brown hair sweeps in a perfect wave over his brow, every strand in place. I've read in books about heroines seeing a man's hair and wanting to run their fingers through it and tousle the strands. The idea seems almost like sacrilege to me. Jeremy is sculpted perfection. Why would I want to dishevel him?

He looks back at me and lowers his voice. "Know what this is about? Why Sofiya wants to see us?"

I open and close my mouth like a baby guppy. It's really not that hard to talk. Until you're put on the spot and someone is looking at you expectantly. My brain finds that too much pressure to function under.

The door swings open, and Sofiya stands on the other side, beaming at us with a glint in her eye.

If my boss wasn't the sweetest woman on the planet, I might be more scared of her. Forget every caricature of an office boss a la *The Devil Wears Prada* and think more along the lines of a Russian Cinderella. Tall and willowy with long, light-blond hair and skin like porcelain with a natural blush highlighting her prominent cheekbones. Even as Sofiya nears sixty-nine, her complexion is flawless. The kindness shining out of her pale blue eyes belies the inner strength I know she possesses.

"There you two are. Come in and sit down." She pivots and heads to her desk.

Jeremy moves to the side so I can enter the office first. I claim the seat on the left, and a moment later he lowers himself into the other chair on my right. It takes all my willpower, but I keep my fingers from fidgeting on my lap. My eyes, however, don't know where to land. My gaze bounces around the office, catching first on a Better Business Bureau award nailed to the wall behind

Sofiya's desk before flitting off to the layer of dust collected on the fake rubber plant in the corner.

Sofiya smiles warmly at us. "How are you two doing this morning?"

Oh, yay. Small talk. My favorite.

I force a smile and say *good* even though my insides are twisted into a knot because I still haven't figured out what this meeting is about, even after three days of obsession.

Jeremy props an ankle over his opposite knee, physically relaxed and showing zero signs that he's worried about the outcome of the next few minutes. "It's been a crazy morning already, but that just means the day can only get better, right? What about you? Did you enjoy the orchestra last night?"

They go back and forth for a few minutes, conversation flowing comfortably between them while I wilt into the office chair's cushioned seat.

"So, you may be wondering why I requested a meeting this morning." Sofiya's words put immediate starch back in my spine.

Jeremy chuckles. "I was just asking Mackenzie that very thing when you opened the door."

Her eyes bounce to me, the curve of her lips suppressed to a smile instead of the wide grin it wants to be. I still, hoping she doesn't expect me to respond in any way.

With a small chuckle, Sofiya sits back. "Well, I won't make you wait any longer. The reason I wanted to talk to you both is because there's a new position opening up in the firm, and with the strengths you two individually bring to the table, I'm confident that either one of you would be an asset in the role. It's a supervisory position, but you both have shown leadership skills in the past. There will be more interaction with our clients than either of you may have experienced, but again, I think both of you are up to the task." She regards each of us in turn. "The hard part, really, is going to be deciding between you two for the job."

My lungs expel air. Keri was right? The last three days of worry were about a promotion? I guess I shouldn't have been so skeptical. I just didn't think I'd ever be a candidate. Not when I can't intelligibly talk to our clients outside of email. But the holiday season is always when employees move up at Limitless Designs.

And for reasons none of us can figure out, the person with the most Christmas cheer gets the advancement.

Every single time.

Sofiya extends her hand first to Jeremy and then to me. "I'll let you know my decision right after the holiday." Her phone rings, and she apologizes before answering.

I glance surreptitiously at Jeremy as he stands. Sofiya has effectively turned my secret office crush into my not-so-secret office rival. No doubt he is overjoyed by the possibility of a promotion. After all, that would be the normal reaction. The hollow pit in my stomach feels more like dread than joy, however.

It only takes that glance to prove what I already know: Jeremy Fletcher is put together, competent, and a shoo-in for this promotion. I am a hot mess and should throw in my red velvet Santa hat here and now.

Jeremy pauses once the office door is closed behind us. The sounds of our coworkers click-clacking away on their keyboards is the base soundtrack to most of my day and instantly brings me a sense of relief. As soon as I get back to my computer, I can bury my head in the proverbial sand of InDesign and finish the brochures for the Milwaukee Wilderness Group.

"Good luck," Jeremy says, his voice a rich timbre that doesn't hold even an ounce of mocking rivalry. Instead, he sounds . . . sincere.

I look up so I won't be talking to his middle button when I respond. I've never had a reason for such proximity before and have certainly never fabricated one. I'm more of the admire-from-afar type. Once upon a time, I'd have been considered a wallflower, which sounds so much better than the truth—that I'm still experiencing the shyness my parents swore I'd grow out of. Thirty-three years old and still waiting for a birthday to come around when I can unwrap the gift of not being awkward in social situations.

I open my mouth, but to my horror, an unintelligible sound slurs from my lips before I can clamp them closed.

Jeremy's brows pull low. But then the corner of his mouth quirks up. "See ya around, Mackenzie." He slips his fingers into his front pockets and strides away.

A flash of canary yellow enters my peripheral vision a second before Keri steps in front of me.

"Well?" she asks, eyes wide.

My shoulders slump. "I'm an idiot."

"Don't talk about my best friend that way." She plants her hands on her hips.

"Even if it's true?"

"Lies!"

I look over Keri's shoulder as Jeremy turns the corner, disappearing from view. This isn't the first impression I've made on Jeremy, but before, I could take comfort in knowing I'd presented myself with quiet professionalism. I was okay with my position of nameless coworker, feeding my hidden feelings without any real-life interaction. But now everything has changed.

Keri hooks her arm through mine and tugs. "Stairwell. Now."

Since our office is on the ninth floor, no one takes the stairs. That abandoned corner of the building has become our echoey space when we need a few stolen moments and don't want to be overheard.

Keri pushes on the metal exit bar to open the heavy door to the stairs. The air is cooler, with no heat circulating in the small but tall space. The latch clicks behind us, and Keri twirls, the yellow skirt of her vintage dress spiraling out over her petticoats. I told her once she reminds me of Mary Tyler Moore from *The Dick Van Dyke Show,* and she'd given me a beaming smile.

"Tell me everything."

I sigh and sit on the top stair heading down to the eighth floor. Keri gathers her skirts and gingerly settles next to me.

"Jeremy Fletcher and I are officially competing for the same promotion."

She nudges my shoulder with hers. "This is good news, Kenz. You should be celebrating, not looking like your cat just died. You know what you have to do to win the promotion. You're practically an honorary elf, so this will be easy for you."

But my favorite parts of Christmas are the Secret Santa parts. Emphasis on *secret.* I can crank up Mariah Carey or Nat King Cole and rock out to them in my car. Bake dozens of sugar cookies and gingerbread men and drop them off at my neighbor's in-house daycare for the children to decorate. Fill up the Toys for Tots bin at the store and imagine a marine in uniform making a kid's day on Christmas morning. Build a snowman in the memory care facility's yard.

None of these things requires me to speak to multiple people or draw any sort of attention to myself.

Christmas should be twinkle lights and snowflake kisses. Magic sprinkled in the air like sugar on holiday cookies. The spirit of the season is supposed to work like a Magic Eraser on the stresses and doldrums of everyday life. It's the something special that happens when Jack Frost nips at your nose and when the nostalgia of music played only one time of year harmonizes with the Salvation Army bell ringers to bring a perfect pitch to the world's favorite holiday.

But instead of a Hallmark Channel marathon of festive magic, Sofiya is taking something good and joyous and making it into her own production of *Christmas Wars: Office Edition.*

"Have you ever wondered why Sofiya always does promotions

around the holidays and then awards the job to the person with the most Christmas spirit?" Keri's accustomed to carrying more than her fair share of the conversation. It's one of the reasons we're such good friends. "I mean, the first year, I thought it was merely a coincidence. But it keeps happening. It's turned into a competition for who can out-Christmas the other person, not necessarily who is better for the job."

"I think it has something to do with her childhood."

Keri looks at me, her bright red lips perched to the side. "What do you mean?"

I pick my words carefully. Too many times I've said something and the meaning came across differently than I intended. "Well, she's kind of like the Grinch."

Keri's forehead scrunches. "But Sofiya is the sweetest. She loves Christmas more than anyone I know."

See? "You're right. She's the best. I didn't mean she's the Grinch because she's grumpy. More like . . ." I pause, searching. "They share a similar history."

She considers this. "I'm not sure I know the Grinch's backstory. Just that he's a mean one, he's a heel, and you don't want to touch him with a thirty-nine-and-a-half-foot pole. Oh, and his heart grows three sizes."

I smile at her. "Well, in the book, no one knows why he has a grudge against Christmas, just that all the carolers and merrymaking and joy are a trigger that sets off his holiday hatred. The movies have attempted to fill in the gap with a tragic tale of an unwanted orphan, abandoned, just wanting to be loved and accepted. Christmas became the symbol of his rejection and loneliness, especially backlit by everyone else's family celebrations and happiness."

She taps her fingers on her knee. "Okay, I'm following. Keep going."

"The Grinch tried to steal everyone's holiday so they could experience the emptiness he felt growing up, while Sofiya—"

Understanding dawns in Keri's expression. "Sofiya overcompensates the lack of Christmas joy in her past by rewarding those who can fill that void." She leans in, whispering even though we are the only two people in the stairwell. "Do you think she even knows she's doing it?"

Maybe other bosses manipulated their employees for personal reasons, but not Sofiya. "She's probably operating on a subconscious level."

"Are you going to talk to her about it?"

That doesn't deserve a response. I give Keri a look I know she can decipher.

"Right. Awkward conversations. What was I thinking?"

Keri doesn't get it because she has no problem talking to anyone. Meanwhile I'd rather spend three hours Googling the answer to a question than three minutes on the phone asking the same question.

"I think I'll just bow out. Jeremy deserves the promotion, plus he'll do a better job than I would. The position requires leadership skills and direct communication with our clients. I'd probably lose the company more accounts than anything. You know how I am."

Keri lays a hand on my arm. "Mackenzie, you can't quit."

"Not quit, just not jump through Sofiya's hoops."

"You might not have a choice." She holds my gaze, her eyes round and soft. She reaches into a deep side pocket, pulling out an envelope, which she gives me.

I look down at the white rectangle in my hand, recognizing the return address immediately as Heritage Hills. My palms grow sweaty, and I fumble with the seal.

"I checked the mail slot this morning before we left," Keri explains, "but I didn't want any bad news to cloud your head before your meeting, so I held on to it."

I flip open the paper and read, my stomach dropping. "Her

insurance won't cover as much as I hoped. Keri, I can't afford my mom's care."

She squeezes my arm. "You can if you get the promotion. It comes with a significant raise. I saw the budget proposal myself."

I sigh as my heart plummets. Whether I like it or not, I have no choice but to play Sofiya's reindeer games.

K eri and I make our way back into the busy workspace of Limitless Designs. The graphic design firm takes up the entire ninth floor, but that sounds more impressive than it is, considering the size of the building. Every business renting space has an entire floor to themselves. It's industrial style, with exposed ductwork and polished cement floors. Very modern and open. Besides Sofiya's office and a conference room, the whole place is one big open space.

The smell of fresh coffee hangs in the air, and I almost make a beeline to the large carafe percolating on the counter of the corner break area. But the acid in coffee will kill my stomach. Still, there's tea.

I stall when Jeremy lifts his head out of the refrigerator, a carton of half-and-half in his hand. I duck my chin to my chest and pivot on my heel. I haven't recovered from my last run-in with him, and I need some time alone to process everything the day has brought.

My feet shuffle to my chair, second to last on the left on our long communal desk that supports six computers and minimal workspace. I lift my noise-canceling Bose headphones—a splurge for some but just as essential a work tool for me as a #2 pencil is for a teacher.

"Mackenzie, can I see you again for a moment, please?" Sofiya stands in the doorway to her office, her hands folded primly.

I choke down my groan and set my headphones back on the desk. As I stand, it feels like half a dozen pairs of eyes are watching me. My cheeks heat, and I stare at the ground as I make my way past my coworkers toward my boss.

I hate being the center of attention. Or not even the center. Just the edge of attention is uncomfortable. I'd rather blend into the background than be the focal point.

I shut the door behind me and take the same seat I vacated less than an hour before. My fingers run across the knitting at the hem of my sweater dress, the material soft but also textured.

Sofiya sits and regards me with a tilted head and a pointed look. "I wanted to check on you. You seemed a bit . . . dazed after the meeting."

Despite being my boss, Sofiya has an openness about her that relaxes me a smidge when we're alone. Talking to her isn't as hard as talking to some other people. Maybe it has to do with English being her second language and the fact that every once in a while, she forgets a word she's looking for or stumbles to get her point across. When I do the same thing, she's patient with me and doesn't let me fixate on whatever stupid thing came out of my mouth.

My shoulders brush the back of the chair, and I freeze before allowing my posture to relax. "I was a little surprised, I admit."

"Why? You are one of the most talented designers this firm has. You deserve the chance at the promotion and raise."

"Thank you." I chew my lip before continuing. "Photoshop and InDesign I'm good at. People, not so much."

"You're better than you think you are, I think." She laughs at herself. "See, none of us is Shakespeare. And good thing, too. We may not be so eloquent, but at least people can understand us." She waves her hand. "Enough of that. You need to get out of your head, not spend more time there."

She bends down and opens a drawer. When she straightens, there's a Tupperware container in her hand.

"I believe in you, Mackenzie. You just need to believe in your-self." She opens the container. Scents of honey, allspice, and black licorice waft into the air. She pulls out a white-glazed cookie. "Have you ever tried a *pryaniki*?"

I sit up straight, my eyes stinging at the memories washing over me. I gingerly take the cookie Sofiya offers. "I have, actually."

These smell better than the ones I had in the past, but the similarity is there. Warmth and cold chase each other down my spine, the way a good memory drenched in sadness leaves a bit-tersweet ache in your chest.

"Really?" Sofiya bites into the soft treat. "I don't have many Christmas traditions, but eating pryaniki is one of them. The director at the orphanage made them for us every year."

"That sounds like a nice memory."

She wipes crumbs from her hands. "Not many outside of Rus-sia have had this cookie. How have you tasted them before?"

I nibble on the end, letting anise mingle with the honey and spices on my tongue. The single bite takes me back to the kitchen of my childhood home. Mom in her apron covered with tiny candy canes, speckles of flour dotting her nose like white freckles, and Tchaikovsky's *The Nutcracker* ballet turning on the record player. "My mom made them."

Sofiya's sculpted brows jump high on her forehead. "She is Russian?"

"No, she just really likes learning about and celebrating other countries and cultures. She always wanted to travel, but being a single mom with a minimum-wage paycheck didn't allow for vacations farther than the shores of Lake Michigan. Since she couldn't travel to other places, she brought those places home to us. Especially at Christmas. Instead of the traditional American spread of honey ham and gingerbread houses, we had tamales and *ponche* or *yiaprakia* and *melomakarona*. We celebrated German Saint Nicholas Day, Colombian Day of the Little Candles, and the Thirteen Yule Lads of Iceland." A smile curves my lips. "If you think coal is bad, it has nothing on rotten potatoes in your shoes."

I take another bite, embarrassed by how much I've shared. Either my brain won't spit out any words or it runs without a filter and doesn't know when to stop. "These are much better than Mom's. She tried, but a lot of times her recipes didn't turn out very authentic."

I stuff the rest of the cookie in my mouth so I can't talk anymore.

"I am not so good in the kitchen myself. I buy these special from a bakery downtown. I tried to make them once and, well, let's just say I know how long it takes the fire department to get to my house." Her eyes twinkle. "Although I did get a date out of the experience, so I can't say it was all bad."

I laugh, wishing I could be more like Sofiya. More like my mom.

"It is good that you have these memories with your mother. Do you still celebrate the holidays together?"

My throat thickens, and I swallow. I curl my fingertips back under my dress hem. "Yes, I do." Although it seems she's a little less with me each year.

Which is another reason I don't want to participate in the promotion contest. Keri may think I'm an honorary elf, but that's because of how special Christmas is to me. Mom always made it the best time of the year, and now it's my turn to recreate the magic of the holiday for her. How can I do that if I'm busy out-Santaing Jeremy here at work?

"That is good," she says, unaware of my inner turmoil. "Family is important."

I want to ask Sofiya who she spends Christmas with. Instead,

I press my lips together and sit there, too afraid I'll say something to make it worse instead of better. Maybe even make her cry. *Goodness, I don't want to make her cry.*

The silence lengthens. Sofiya looks a little sad. A little lost.

The longer I don't say anything, the thicker the air gets. My pulse starts to hammer against my ribs.

My brain rattles for something to say, and my gaze darts around the room, hoping for inspiration. Anything will do. My thought waves are like an analog TV without an antenna—static.

Sofiya seems to shake herself from her inner musing, and her eyes focus on me as she steeples her fingers. "Anyway, on to the other reason I called you in here. We've just acquired a new account for a start-up company needing pretty much everything. Logo and website to begin with, but they're also talking about campaign art and layout for a magazine ad."

"That's great."

She levels her gaze at me, and I swallow against the brunt of her full eye contact. "I want you to take the lead on the account."

"Me?" My voice squeaks. "Are you sure someone else wouldn't be a better choice?"

"Yes." She's firm in her reply. "It's time to stop hiding in the corner. I know you can do this. Now's the opportunity to prove it to yourself."

I don't want to prove anything. I like my corner. But I smile tightly and keep those thoughts to myself.

"The CEO will be coming by in three days to go over your preliminary vision board." She gathers a manila folder and passes it over her desk to me. "Here's all the information about his company. He said he was open to any of our ideas, so you have full creative rein."

I open the folder and read the top page. MedHealth Transports. The company offers a range of medical transportation services from picking up and delivering prescriptions to couriering lab specimens and medical equipment. An Uber for all things health related.

"I know you'll do a great job," Sofiya says.

I stand, my knees a little wobbly. "I, umm . . . I guess I'll . . ." I hold up the folder and give it a little wave before I turn and retreat.

Today is turning out to be one burned-out bulb after another on a strand of tangled Christmas lights. If I could throw the whole thing away and buy a new strand, I would. Instead, I'm stuck figuring out how to change these stupid bulbs, or my Christmas—and my life, apparently—is going to be about as bright as Times Square in a blackout.

A re you about ready to head home?" Keri has her oversized bag hanging from her shoulder.

"Just one second." I save my current designs.

I've narrowed down my font options for the MedHealth Transports logo to five. My favorite is a simple serif called De Valencia. The lettering is in all caps and has a sleek, modern look with clean lines and easy readability. This font can stand on its own. But clients like options, so I've picked out a couple of other serif fonts and a script font in case the client thinks simple and clean is "boring" and wants something fancier. A monospace font rounds out my picks.

Keri leans over so her face is beside mine. She points to the screen. "I like this one."

It's a sans serif called Matchbook that features tall, skinny letters. I thought the initials of the company looked good in front of two slightly overlapping diamond outlines. I've also brainstormed a car with the medic cross on it as a possible logo. Sometimes the most on-the-nose ideas are the ones the clients like best. No one wants their consumers to be confused on what their brand or products are.

I close out of the program, log out of the system, and shut the computer down for the night. I still have a lot to do before the client meeting in three days, but narrowing down these font choices is a good start.

"I know it's not really in the same direction, but do you mind if we stop on the way home to see my mom?" Without Keri, I'd be solely reliant on the city's public transportation to get anywhere. I don't usually feel bad about hitching a ride since we're housemates and coworkers, so she's already heading to and from work, but these extra destinations make me feel like a moocher.

She nods at my forehead. "Stop with the worry eyebrows. You're not an inconvenience, so stop thinking you are."

I grab my clutch from beside the keyboard. "I don't know how you do that. It's kind of creepy."

"I'd say it's my superpower to read minds, but your face just says what your mouth is too reluctant to."

"Really?" I rub my cheeks and work for a neutral expression. "Okay, what am I thinking now?"

"That you want to trade Secret Santa names with me," Derek interrupts from his desk space to my left. The long communal desks and open space may create a synergetic work environment, but they don't allow for private conversations.

Keri smirks and juts her chin at him. "Who'd you get?"

I look between them. "Isn't the whole point of Secret Santa *not* to know who the gift giver is?" Besides, I drew Rosa's name and have already mentally purchased her gift—a Time-Turner necklace like the one Hermione used to take twice the number of classes at Hogwarts. It's cute, with a miniature spinning sand clock in the middle of a decorative pendant. Rosa's a huge Harry Potter fan. One time, I caught her whispering "alohomora" while she waited for the elevator. Derek had been standing on her other side and asked her what she'd said. I'd leaned over to Rosa and whispered, "Muggles."

Derek's smile is mischievous. "Half the fun is playing detective to figure out who has whose name. Then you can trade for the person you wish you'd gotten."

Keri laughs. "Let me guess. You wish you'd gotten Annabelle's name."

Derek perks up, not unlike a dog who's just heard the word *walk*. "Are you her Secret Santa? Will you switch with me? I'll bring you a peppermint mocha every day for a month."

"Down, Fido." Keri's still laughing. I guess I'm not the only one to see the puppy similarity. "I'm a supporter of office romances." She slides her gaze to rest on me for two beats before looking back at Derek. "I'll switch. Who do you have?"

Derek beams, then readjusts his weight in his swivel chair and breaks eye contact. "I have Frank," he mumbles.

"Come again?" Keri obviously didn't hear Derek, but I did. I push back my chair, inching away so I don't get caught in the crossfire.

Frank isn't any of the female employees' favorite. What he considers a compliment—usually how a part of our anatomy looks in an article of clothing we're wearing—we consider highly inappropriate. He also feels entitled to our time, conversation, and personal space. If harassment were a flavor, Frank would be vanilla, and unfortunately we've all experienced worse, so we deal with his vanilla and count down the days until his retirement. Currently one hundred and seventy-three. There will be a big party, but it's more for us than for him.

"Frank," Derek repeats louder. "I drew Frank's name."

Keri presses her lips together so tightly they disappear. Her nostrils flare as she takes in a deep breath. "I was going to do an even swap, but I think I'm going to need those peppermint mochas if I'm forced to shop for Frank."

"He's—"

"If you're going to finish that sentence with the words *not so bad*, the deal is off."

Derek holds up his hands in surrender. "I was going to say he's the worst."

"Good." She nods her head once. Conversation closed. She takes another deep breath, this one to cleanse her mind of thoughts of Frank, if I know her at all. She forces a smile my way. "You ready now, Kenz?"

"Ready." I shove my chair into its spot and palm my clutch. "See you guys on Monday."

Derek nods, and Lincoln, the only other coworker who's stayed late today, absently lifts a hand as he stares at his screen.

"Thanks again for being willing to stop at Heritage Hills. I really appreciate it," I tell Keri as we head to the elevator.

She makes a shooing motion with her hand. "What are friends for? Besides, I'm not being completely magnanimous. Remember the nurse that helped me last time when I got lost? Alejandro." She says his name with an exaggerated accent, rolling her R hard, but she does it with this flirty, dreamy look on her face. With the fifties-style A-line dress she has on plus her pin curls done like Betty Grable, she looks like someone's rebellious daughter from Miami falling in love with a neighbor from the Caribbean south. Very *West Side Story* meets the Cuban Missile Crisis. "I'm hoping he'll be there again. Last time I definitely picked up a vibe."

In theory, I know what she means. Intellectually, I realize that people send out signals to those they are interested in. Like radio waves or something. My internal antenna, however, is either broken or has never developed because I can never tune in to the right frequency to pick up those signals . . . or send them, for that matter.

I am about to ask what Alejandro said or did specifically that could be considered a vibe when my gaze snags on a familiar profile.

Strong jaw and cleft chin. Straight nose. Perfectly styled hair. Jeremy waits for the elevator with one hand in his pocket, the other cradling his phone as he stares down at it. He looks up as we approach, and the force of his eyes in my general direction causes my steps to slow. I unconsciously drift to place myself in Keri's shadow.

Jeremy glances at his phone one last time before slipping it into his pocket. The elevator doors open, and he offers us a smile. "Ladies first."

Keri snaps her fingers. "Oh, shoot. I left my lunch container in the refrigerator. Don't want to leave it over the weekend and have it grow mold."

I feel a hand on my back, and then I'm stumbling forward. I grab the side of the elevator for support, turning to glare at my supposed best friend.

Her smile is sweet and innocent. "I'll see you downstairs, Mackenzie. Have a nice weekend, Jeremy."

"You too," Jeremy says as he follows me into the soon-to-be enclosed space. The doors slide shut after he presses the button for the bottom floor.

The spicy scent I'd picked up on him earlier in the day is stronger in our cramped quarters, and now I can identify the undertones of citrus. Orange, to be exact. It's fresh but also warm somehow.

"So." Jeremy leans his shoulder against the elevator wall and regards me. "Crazy day, huh?"

I peek up at him through my lashes and nod. The numbers indicating which floor we're on slowly count down, but not fast enough.

Outwardly, I stand still and try to keep my gaze from becoming a butterfly, flitting about the elevator but never landing on one thing. Inwardly, a civil war has been declared between the person I wish I was and the person I really am.

The person I wish I was would enjoy this one-on-one time with an attractive and available man. She'd look him boldly in the eye and smile. She wouldn't feel nervous or grasp for the simplest thing to say. She might even punch the emergency stop button and do something daring like ask him on a date. (Okay, in the back of my mind I was thinking grab him by the shirt and kiss him senseless, but apparently even my imaginative alter ego isn't that intrepid.)

The person I am, however, is going to have a bruised rib from how hard my heart is pounding against it. If only I knew how to make small talk or if maintaining eye contact didn't make me so uncomfortable. If only there was a third person in this elevator to take the pressure off of me. Then I could slink back into the shadows.

"Did you have any idea the meeting this morning would be about a promotion?" Jeremy continues to lean against the wall casually.

I shake my head. Yes, Keri had suggested it and past patterns show Sofiya will promote someone at the end of the year, but no, I didn't think I'd be considered.

"Any fun plans this weekend?" He switches topics.

I plan to make some peppermint bark fudge for the staff at Heritage Hills. Would he think that was fun? I lift my hands palm up and shrug.

The elevator settles, and then the door opens. I give a little wave, tuck my head, and skedaddle, the tiny general inside my head yelling a swift retreat.

"Mackenzie."

Jeremy's voice makes me stop and turn, my clutch held against my belly.

"Next time, how about not dominating the conversation and letting me get a word in, yeah?" He grins and waves, then leaves.

Next time. What a horrifying and thrilling notion.

It takes a few minutes for the elevator to travel back up to the ninth floor, collect Keri, and travel back down again. When the doors open, her face can barely contain her excited smile.

"So?" she asks.

I start walking, and she has to jog a couple of steps to catch up to me. "Never do that again."

"What? Why?" She puts a comforting hand on my arm. "Whatever you said, it couldn't have been that bad."

I slow my steps. "I didn't say anything."

"Nothing at all?" She blinks. "You guys rode down in complete silence?"

That probably would have been easier and less embarrassing. "No."

Understanding dawns in her eyes. "So, he talked and you . . ."

"Nodded and shrugged like an idiot."

Keri's grip on me tightens until I'm forced to stop walking.

"You are not an idiot." She enunciates each word slowly. "You need to stop talking about yourself like that."

"I'm sorry."

"Don't apologize to me. Apologize to yourself."

I stare at her.

She stares back and crosses her arms. "We're not leaving until you apologize. Say, 'Mackenzie Delphine Graham, I'm sorry for filling your head with nonsense about yourself. You are kind and caring, and anyone would be lucky to have you in their lives.'"

I snort, but the icy stare Keri wears refuses to melt. Good gracious, she's serious.

"Fine." I repeat what she said, but the words lack conviction. I may be kind and caring, but I am also a social screw-up.

She hooks her arm through mine and pulls me along. "Let's go see your mom."

I hip-check her, glad not to be on the receiving end of her glare anymore. "And Alejandro."

She shimmies her shoulders and waggles her brows suggestively before dissolving into a fit of giggles.

The cold air is a shock to the system as we step out of the

building. I zip my fleece-lined jacket up higher, stopping just below my chin. My breath puffs out, evaporating in white wisps before my eyes. The sky is dark above us even though it's only six o'clock. Winter days are short here in Wisconsin. Keri and I catch the sunrise and about an hour of light in the morning, but the sun clocks out every day before we do.

We climb into Keri's Subaru and fifteen minutes later turn into the parking lot at Heritage Hills. My stomach sinks to my toes, the familiar guilt weighing me down. I try to mask my expression before Keri notices. She's already gotten after me enough today. Besides, I know what she'll say. That Heritage Hills is the place my mom chose. That even though I may not like her decision, it was her choice to make.

And I know that, deep down. Before her mind became too far gone, she wanted to have as much control over her own future as she could. I protested, pleaded for her to let me take care of her, but she wouldn't listen. She made a different choice, and I have to live with that.

The facility reminds me of a small apartment building, three stories tall with windows banking the perimeter so each room can get natural light. In the spring and summer, flowers line the walk up to the entrance, inviting guests and residents alike. Now knee-high illuminated candy canes replace the dormant floral landscape. Two evergreen wreaths hang from the double doors, and cellophane-wrapped poinsettia plants stand sentry on either side.

A hint of pine scent welcomes as much as the warmth when we enter, and I notice a live Fraser fir in the common room that hadn't been there the other day.

"Tell your mom I said hi," Keri says, her focus across the room.

I follow her line of sight to a certain nurse with muscular forearms tucking a crocheted lap blanket over the legs of an elderly resident in a wheelchair.

"Have fun with your vibes," I tease.

She's not flustered in the least as she winks at me. "I plan to."

Mom is on the ground floor, so I make my way to the west wing, where her room is. I lightly knock on her door. "Mom, it's me," I say before slowly opening it.

"Mackenzie?" Mom turns from where she stands bent over a table, puzzle pieces organized in a linear fashion. Her eyes mist. "It's so nice to see you."

I was here a couple of days ago, but that was a bad day. She hadn't recognized me, and my presence only agitated her. I left before she got so worked up she needed medication to calm her down. I don't know if she remembers that or not.

These days, I never know what she remembers and what she doesn't.

"You look good," I tell her as I carefully give her a hug.

"I feel good," she answers, squeezing me back with strength she hasn't possessed in a while. "How are you? How's work?"

I set my clutch on a side table and peer at her puzzle. It's a Thomas Kinkade painting of a Christmas cottage all lit up, snow on the ground and hanging heavy on the pine tree boughs. A snowman stands adjacent to a stone bridge, and the image makes me think of a family all cozied up by a warm fire in that cottage, sipping hot chocolate and feeling secure.

"Mackenzie?"

I look up at Mom and realize she's asked me a question. "Work is good. I'm being considered for a promotion, actually."

Her smile brightens. "That's wonderful."

I pick up a puzzle piece and test it against another. Not a fit. "I'm not sure if I'm the right person for the job, to be honest."

She studies me. "If it's any constipation, I think you'll do great." Her brow furrows. "Why are you making that face?"

I guess Keri was right. My face really doesn't need my mouth to communicate. I try to keep my lips in a straight line but fail to keep the humor out of my voice. "I don't know what you're talking about."

"That's the face people get when I say something wrong. What did I say?"

"It's no big deal."

"Kenz."

"You just said *if it's any constipation* instead of *if it's any consolation.*"

Her mouth twitches. I'm not sure if it's a precursor to laughter or crying.

I rub her back. "Mom, it's okay."

She snickers, then full-on belly laughs. "Well, you can't blame me. Around here, constipation is a frequent problem."

I watch her, almost afraid to join in her merriment. A part of me feels that laughing would be callous or making fun of her condition. It feels disrespectful.

"Oh, come on, Mackenzie. It was funny. Laughter is good for you. It releases stress. You don't want to keep everything bottled up inside. You'll get stopped up." She elbows me at her joke.

I shake my head at her but let myself feel the joy of the moment. At fifty-eight, my mom is the youngest person at Heritage Hills. One of the youngest people on record to suffer from Alzheimer's. Just to look at her, you'd say she didn't belong. That is, until you talked to her and she thought she was a senior in high school getting ready for the prom. Or you introduced yourself and ten minutes later she asked you who you were. Or she didn't remember her own daughter.

But at this moment, her blue eyes sparking with intelligence and laughing like she used to . . .

This is a moment to cherish.

Mom smiles as she picks up a border piece and connects it at the bottom of the puzzle, humming.

"Is that 'All I Want for Christmas Is My Two Front Teeth'?" I ask.

"Yeah. Except we've changed the lyrics." She starts to sing.

"'All I want for Christmas is my mem-or-y, my mem-or-y, my mem-or-y.'" She grins. "Clever, right?"

My eyes sting, and I blink back tears. Forget the woman I wanted to be in the elevator. I want to be like this woman right here. My mother. Laughing in the face of her weakness and being stronger for it.

4

Jeremy Fletcher had a plan. Well, really he had a number of plans. Five years. Ten years. Twenty. But the current one was working out exactly how he had designed.

He glanced at the digital calendar on his laptop. Monday he'd start his campaign with pomander balls. (He'd been calling them spikey oranges until he learned after an internet search that they had a real name.) He'd already purchased a crate of oranges at the wholesale mega store. He owed Nathan and Natalie credit for the idea. They'd come home from school with an orange each, both stabbed with cloves. A mutilated murder of the mandarin variety.

But he had something a little more aesthetically pleasing in mind. He wanted to impress the head of a graphic design firm, after all. If he could arrange the cloves in patterns, maybe even score off some of the fruit's rind in scrolls and lines, then the pomander balls would both smell and look good. He'd grab Sofiya by two of her senses at once, and she'd be reminded twice as often of his effort and how much he deserved the promotion.

Making one ball for Sofiya would score him a point, but the tally marks would multiply if he came into the office on Monday with a pomander ball for each of Limitless Designs's employees. A sign that he had the thoughtfulness to be a leader. That he appreciated and cultivated a team environment. That he was the person she should choose.

Would Mackenzie have a similar plan of attack? Just the idea of the diminutive woman going on the offensive made him smile. She wasn't necessarily small, but she sort of shrank in on herself at times. Like in the elevator, for instance. He'd tried to cajole her out of her shell a little, but she hadn't said a word. Only cast furtive glances his way. If he wasn't mistaken, her breathing had even quickened. His ego would like to say that was because his charming self had affected her, but the likelier culprit was that she was shy and timid by nature. He couldn't wrap his mind around Sofiya seeing Mackenzie commanding a conference room or handling a particularly difficult client.

Feet pounded on the stairs from the second story of the house. Jeremy closed his laptop and mentally switched gears from work to homelife. He watched his niece and nephew descend, backpacks slung low at their hips. He tossed each of them an orange, which they caught in midair.

"You guys sure you don't want to stay and help me with these?" he asked, already knowing what their reaction would be. What eleven-year-old wanted to spend Friday night at home with their parental when they could be playing video games or—he shuddered—spending countless, mindless hours on YouTube watching *other* people play video games?

Sure enough, the preteens scoffed. "Unlike you, Grandpa and Grandma let us eat as many cookies as we want." Nathan tossed the orange back to Jeremy.

That was the difference between parents and grandparents, because when Jeremy was a kid, there had most definitely been a one-cookie rule.

"And let us stay up late," Natalie added.

"Plus, Grandpa said we can watch a *real* Christmas movie. *Die*

Hard." Nathan grinned so wide it was almost painful to have to burst his bubble. Almost.

Jeremy pointed at him. "No R-rated movies."

Nathan sucked his teeth in frustration. "C'mon, Uncle Jeremy. I'm not a baby."

"You know the rules."

Nathan's body sagged, a sullen expression taking over his face. "If you had your way, we'd only be allowed to watch *The Polar Express* on repeat."

Natalie shrugged. "I like *The Polar Express.*"

"You would," Nathan mocked. "You *are* a baby."

"I'm thirty-four, and I like *The Polar Express.* 'Hot choc-o-lat!'" Jeremy danced his fingers with jazz hands like Tom Hank's cartoon character in the movie.

Nathan rolled his eyes. "Whatever."

Middle schoolers were a tough crowd. Jeremy remembered when Nathan would have died laughing at his goofy antics. Not for the first time, he wondered what his sister, Heidi, would have done or said.

But she wasn't here. She hadn't been for eight years. Not since—

Jeremy clapped his hands once. The sudden noise disrupted the morose trail his thoughts had started to hike and put an end to the current conversation. "You two remember your toothbrushes? Pajamas?"

"Yep," they chorused.

"You sure you don't want me to drive you?"

Natalie kissed his cheek. "It's only a few blocks. We've got our headlamps and our cell phones. Stop worrying."

A small lump lodged in his throat. "It's only because I love you so much that I worry."

She smiled, looking much too grown-up. The days were long with kids—*so very long* at times—but the years somehow flew by. It defied the laws of physics. Pretty soon, though, they'd be in high school. Then college.

Oof. College tuition for two at the same time.

Good thing he had these plans in place.

"We love you, too, Uncle Jeremy." Natalie smiled sweetly at her uncle, then turned and gave Nathan a pointed look. He mumbled something that might have resembled a heartfelt sentiment if anyone could hear or understand the words.

As soon as the twins left, Jeremy retrieved his phone and opened the tracking app. He watched the two dots that represented his niece and nephew move along the map until they finally stopped at his parents' house.

He put his phone away, then lined up his pomander ball–making supplies on the low coffee table. If he was going to spend the evening making arts and crafts, he was at least going to do it while sitting on his comfy leather sofa and watching the football game he'd missed the night before because Nathan had hockey practice.

He'd just slipped the paring knife out of the wooden knife block when the doorbell rang. Three of his good friends—Alejandro, Lincoln, and Jill—stood on his doorstep.

"What are you guys doing here?" he asked, dumbfounded.

Jill blew into her hands. "Can we do the questions inside? It's freezing out here."

Jeremy took a step back and opened the door wider. Lincoln clapped him on the shoulder as he passed. "Do you have anything to eat?"

Jeremy shut the door, then trailed his friends to the living room, where Lincoln had already started peeling an orange. Jill unwrapped a fuzzy scarf from around her neck, then settled next to Lincoln.

"So, what are you doing on a child-free Friday night?" Alejandro eyed the fruit and spicy cloves.

"Same thing he does every night, Pinky." Jill paused for effect. "Trying to take over the world!"

Great, now he'd have the *Pinky and the Brain* theme song from *Animaniacs* in his head all night.

"Not the whole world," Lincoln clarified. "Just Limitless Designs."

"What's your evil master plan?" Jill asked, hugging a throw pillow. "And, more importantly, do you have a sinister laugh to go with it?" She leaned forward and snatched an orange from the crate. "Seriously, are your coworkers a band of pirates and you're trying to save them from scurvy?" She arranged her face to look serious and concerned as she addressed Lincoln. "Babe, tell me the truth, does he make you walk the plank at work?"

"Aye," Lincoln said in a horrible pirate accent.

"For your information"—Jeremy snatched the orange from Jill as she tried to toss it from one hand to the other—"I'm working on securing a promotion."

"With citrus fruit?" Alejandro sounded incredulous.

"I do have a—"

"He's going to say *plan*," Jill interrupted gleefully.

Jeremy rolled his lips between his teeth and started over. "There's a method to my madness."

Lincoln pointed at Jill. "He's finally admitted it. He's crazy."

Jeremy sighed. "Is there a reason you guys came over?"

"Giving you a hard time is reason enough." Lincoln grinned.

"Great," Jeremy responded in a monotone.

"But we also know you and your type-A personality. So we knew, even though you have a rare kid-free night, that you'd still be here at home, working on something or other. And given your meeting with Sofiya, I figured that something would have to do with the promotion."

"So we are here to make you a deal," Alejandro added.

Jeremy lifted his hand to run his fingers through his hair but stopped himself, crossing his arms over his chest instead. He used to have untamed hair, wild and free, and he'd run his hands through it when he felt frustrated, even pulling the ends a bit when he was at his own end—of patience. But that was before he'd gotten organized and ordered. A place for everything and everything in its place. Including his neatly trimmed, gelled-into-submission hair.

"What kind of deal?"

"We help you out with whatever you've got going on here this Friday night." Lincoln waved his hand over the pomander ball supplies.

"And you help me out with something I have going on next Saturday night," Alejandro finished.

The last time Alejandro had asked Jeremy for help, it had been to call out numbers for bingo night at Heritage Hills. Calling out *B4* and *I17* in a booming voice hadn't been so bad, plus the residents had loved having Nate and Nat there to help them with their cards. Even if one little old lady had mistaken him for a younger version of her deceased husband and gotten a little frisky, Jeremy could risk a butt pinch for help with these pomander balls.

"Deal."

"Plan, let me introduce you to wrench." Jill's face could barely contain her grin as she picked up a fruit and jabbed three cloves across the center in quick succession.

"What do you mean?" Jeremy asked, but Jill just grinned wider. He turned to the guys. "What does she mean?"

Lincoln and Alejandro shrugged.

Jill shoved in four more cloves. She seemed to be making an equator in the sphere. "Dating and marriage are not a part of your five-year plan."

"Don't listen to Jill," Alejandro reasoned. "I'm not marrying you off next week." He laughed, but it sounded choked. "How absurd."

Jeremy stared him down.

Alejandro threw his hands in the air. "Fine. I need you to go on a double date with me."

"No."

"You already agreed. Plus, I really like this woman. She comes with her friend whose mom is a resident at Heritage Hills. We've been flirting back and forth the last couple of weeks, and she agreed to a date—but only if I could bring a buddy for her friend."

"Why don't you both leave your friends alone and go out by yourselves?" Jeremy grumbled.

His pals might tease him about his many plans, but they were there for a reason. He'd thought long and hard as he'd ordered out his life. What was best for Nat and Nate. What goals were achievable and which were pipe dreams. Plans weren't silly. They were essential to being a responsible adult, especially an adult raising two kids on his own.

"It's one date, Jeremy," Alejandro deadpanned. "It's not like you're going to fall in love with this woman."

Nope. Because love wasn't anywhere on the schedule until the twins turned eighteen and graduated high school. No matter what his friends said, there'd be no deviation on that point of his itinerary.

5

I mentally rehearse my presentation for the hundredth time, going over what I want to say, then Mr. Mitchell's response, then my reply. I've done this for as long as I can remember—have whole conversations with other people in my head. The discussions usually happen when I'm angry or upset at someone. I'll confront them in my thoughts with full dialogue on both sides.

I can't believe you did such and such.

And then I'll answer myself as if I were the other person.

You're angry with me for such and such? What about you and this and that?

And back and forth I'll go, lobbing dialogue like a tennis ball over the net until I've resolved the issue with the other person in my mind or I've worked myself into a state of exhaustion. Either way, it allows me to have the discussion without any real confrontation. Win, win.

Omitting, perhaps, the small likelihood that the words I imagine the other person saying aren't what they'd actually say, my process works great.

Except now I can't have the conversation only in my mind

and be done with it. This time I physically have to walk into the conference room and verbalize the words I've been practicing.

My pulse beats like a timpani drum in my chest. Just thinking about standing in that room, all eyes on me, is enough to turn my circulatory system into the percussion section of a concert band.

It would be so much easier if Mr. Mitchell were like my free-lance clients. Then I could email him my preliminary designs and converse about his account in the preferred manner of anyone born after the disco decade—with our fingers on a keyboard. But Sofiya insists on maintaining a personal touch with clients, so like it or not, I have to walk him through his options in person.

I put a hand to my sternum and will my heartbeat to slow down. What I need is a distraction. If I keep replaying the pre-sentation in my mind like the FBI looking for evidence of a crime on a surveillance tape, I might make myself sick.

"Alexa, play Shania Twain." Nothing says woman empower-ment like '90s Shania.

The female digital voice responds, and then strands of "Any Man of Mine" play through the speakers. I grab a pair of leopard-print flats from my closet in the country star's honor. I'll never have her confidence to walk into a room and own it, but maybe in these I can walk without stumbling and making a fool of myself.

People say to make goals realistic. That's about as good as I can do.

Besides, the shoes pair nicely with the black pencil skirt and hunter-green twist-front pullover I'm wearing. I may not feel confident, but I can at least try and project that image. Sofiya believes in me, at least.

And Mom is counting on me.

I check my appearance one final time in the mirror, then step out of my bedroom at the same time Keri exits hers. The folds of her billowy skirt brush against my leg, drawing my attention.

The material is green but not solid. More like . . . pine branches? Which makes sense, considering the yellow pom-poms swagging in three layers of flounces and the striped candy canes and ornamental globes hanging in each pleat. Keri is wearing a crazy Christmas tree skirt. And pulling it off better than most people do their overpriced designer jeans and Ugg boots. She looks like a mash-up of June Cleaver and a young Mrs. Claus.

She catches me staring and does a little pirouette in the middle of the hall, causing her skirt to bell out. "Like it? I'm wearing it for you."

That makes me pause. "For me?"

"Yeah. I figured you spent all weekend working on the designs for your meeting today, so you didn't have any time to figure out how to bring the holiday spirit to work and get a head start on beating Jeremy."

"I wish this wasn't a competition with a winner and a loser."

"Yet that's exactly what Sofiya made it. Like it or not, Jeremy is now your rival." She shimmies her shoulders playfully. "Doesn't mean you can't play a little dirty."

"I'm going to ignore everything you just said." I walk away from her and collect my laptop and charging cord, sliding both into their traveling case. I look back at Keri. "What do you mean you're wearing the skirt for me, though?"

"Isn't it obvious?" She slings her purse strap onto her shoulder. "I'm going to tell everyone you picked out my outfit for a bit of holiday cheer."

I barely stop myself from groaning. "Please don't."

Her lips pout. "You don't like my skirt?"

I open the front door and usher Keri out. "I love your skirt, but you take the credit for it."

"Kenz, I just think—"

"Please." There it is. That note of desperation. That chord in my voice that says I can barely handle what's on my plate right now, so please don't dish me up any more.

She smiles softly. "Okay."

"Thank you."

We drive across town butchering Shania Twain's music with our off-key singing. Somehow, I don't think the country legend would care. I like to think she'd smile and wink, then offer us a tube of her famous matte red lipstick.

Every mile closer to work, my voice gets wobblier. When Keri pulls into a parking space, I'm ready to march into Sofiya's office and beg her not to make me do the presentation. I'll give her all the designs, and she can go over them with Mr. Mitchell.

Keri shuts off the car, then turns to me. She grabs one of my hands and squeezes. The pressure is oddly comforting.

"Listen to me." Her voice is low and calm. "You're going to go in there and let your amazing work speak for itself."

"Well, I do have to say *something*." I force my lips to turn up into a false smirk.

She smiles at my attempt at humor. "Don't overthink every word."

Too late.

"Don't let your head fill with worry about what everyone else in the room is thinking about you. Their opinions don't matter."

I wish that were true, but I've always been a people-pleaser, and I want everyone to like me. Not in a popular way, just in a nice way.

"And for the love, when this is over, don't analyze every word you said and then beat yourself up for years to come about any small statement or tiny infraction you dream up."

I laugh despite myself. "It's like you know me or something."

"I do." She scrunches her nose at me. "That's why I *know* you're going to kill it and everyone will love you."

I wish I could say the pep talk erased my nervousness, but even before we step off the elevator, I'm back to sweaty palms and my pulse pounding in my ears.

Jesus, I have faith that You can take this spirit of fear inside me away. I know it doesn't come from You because You are Love, and the Bible says love casts out fear. Cast it out of me now. Replace it with power and a sound mind like You promised in Second Timothy.

The prayer does little to calm the anxiety bubbling within me like a hot spring. How many times in my life have I prayed a similar prayer? Too many times to count, that's for sure. And yet here I am. Still a bundle of live-wire nerves. I know the problem isn't with God. I know He has the power to take my anxiousness away and calm my hyper-productive mind. No, the problem isn't God. It's me.

"If you have faith as small as a mustard seed . . ."

If. The key word there. I *think* I have faith. I mean, I pray and I read my Bible and I believe that Jesus is Lord and all powerful. But I must not have *enough* faith. If I had enough faith, then I wouldn't still be struggling with the tightness that cinches like a band around my chest or the bully of worry that chases all other thoughts out of my head and causes my heart to race for its life.

I have faith. I have faith.

A wall of spicy citrus hits me in the face as soon as Keri and I walk into the office. I recognize it immediately as the same scent that had clung to Jeremy in flirtatious hints on Friday. Why was his smell permeating the entire office now?

"Hey, guys." Rosa greets us. "Come look what Jeremy brought everyone."

She walks to one of the communal desks, and we follow. There, all lined up like rotund soldiers, stand a line of pomander balls studded in intricate designs. I know their proper name because of a class field trip to Colonial Williamsburg when I was ten. If I remember correctly, people started making and wearing them to stave off the stench of sickness.

Which is good, because I think I might hurl.

Not until this moment do I realize I harbored a hope that Jeremy wouldn't participate in Sofiya's little game. I'd secretly crossed my fingers that he'd come to the same realization that I had—that if neither of us jumped through Sofiya's hoops, she'd be forced to promote one of us based off our work alone.

I guess that isn't the case.

But maybe I can still get away with not turning the next few weeks into a full-blown Christmas competition. If I ace this presentation—

"Don't you just love the way these smell?" Sofiya holds up a studded orange and breathes it in. She exhales, then looks at me. "Ready for the meeting?"

I swallow, and the lump in my throat tastes a lot like trepidation. "As ready as I'll ever be."

She beams. "Good. Lincoln is already in the conference room. If you give him your jump drive or laptop, he'll set everything up for the large wall monitor."

I scurry off toward one of the only rooms with a door, hoping I can shut out the reminders of Jeremy and the conflicting feelings he's stirring inside me.

Lincoln is quick to set up all the required technology, and before I'm ready, my coworkers trickle in. Soon Sofiya arrives, escorting a grey-haired man with a bushy but well-groomed mustache into the room. He's tall and lean with a navy-colored suit that fits his shoulders just right.

Sofiya thinks so too, if the way her hand lingers on his forearm is any indication.

"Good morning, Mr. Mitchell. It's a pleasure to have you here with us today." There. Nothing too awkward or embarrassing in that, was there? Although maybe I shouldn't have used the word *pleasure*. Yes? No?

I shake his hand and offer him the seat at the head of the oval table. I jump into my practiced presentation, my voice solidifying from its shaky start as I progress. So far, things are going relatively smoothly. The slides help me stay focused, and Mr. Mitchell asks questions. Questions are easier to answer than keeping a running monologue going.

"That's why I think we should go with something sleek and modern for your logo." My favorite mock-up is on the screen, and Mr. Mitchell studies it.

He leans forward. After a few moments, he smiles. "I have to say, I'm impressed. I didn't think I'd love something so simple, but your design is flawless. Well done."

My neck heats under his praise.

First brain cell: *Respond by commenting on what a lovely compliment that was.*

Second brain cell: *No. A simple thank-you is best.*

The message they send down to my mouth, the one I actually say: "I love you."

Time stands still. Did I just—?

Kill me now, I did.

I slap a hand over my mouth, my face on fire for a different reason. Mr. Mitchell's eyes widen in surprise, and the room is so quiet it seems like everyone is holding their breath.

My hands move to my cheeks, but I really want to cover my eyes and hide behind my palms. "I'm so sorry. That's not what I meant."

Someone covers a snicker with a cough.

"I meant to say *what a lovely compliment, thank you,* and it came out all wrong and instead I said *I love you.* Of course, you know that because you're sitting right here and heard it." My gaze sweeps the room. Everyone is staring at me. My hands are shaking. I cackle a nervous laugh. "I don't love you, obviously. Not that you don't seem like a perfectly nice man, but we just met. I mean . . . umm . . ."

Someone save me from this mortification.

Jeremy rises from his seat at the middle of the conference table. Every hair is in place, his shirt appears to have been ironed, and his brown leather loafers even look like they've been shined. His put-togetherness makes a neon sign of awkwardness flash above my head.

"Why don't I show him the website options?" He holds out his hand.

Keri wags her head at me, mouthing the word *Don't.*

But I can't come back from this. It's not possible.

In defeat, I hand over the remote clicker and sit down, slouching even. Jeremy can easily walk Mr. Mitchell through some of the websites we've designed in the past and talk to him about content—especially the role of search engine optimization, usability, aesthetics, visibility, and the importance of interaction.

In the meantime, I'll sit here and do exactly what Keri told me not to—relive my faux pas and punish myself for my idiocy. I can't help but think that if only I were a better Christian, I wouldn't be having these issues.

6

You have got to be kidding me.

My fingers strain, spinning the cardboard toilet paper dispenser. A single thin strip of paper about two inches in length comes off at my tug. Not nearly enough to do the job.

I strain farther, spinning the roll in vain.

Useless.

I sit up and look around, but there isn't a spare roll hiding in the stall anywhere.

My kingdom for three-ply!

I can't even text Keri to come snag me a few squares from the neighboring stall because my pencil skirt doesn't have pockets, which means I don't have my cell phone.

And I'll become a skeleton perched on a porcelain throne before I yell and hope someone hears me through the walls.

My mouth has gotten me in enough trouble today. My name is on the tips of enough tongues. I just want to go home and forget that today ever happened. Not that I can. I'll be reliving and berating myself for my verbal slip-up for the rest of my life.

"Don't worry about it," Keri had tried to reassure me earlier. "It wasn't that bad."

"Not that bad? I told him I love him."

She grinned. "He wasn't offended or anything. In fact, I over-heard him joking with Sofiya about it."

I groaned.

"Stop beating yourself up. Don't blow the morning out of proportion. It wasn't a big deal."

Except it feels like failure, and failure is a big deal. Not only that, but I can't figure out how to react to Jeremy taking over. On one hand, he rescued me when I was drowning in mortification. At the time, I'd wanted nothing more than to dissolve into the wall and disappear. But what were his motives? Was he being nice? A good guy? Or was he taking advantage of my weak moment and swooping in for the kill, proving he should get the promotion instead of me?

I hate that I even consider such a thing, and last week I wouldn't have. I'd probably have noted the incident in my ongoing mental list of why Jeremy Fletcher is such a great guy. But things have changed, haven't they? And that change is making me look at the situation from an angle I never would have before.

Keri's right. I need to get out of my head.

I also need to get out of this bathroom.

The sound of the door being pushed open disrupts the silence. *Hallelujah!* I lean down to try to catch a glimpse of the woman's shoes beneath the stall door. I hope for Keri's black Mary Janes but am met with an unfamiliar pair of white-and-black-checked Vans.

This is going to be embarrassing, but I don't see a way around it. "Hello? Umm . . . can you grab me some toilet paper from the other stall, please?" I wave my hand under the stall divider.

"Sure." The voice is younger than any of my coworkers'.

A wad of white tissue lands in my palm. "Thank you." See, I *do* know how to say it correctly.

I'm at the sink washing up when my rescuer emerges from the other stall. She's young, not quite a teenager, and I wonder who she belongs to.

"I love your hair." She looks at me through the mirror as she lathers soap on her hands. "How did you get it like that?"

I touch the braided crown at the top of my head. "It's just a simple inside-out French braid, and then I loosen the hair to make it appear thicker."

She nibbles on her bottom lip, her braces glinting in the overhead lighting. "I don't know how to French braid."

"Do you . . . do you want me to show you?"

Her eyes go wide. "Would you?"

I dry my hands and toss the paper towel in the trash. "Sure." I stand beside her. "Should I do yours or mine?"

"Oh, mine, please." She reaches back and pulls out the elastic band holding up her ponytail.

"My name is Mackenzie, by the way," I say as I gather the hair at the top of her head and divide it into three strands.

"I'm Natalie. My uncle works here. Maybe you know him? Jeremy Fletcher?"

My fingers pause. "Sure. I know him."

"He's great as a parental, but braiding is outside his wheelhouse, and Grandma's arthritis keeps her from being able to do it."

Parental?

"Mm-hmm." Words are beyond me at this news bomb, but I manage the hum as I gather more of her hair to add to the braid starting to march down her head.

"So it's basically a regular braid, you just add a portion of hair on both sides after each twist?"

"Yeah. It's a little awkward to do on yourself at first, but you'll get the hang of it with practice."

The door to the bathroom opens a fraction. "Natalie?" A male voice enters the female-only domain. "You didn't fall in, did you?"

"No, Uncle Jeremy." Natalie's cheeks redden. She looks at me through the mirror again. "Sorry."

I smile, though I feel I'm on a two-second delay. "So, Jeremy is your . . . parental?" Man, do I feel old using that term.

"Yeah. My parents died in a car accident when I was three, and Uncle Jeremy has been taking care of my brother and me ever since." She says it so matter-of-factly that I don't know how to respond at first.

"My dad died in a car accident when I was young too." Not what I'd planned to say. While she seems to have no problem talking about her parents' death, I rarely ever talk about mine.

"Sucks, right?" She eyes my progress with her hair. "Oh, you're almost done."

I tie the end with the elastic band. "Done."

She beams. "Thank you!"

Keri walks in, purpose in her stride. When she notices Natalie, her step hitches. "Oh. Hello." She turns her gaze to me. "You've been in here forever. I was starting to worry."

I lean toward Natalie. "My parental."

She giggles.

Keri ignores my comment. "Why were you taking so long?"

"I was stranded in a deserted stall with no TP in sight until this young lady heard my SOS and rescued me."

Natalie's grin widens even more.

Keri shakes her head. "And this young lady is . . ."

Natalie holds out her hand. "Natalie Keller."

One of Keri's brows raises. "Jeremy's niece?"

I stare at her, wondering how she knows about Jeremy's niece. And by her surprised tone, she *knows*. Why didn't she tell me the guy I thought couldn't get any better actually *was* better? A man who'd stepped up to the plate to become an instant father and take on the responsibility of raising his niece and nephew? How could a girl not swoon at that? Forget bouquets of flowers and expensive grand gestures. A man who demonstrates his dependability is one that makes me go weak in the knees.

"Thanks for showing me how to French braid, Mackenzie. It was nice to meet you." Natalie offers a small smile.

I smile back. "You too."

Keri gives me a look I can't decipher as soon as Natalie walks by her.

What? I mouth.

She rolls her eyes and shakes her head, then spins on her kitten heels and follows the tween out of the restroom. The caboose that I am, I leave last.

"That was something else in the conference room earlier, am I right?"

Lincoln's distinct New Orleans accent stops me in my tracks. His voice is loud and clear, and I realize he must be standing on the other side of the large potted bamboo palm to my right. I take half a step back, not wanting to discomfit him by making him aware that he's been caught talking about someone by the person he's talking about.

"It was like watching a newborn giraffe try to take her first steps."

Jeremy's rich tenor makes me suck in a sharp breath. He's talking about me behind my back too? But being compared to a baby giraffe isn't that bad. Baby animals are cute, at least.

"All gangly limbs and awkward movements, weak legs shaking until she falls flat on her face. You can't help but feel sorry for her."

Okay, that was *not* cute. I take another half-step back, but my retreat is thwarted by the wall at my shoulder blades. A thousand thoughts flood my mind at once.

This is why I don't like attention drawn to me.

I told Sofiya I couldn't do it.

Jeremy Fletcher thinks I am weak, awkward, and someone to be pitied.

A warm hand closes around my wrist, drawing my attention back to time and space. Keri's expression is somewhere between comforting friend and avenging warrior princess. Where I had been taking steps back, she takes one forward. This time it's my hand that reaches out and clasps her wrist.

Her storming out from behind the palm and letting Lincoln

and Jeremy have a piece of her mind isn't going to do anything more than add fodder for those who want to gossip by the non-existent water cooler. I'd rather ignore everything I just heard than add more flames by letting a confrontation happen.

I tug Keri in the opposite direction of the guys. Maybe they won't notice and we can get away before we accidentally eavesdrop any more.

"Can we stop by that candy shop on the corner and pick up some saltwater taffy on the way home, Uncle Jeremy?"

I'm not too far away to miss Natalie's question.

Or Jeremy's reply. "Sure. You deserve a treat after getting those braces on."

My feet stumble. Braces and chewy candy do not mix. Two years of orthodontics had drilled the "can't eat" foods into my memory. Saltwater taffy was high on the no-no list.

Overlook it. They're smart. They'll figure it out without your help. You don't want more attention today, remember? Talking will only make them all stare at you again.

But poor Natalie would be in pain. . . .

I sigh and pivot. "Sorry, I couldn't help but overhear." Everything. I heard everything. "But you really shouldn't eat hard or chewy things while wearing braces."

"Oh yeah." Natalie frowns. "I forgot the orthodontist said that. Thanks, Mackenzie."

My gaze slides to Jeremy's of its own will. A glutton for punishment. His eyes are the same rich, deep brown they've always been, but now the soft gentleness I previously found myself being pulled into looks an awful lot like pity, and maybe a little like guilt.

I lower my gaze, my limbs feeling heavy.

Don't do that. You're better than that.

Am I, though? Most of the time, I don't think so.

M y emotions brewed all last night. So much so that I couldn't sleep. Anger, frustration, and hurt built pressure like a volcano behind my breastbone, ready to explode. Instead of drifting off to sleep, I stared up at the ceiling, the fan in the center clicking with each rotation.

Not only did I have the immense pleasure of reliving the embarrassment from the conference room (seriously, who blurts out *I love you* in a work meeting to a client?), but the reel that refused to hit pause in my mind was a double feature. One embarrassment after another. And this time I couldn't console myself with Keri's words that my mind was making the situation out to be worse than it was. Not when I have Jeremy and Lincoln's conversation to bring credence to what I already know.

I'm a hopeless case of social ineptitude.

Even arguing with Jeremy in my mind didn't help. Conjuring up a mental image of him and telling that image that he'd hurt my feelings and that I didn't want his pity hadn't calmed me at all. Maybe because the retort I put in mental-image-Jeremy's mouth wasn't apologetic. Instead of apologizing, he justified his words by saying he'd only been speaking the truth. In fact, he'd even been antagonistic, daring me to prove he was wrong.

I don't get angry often, but I admit I was then. That anger pushed me to meet imagination-Jeremy's challenge. Which led to a bit of online sleuthing. I needed some weapons in my arsenal if I had any chance of convincing Sofiya I was competent enough for the promotion.

It turns out I'm not the only one on the planet who gets tongue-tied in front of other people (go figure, right?). Whose heart races and head spins at the idea of social interactions outside their comfort zone. Some people have found a few different things that help in those situations.

Things like cosplay.

I read a discussion in an online forum from people who ex-perienced social anxiety like me. Some of the commentors said when they dressed up in cosplay and attended comic cons or other fandom conventions, their anxiety disappeared. When they put on the costume of whatever character they were dressing up as, they became that persona. They no longer worried what people would think about them personally, because any judg-ments they might run into would be projected onto the character they embodied, not themselves. They also sort of borrowed the character's personality. So if the character was bold and confi-dent, then they became bold and confident because they saw themselves as the character.

The concept fascinated me. Not that I didn't want to be me, but . . . yeah, I guess there are parts I want to change. The inability to converse in the simplest form of communication—small talk—for one. The way a crowd of people makes me want to shrink inside myself. The nagging voice inside my head that makes me hyperaware of my every word and action and how those around me will perceive them.

I try to lay all these things at the feet of Jesus, but they're like too-wet dough. I clean the mess off one hand only for the dough to stick to the other. I swipe at the clingy gluten strings only for them to adhere back to the first hand again. I can't get rid of my anxious feelings to save my life.

So I fight. I fight the good fight of faith like Paul says to do. Day after day. But the more I fight, the more it feels like the reflex in my brain switches to flight, and I find myself running farther and faster in the wrong direction.

The running needs to stop. Instead of flight, I need to choose fight for once in my life. Because I'm not just fighting for myself, I'm fighting for my mom.

Which is why I now stand in front of my closet, reaching for a dress in the back that I inherited from my mom from her younger days trying to revive disco and go-go dancing. Instead of the bright colors and groovy patterns reminiscent of the trend, the dress is mostly solid red with a thick black collar, but it still boasts that classic retro silhouette. Thankfully it's long-sleeved, and a pair of thick tights and knee-high boots will keep me from freezing. Plus, the dress is normal-looking. Even when I add a Christmas tree brooch over the area of my heart, no one but me will know that, along with donning the outfit, I'm also donning the bravery and moxie of an intergalactic member of Starfleet. There's no room for trepidation and self-doubt aboard the starship *Enterprise*, and I won't allow any in myself today. Maybe this isn't *where no man has gone before*, but it's definitely outside my comfort zone.

I finish clasping the brooch to the dress and check my reflection in the mirror. I am no longer Mackenzie Delphine Graham. I am Nyota Uhura, intrepid communications officer serving in the twenty-third century.

"Keri," I call as I exit my bedroom and square my shoulders. "Are you almost ready? We need to make a stop on our way to work."

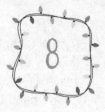

8

U ncle Jeremy, do you know where my shoes are?" Nathan yelled from upstairs.

Jeremy paused, butter knife in one hand and a slice of bread in the other. "Did you check the bathroom?" Heaven forbid either kid's things were where they belonged, so he wouldn't even bother suggesting the logical place to find shoes—the closet.

"They aren't there," Nathan yelled again.

Jeremy sighed and set the bread and knife on the kitchen counter alongside a package of deli meat and American cheese squares. He glanced out the small square window over the sink, noting the lightening of the sky. When he'd woken up, it had still been pitch-black outside. It was still supposed to be barely dawn when the twins climbed onto the bus for school, but already the darkness had started to make room for the light, like someone slowly turning a dimmer switch on for the world.

Which meant they were late. Again. No way he could find Nathan's shoes and finish these sandwiches for the kids' lunches and still have time for them to catch the bus before the driver pulled away from their stop.

Jeremy's feet landed heavy on the risers as he marched up the stairs to the second story. A huff of frustration followed by a banging sound came from the bathroom.

He detoured that direction. Natalie stood before the mirror, hands twisted in her hair and her face screwed up in disgust.

He leaned against the doorjamb. "What's up, buttercup?"

Natalie's hands lowered in defeat, her hair tumbling in disarray around her cheeks. "Mackenzie showed me how to French braid yesterday. She made it look so easy, but every time I try, my hair just looks like garbage."

Jeremy tried to bypass the surprising part of that statement. The part having to do with Mackenzie. He had a distraught pre-hormonal young lady on his hands, and experience had taught him that sometimes dealing with kids at this age was like carrying a stick of dynamite. He had to go slow and handle with care, or there could be an explosion.

But he'd been thinking about Mackenzie all morning. Which might be a contributing factor to them all running late. His movements had been lethargic as he'd gone through his morning routine while wondering if Mackenzie had overheard what he said about her the day before.

Should he assume she had and apologize off the bat? It had been poorly done, he and Lincoln talking about her behind her back that way. Or should he wait it out and see how she acted today at work? If she hadn't heard them, then he didn't want to bring it to her attention and unnecessarily hurt her feelings.

The clincher, he'd decided, was how to decipher if she'd heard or not. With other people, if they were standoffish or in any way tried to avoid him, then he'd assume he'd offended them and needed to make amends. But Mackenzie naturally kept to herself, hardly ever interacting or conversing with anyone other than Keri besides a few words here or there.

He still hadn't figured out what he should do.

"You agree, then." Natalie sounded hurt. "My hair is garbage."

Shoot. He'd allowed himself to get sidetracked, and look what had happened. He pushed himself off the doorjamb and slung an arm around Natalie's shoulders, squeezing her into a side hug. "Your hair is not garbage. It's beautiful. *You're* beautiful. But maybe we should practice the braid sometime other than when we're running late for school, hmm?"

He moved behind her and picked up her hairbrush. When she was in elementary school, he'd been on hair duty every day. But back then she'd been happy with kitty-eared headbands and oversized bows with ponytails. He'd already been told she was too old for such things now, so he knew not to suggest either. Honestly, he was surprised she was letting him run the brush through her strands now, but he wouldn't say anything to ruin the moment.

"How about something like . . ." He parted her mane down the middle, then sectioned off two small portions of her caramel-colored hair around her face. Pulling those to the back of her head, he secured them loosely with a simple gold barrette. "This?"

Natalie turned her chin first one way and then the other, inspecting his handiwork. Then she smiled and reached for her toothbrush.

Crisis averted.

"I still can't find them," Nathan now yelled from downstairs.

Short-term victory.

Jeremy opened the door to Nathan's room. Discarded clothes littered the floor, an empty laundry basket alone in the corner. No wonder Nate couldn't find anything in here. Jeremy bent down and picked up all the dirty clothes, depositing them in the hamper. No shoes under the mess, however.

He trudged back downstairs. Nathan sat at the table, eating a large bowl of cereal, milk dripping from his suspended spoon.

"What happened to your black pair of sneakers? Can't you

wear those instead of the blue pair?" Jeremy looked toward the front door, hoping to see the Adidas sitting there.

"Can't." Nathan slurped. "The blue ones are the only shoes I have that fit."

"The *only* ones?" Surely not. Jeremy had bought Nate two new pairs a month ago.

Nate took another bite. "Yep."

They were apparently going shoe shopping after work.

Jeremy made his way into the living room and lowered himself onto his hands and knees to look under the couch. Dust bunnies, a candy wrapper, three dirty socks that looked like Nathan's, and there, a pair of shoes. He grabbed the Adidas and socks, then rose to his feet. He held the shoes in one hand and the socks in the other.

"How'd those get there?" Nathan sounded genuinely confused.

Today was not the day; right then not the time. They were late, and Jeremy didn't have the energy.

He quickly finished making everyone's lunches, and then they all piled into his SUV.

The sun had already crested the horizon, the early-morning light erasing the warm color palette of deep golds and rich oranges. The sky had transformed into an azure blue. If they weren't so late, he'd appreciate the beauty. As it was, he doubted he'd be able to get the kids to school before the bell rang.

Thankfully, the traffic lights seemed to be on his side, turning from red to green and shaving time off their commute. He pulled into the drop-off lane with three minutes to spare.

"Have a good day, guys," he said as the twins grabbed their backpacks.

"You too." They both gave him a peck on the cheek, and then he watched them walk into the school building.

After a glance in his rearview mirror, he pulled back onto the street to head to work. He'd have to thank Sofiya for outfitting the office with a Keurig. He hadn't had time for a cup of coffee, and he desperately needed some caffeine. He found an empty parking spot on the street that didn't require parallel parking and navigated his SUV into the space.

It sounded crazy, but now that he was at work, he felt like he could slow down for a minute and relax. Get that cup of coffee, check his emails, and take a moment to breathe instead of rushing around like a crazy person. He'd tried numerous times to get Nathan and Natalie more organized so things weren't always so chaotic, but those plans and systems never lasted more than a couple of days before the kids slid back into their disorderly ways. He'd finally given up and told them to keep their bedroom doors closed so he didn't have to see the disarray and lose his mind that nothing—literally nothing—was in its place.

The doors to the office building slid open automatically, a welcoming wall of warmth beckoning him inside. The first floor was nothing more than a lobby with the elevator along the back wall, restrooms to the left, stairwell to the right, and a pedestal with a glass case housing a list of businesses on each floor.

He took a step, and something crunched under his foot. He was used to the clacking of heels, but not a crunch. Hopefully no one had broken glass and then not cleaned it up. Gingerly he raised his foot in case the crunchy culprit was something sharp.

Pine needles? Why were pine needles on the floor of the lobby? His gaze rose. A trail of spikey coniferous leaves led toward the stairwell.

What in the world?

Curiosity getting the best of him, he opened the door to the stairs. More green needles littered the risers heading up to higher floors. Scuffling sounded above his head, and he looked up the narrow chute of space that the stairs wrapped around.

Pine needles rained down, and he closed his mouth in the nick of time to keep himself from choking on them.

"Why couldn't you have used an artificial tree?" a feminine

voice asked. "It would've come in a box that would fit in the elevator and would have been easy to carry."

A second person grunted. "Sofiya wants," she panted, "an authentic Christmas experience. How is a fake tree authentic?"

Mackenzie.

It kind of scared him that he recognized her voice right away. He probably wouldn't have last week, they'd had so little interaction. Then again, last week almost seemed like a lifetime ago. Maybe because of the competition, he was keenly aware of the way she softened the "r" sounds in her words. It made him think maybe she was originally from the South, although her accent—if he could call it that—wasn't strong.

He couldn't think of any other reason he'd picked up on such details. She was pretty, yes, with her wildly long hair and equally long eyelashes that she liked to hide behind. Not to mention her small, shy smile that beguiled him. That hint of an upturn to her soft-looking lips that made him wonder what went on in that head of hers.

"Ouch! Tanner just poked me in the eye."

Tanner?

A thump sounded, followed by "Tanner?"

He'd thank Keri for echoing his thoughts, but then he'd make his presence known. Not that he had anything against offering to help the ladies, even if one was technically his rival, but the whole situation held the forecast of entertainment.

"Oh good, we're resting," Keri panted.

"Just for a moment." Mackenzie sounded a little winded as well. "And doesn't he look like a Tanner to you?"

"It looks like a tree," Keri drawled.

"When I saw him in the lot, I thought he was gorgeous with all of his lovely branches, and the song 'O Tannenbaum' came to mind. Then his branches got frisky and started poking me in inappropriate places. I didn't want to call him Frank, so Tannenbaum got turned into Tanner."

"I'm not sure how to respond to that except to say thank you for not naming it Frank. One Frank in the office is one too many."

"Speaking of Frank, any ideas on what you're getting him as a Secret Santa gift?" The acoustics in the stairwell made Mackenzie's voice echo.

"I was thinking *An Idiot's Guide on How Not to Be a Male Chauvinist Pig* would be a great present. What do you think?"

"Definitely a 'we gift' for everyone. Ready to start again?" Mackenzie asked.

"Only two more flights, right?"

"Yeah. We're at the corner now, so we'll need to turn again."

"Don't do it," Keri warned.

"Pivot. Pivot. PIVOT!" Mackenzie got louder and pronounced the two syllables more harshly with each repetition.

Keri groaned while Jeremy barely contained his laughter. Ross's iconic moving-of-the-sofa scene from *Friends*. Who would've known Mackenzie hid such a sense of humor behind her quiet demeanor? Why didn't she let more people see that side of her? What other delightful gems did she conceal behind her shyness?

"Shut up. Shut up. SHUT UP!" Keri answered in a horrible Chandler Bing impersonation. "There. Is it out of your system now?"

"Not quite." Mackenzie sounded cheeky. "There are two more turns until we get to our floor."

Keri groaned again, but this time Jeremy couldn't hold back all of his laughter. A tiny chuckle escaped. He pressed himself under the stairs leading to the second floor in case either Keri or Mackenzie had heard him and looked over the railing to investigate. But the ladies must not have heard anything over the noise they made lugging up the tree.

Exiting the stairwell, he took the elevator up to the ninth floor. As soon as he stepped into the office, he noticed the tree stand over by the large window letting in the morning sun. There seemed to be a buzz of excitement humming on every particle of air. He made his way over to Lincoln, who leaned a hip against the counter of the kitchenette/break area, coffee mug in hand.

"Looks like you're about to be showed up, my friend." Lincoln grinned over the rim of his cup.

Jeremy selected a dark roast k-cup and popped it into the Keurig. He wasn't worried over a cut fir. He had an entire calendar of holiday delights to help secure his position. "Those pomander balls took hours to create. Mackenzie just bought a tree from a stand. It's not like she went out into the woods and chopped it down herself."

"Yeah, but have you noticed Sofiya?" Lincoln pointed toward the door leading to the stairwell.

Their boss stood in knee-high leather boots, bouncing on the balls of her feet so that her heels clicked on the wood floor every time she lowered onto them. Her hands were clasped together under her chin, a childlike expression of expectation and exuberance on her face. She was the embodiment of a kid at Christmas.

Annabelle entered their circle, followed by Derek, her ever-present shadow. "I can't believe Sofiya has never had a real Christmas tree before. My parents always took us to the tree farm when we were kids and let us pick out our tree. What about you guys?"

"I was a Boy Scout," Derek said. "Our troop sold trees every year."

"Never had a tree, huh?" Lincoln looked at Jeremy, then swung his gaze to Sofiya. "What do you guys think? If Jeremy and Mackenzie were keeping score, who'd be up in points now? Jeremy with his oranges or Mackenzie and the live tree?"

"They're pomander balls," Jeremy retorted weakly.

Annabelle's eyes filled with commiseration. "Sorry, Jeremy, but look at Sofiya. Obviously, she's always wanted a live tree, and now Mackenzie is giving her one. She's literally fulfilling a Christmas wish. How can you beat that?"

"Make it snow?" Derek suggested.

They all turned to stare at him.

"What? Everybody wants a white Christmas. People even write songs about it."

The door to the stairwell opened, and Sofiya squealed and clapped her hands. Actually squealed. In delight.

Fraser firs trumped citrus fruit.

"So all I have to do is figure out a way to control the weather," Jeremy deadpanned. "Thanks for the suggestion."

Both Mackenzie and Keri's cheeks were pink, lines of exertion running along their foreheads. Guilt pricked at Jeremy's conscience. He should have done the gentlemanly thing and offered to help carry the tree up the stairs.

He stepped forward and grabbed the trunk from Mackenzie. "Here. Let me help."

She looked at him with her too-large eyes. Something he couldn't unravel wound through her amber irises before retreating. He waited for her gaze to skitter away like it always did. For her to tuck her chin or turn her head, but she didn't. She held his gaze.

Two beats. Three.

A tug of the tree in his hands broke the invisible connection. He turned to find Lincoln on the other end. Keri wiped her hands on a Wet Wipe Rosa had given her from her purse.

Jeremy and Lincoln finished carrying the conifer across the office and secured it in the stand. Jeremy pushed himself off his knees and stood. Sofiya crowded Mackenzie, gushing her joy about the tree. Mackenzie's smile seemed wider than normal. More confident.

Jeremy couldn't help but be happy for her, even if it meant his name lay at the bottom of the imaginary leaderboard of their competition. Warmth spread across his chest, a feeling of almost pleasure at the slight changes he noticed in Mackenzie.

Don't get invested, he warned himself. After all, her lack of self-assuredness and poise gave him the edge over her. And he needed the promotion to accomplish his career goals as well as to provide for the twins' future.

Rooting for his rival wasn't a part of his plans.

9

Sofiya had been beaming at Mackenzie for the last ten minutes. Six hundred seconds of Jeremy watching whatever lead he thought he'd had over Mackenzie getting smaller and smaller in the distance.

But he wasn't out of the race yet. Mackenzie might beat him at a sprint, but he had a marathon of Christmas cheer in his back pocket. In fact, he'd already ordered an assortment of Christmas cookies to be delivered around lunchtime from the little bakery on the corner.

Sofiya gave Mackenzie a hug before heading back to her office. Jeremy should take his cue from his boss and start the workday as well, but he couldn't seem to get his feet to move to his desk. Instead, he stayed rooted to his spot lounging against the break area granite counter, staring at Mackenzie over the rim of his coffee mug.

She had all her gloriously long hair piled on top of her head. He had no idea how the thick mass stayed up there—he didn't see an elastic band in sight. What he did notice, however, was the slope of her slender neck. The creamy white skin usually hidden by her luscious mane, exposed. She began to shrug out of her dark grey wool coat. She turned, her profile to him, the delicate outline of her jaw showing off the graceful lines of her soft features.

He really should look away. If Mackenzie or any of his other female coworkers caught him practically ogling her, they'd lump him into the same unflattering category as Frank.

Just as Jeremy began to lower his gaze, Mackenzie turned once more, this time facing him fully. Her outfit caused his eyes to stop their downward track.

Was she really wearing . . . ?

No, it couldn't be.

He looked closer. What in the United Federation of Planets?

It wasn't the real deal, but close. She had on a red knee-length dress with a thick strip of black around the collar. Pinned over her heart lay a gold Christmas tree brooch that looked like the Starfleet insignia from a distance. While her dress resembled the uniform of the *Enterprise*, Mackenzie Graham hadn't shown up to work in cosplay. Her outfit had to be coincidental. Even if she were a hardcore Trekkie, he'd never noticed her wearing anything but everyday professional clothing. Nothing out of the ordinary or even anything with too much style. In fact, he wasn't sure he'd ever have noticed what she wore except that she always hung out with Keri. And Keri Stratham never dressed like anyone else in the room.

Maybe Mackenzie wasn't a Trekkie. Maybe the opposite was true. Maybe she knew nothing about the show and therefore didn't realize she looked like one of Captain Kirk's Starfleet officers. Maybe he should walk over to her and flash the Vulcan salute. Nothing like a little *live long and prosper* between friendly rivals.

Grinning, he pushed off the counter and drained the last of his lukewarm coffee, then rinsed the mug out in the sink.

Mackenzie had dragged a plastic bin over to the tree and was kneeling beside it, pushing Christmas decorations aside as if she were looking for something specific when he approached.

"I come in peace."

Her chin tilted, her round eyes meeting his. A slight V pattern formed between her brows. Did she really not know the famous quote?

Her hand left the side of the bin, her fingers rubbing the gold Christmas tree brooch.

Beam me up, Scotty.

But if Mackenzie hadn't known the words of Spock, maybe she wasn't touching her insignia-looking jewelry as a way to transport herself out of his presence. Although the look of discomfort about her made him think she'd rather be someplace else.

What had seemed like a fun way to let her know there weren't any hard feelings on his side but also to warn her he wasn't giving up hadn't gone the way he'd thought it would.

He let out a puff of breath. "What I meant to say was, good idea with the tree. I'd scheduled decorating the office for tomorrow, so I hope you don't mind if I bring in some stuff to spruce up the place."

She blinked up at him. While she maintained eye contact better than she had in the past, words still hadn't made it past her lips. He felt the need to fill the silence. Maybe if he kept talking, she'd get comfortable enough to say something back.

"You know, spruce it up with actual spruce. My parents have a tree in their backyard. I thought I'd cut some branches and deck the halls, so to speak. Not exactly boughs of holly, but it'll still look good, don't you think?"

Mackenzie's cheek twitched. Was there a hint of a smile?

Jeremy pressed, hoping if he kept rambling, his inane words would push past the last of her restraints and she'd release whatever was holding her back. Although why he cared, he didn't know. His actions were counterproductive, yet he continued anyway.

"Unless you think that would be cheating? I'd never want to be accused of stealing your ideas or winning by unscrupulous means." He rocked back on his heels. Perhaps a little trash talk. Just a hint. Maybe the offense would be enough to send her on the defense. To verbally fight back. "Because I *am* going to win, Mackenzie. Fair warning."

She rose slowly, both in stature and to the bait. He bit the inside of his cheek to keep his grin from stretching across his face. Anticipation thrummed just under his skin. He had a feeling that wit and intelligence were bottled up inside her compact figure, waiting to be unleashed.

"Jeremy, can I see you in my office, please?" Sofiya's voice interrupted whatever Mackenzie was going to say, her yet-to-be-formed words dying on her pert mouth.

Disappointment stole the lightness from Jeremy's center. Mackenzie turned fully away from him and focused once more on the bin of decorations.

This wasn't over. Against all reason, he wanted her to like him. To be his friend. Or maybe not even that—they were opponents, after all. Pitted against each other. Friendship might be too much to ask. But getting her not to be so nervous in his presence wasn't. He had no idea why she acted skittish around him. Had he done something to make her uncomfortable?

Even if she had overheard him and Lincoln talking yesterday, her uneasiness in his presence went further back than the last twenty-four hours, so the cause, whatever it was, had to be something else entirely.

Then again, maybe the issue wasn't him personally. Maybe he reminded her of someone she had a reason to be nervous around. Either way, he'd made up his mind. Mackenzie was going to get used to him, one way or another. He'd prove to her that he was a nice guy and she didn't need to be on her guard around him.

Well, at least personally. Professionally was another story. But that was a different can of worms.

He walked into Sofiya's office.

"Go ahead and shut the door behind you," she said.

That didn't bode well. He did so, then took the seat across from her desk.

"I've received a communication from Shiloh Press about the book cover they commissioned from us." She clicked her mouse, presumably to bring up the email.

Jeremy cleared his throat. "Yes. I sent them five different designs I thought expressed their notes and vision board."

Sofiya folded her hands, the manicured nail of her index finger tapping her opposite knuckle. "They aren't pleased, Jeremy."

Mentally, he brought up his designs. The work he'd done on Photoshop to manipulate the stock image had been meticulous. No one would be able to tell the photograph had been remastered at all. What about the final product did the editors at the publishing house not like? The colors were sharp and vibrant; the lettering easily legible even in a thumbnail size.

"Their main points of issue are with the compositional flow and the lack of negative space in your layout to enhance the key elements." She swiveled the monitor so the screen faced him. The first of his designs projected from the center. "The color palette you've chosen is pleasing, and I think it fits the genre and tone they asked for, but you've concentrated the color mostly here in the top left corner. If you repeated those tones throughout the cover, then you'd cause the eye to bounce around, following the lead of your pigment."

Okay, he guessed that made sense.

"Also, as for white space, I agree with their assessment that you've tried to do too much. There are too many fixation points that compete instead of harmonize. In this case, less would be more." She swiveled the monitor back to face her. "They've added more notes, which I'll forward to you, and would like to see improvements and edits by end of the workday tomorrow."

"Yes, ma'am." He gripped the armrests of the chair, preparing to launch himself out of the seat and get right to work.

"I know you've got it in you, Jeremy, or I wouldn't be considering you for the promotion."

Unspoken message: *Get this right. Your future job depends on it.*

He walked out of Sofiya's office and let himself fall into his office chair, then shook his mouse to wake up the computer. Movement from the corner of his eye snagged his attention. Mackenzie stretched on her toes to hang an ornament high on the tree. He had to admit the fresh-cut fir had been a great idea. Not only did it look amazing, it smelled good as well. In fact, the pine scent covered any lingering whiffs of citrus and clove from the few pomander balls that remained around the office.

The green branches now looked like they'd received a fresh dusting of snow. Unless he'd missed something in Sofiya's office, a personal snow cloud hadn't developed and dumped fresh powder on the pine. Mackenzie had also wound a fuzzy white garland of some kind around the whole thing. Whatever the garland was made out of gave the tree another layer of texture, a soft and dreamy quality. In contrast, what looked like frost-covered twigs poked out of the branches here and there. Glass snowflake ornaments caught and reflected the light, as did shiny silver-blue balls.

Everything looked perfect. In its spot. Just the way Jeremy liked it. And yet he wanted nothing more than to go over there and mess it all up.

Not because he wanted to sabotage Mackenzie or bring chaos to the beautiful order. He wouldn't *leave* the tree messed up. But he'd been so close to getting her to talk to him earlier that he could still taste the sweetness that victory would give.

His gaze flicked back to his computer screen. He only had today and tomorrow to figure out all the areas where he'd gone wrong with the design and fix them. He should really get to work.

Tink. An ornament fell to the floor and rolled to his feet.

Those designs wouldn't go anywhere.

Hiding his grin lest his mischievous intent show on his face and alert Mackenzie, he picked up the shatterproof orb and walked toward the tree that belonged in an enchanted winter forest.

"Need some help?"

Mackenzie startled, a piece of hair falling from the pile on her head to curve around her jaw. She shook her head slightly, dislodging her loose bun to settle off center. After giving him a timid smile, she went back to arranging one of the frosty sticks in the middle of the tree. She must have spray-painted them then rolled them in glitter.

"I'll just . . ." He held up the sparkly sphere and pointed to the other side of the tree.

She ignored him.

He went around the trunk to a spot still devoid of much decoration. The bin of ornaments sat nearby on the ground. After hanging the one in his hand, he retrieved a few more and hung them in a clump with the first one. It looked as if a toddler had been trying to be helpful.

Mackenzie walked around the tree's circumference, stalling when she noticed him standing there. Then she caught sight of his wad of baubles. He placed his hands behind his back and tried to morph his face into the expression of fake innocence Nate still tried to pull off from time to time. Maybe with a dash of *I'm so pleased with my accomplishment* thrown in for good measure.

Mackenzie stared at the wreckage. She peeked over at him.

Jeremy beamed.

She gave a wobbly smile. Without a word, she stepped around him and attached a star to a branch.

He moved to another section of the tree and continued his horrendous decorating assault. When he went back to the bin for more ornaments, he noticed his clump of globes had been removed and hung from more pleasing locations. He peeked around the branches. Mackenzie was busy putting a new hook into a silver star. Quickly, he gathered the spheres back together and rehung them in their original wadded position. Rustling alerted him that Mackenzie was heading his way, so he dashed around the tree and out of view.

"Seriously?" she muttered under her breath. That was all. Just one word. Then she rearranged the globes for the second time and went back to intricately creating a masterpiece.

After thirty minutes back and forth where he'd screw up the flow with an ornamental train wreck and Mackenzie would fix the damage without a word, Jeremy shook his head. He'd learned two things from the experience. One, pushing Mackenzie or baiting her wasn't an effective way to get her to open up and start talking. Two, he'd never encountered a more patient or long-suffering person in his life.

How many hours did it take a person staring at a computer screen to go cross-eyed, for his vision to blur, for him to momentarily lose his will to live? Jeremy didn't know, but he figured he was nearing the answer.

He dragged his palm over his face, blinking rapidly as if that were the reboot button for his eyes to restart and the bug in his brain to magically be gone.

He'd been staring at this design too long. The details were all blurring together. He'd reduced the number of elements in the overall layout so the eye would know where to focus, and he'd cleaned up the color saturation problem, but the design still didn't seem polished.

"I have a delivery for Jeremy Fletcher."

Jeremy's head snapped up. It wasn't quitting if he *had* to step away from his computer. Besides, coming back to it with fresh eyes might be exactly what he needed to do.

He sprang up from his chair, the caster wheels propelling it out a good five feet. He quickly wheeled it back to its home at his desk so no one would trip, then hurried to the delivery person holding two white bakery boxes. After pressing a couple of bills for a tip into the young man's hand, he took the three dozen cookies to the break area, set them down, then lifted the box lids. Delicious-looking treats stared back at him. Little Santas with vibrant red hats and suits. Deep blue snowflakes with intricate piping details. Lastly, forest-green Christmas trees with golden stars on top. His mouth flooded in anticipation of the much-needed sugar boost.

"Wow. Those look good."

Jeremy peered over his shoulder, surprised to see Jill. He turned and gave her a one-armed hug. "Hey. What are you doing here?"

Lincoln appeared, shrugging into a black leather jacket. "We're headed out on a lunch date."

Jill threaded her arm through her husband's. "You could stand to experience a little midday romance yourself." She gave Jeremy a meaningful look.

Jeremy picked up a cookie. "I expect to feel a lot of love for this baked good, so I'd say I'm all set."

"Are those cookies?" Derek did a poor job restraining the expectancy from his voice.

"I ordered Christmas cookies for everyone. Help yourself and enjoy."

"Sweet." Derek palmed a snowflake, but instead of taking a bite, he placed it on a napkin and carried it over to Annabelle's workstation. "You remind me of this snowflake because there isn't another woman out there like you."

An elbow to the ribs made Jeremy's breath whoosh out of him. He stopped watching the sappy scene unfold and glared at Jill.

"*That's* midday romance. Don't you want that?" she asked.

"To spout off corny one-liners? No, thank you."

She threw her hands in the air. "I give up."

Lincoln reined her in by tucking her into his side. "Don't give up yet, sweetheart. He still has to go on that double date with Alejandro."

"But he's so stubborn he won't even try to like her even if she's perfect for him."

Jeremy crossed his arms. "You guys realize I'm standing right here."

"Mommy and Daddy are talking, son." Lincoln patted him on the head.

Jeremy swatted his hand away. "Tell me again why I'm friends with you two."

"Because you don't have a choice," Jill said smugly.

Jeremy laughed, and some of the tension he'd felt analyzing his cover design all morning started to seep out of him. "Get out of here, you crazy kids." He shooed them away and watched the couple head to the elevator.

"Did I hear something about cookies?" Sofiya sidled up next to him.

Now was the perfect time to score some extra points with his boss. He moved his hand over the boxes like Vanna White. "What would you like? Santa, snowflake, or tree?"

"Let's go with—" she considered each option, then pointed— "a snowflake."

He grabbed a napkin and handed Sofiya a cookie. "I wish I could take the credit, but I know my limitations, and baking exceeds those."

She chuckled lightly. "Knowing one's limitations is an asset as long as a person is willing to try to expand those limitations and not get boxed in by them. However, I am also not an accomplished baker." She took a delicate bite. A noise of appreciation hummed in her throat. "This is good." She dabbed at her lips with the napkin, swallowed, then smiled.

Jeremy froze. Why were Sofiya's teeth blue? He watched her lift the snowflake cookie—the *blue* snowflake cookie—to her lips. Watched her teeth sink into the icing.

He punched back a groan. His brilliant idea of professional Christmas cookies had backfired and stained his boss's teeth.

The boss he desperately needed to impress. He didn't want to tell her, but letting her go through her day with blue teeth would make things even worse.

"Sofiya," he started.

"Jeremy," Keri interrupted. She looked almost gleeful as she pulled Derek and Annabelle behind her, their hands covering their mouths. "I hate to be the one to break it to you—"

Then why couldn't she contain her smile?

"Actually, that's not true. I'm getting immense satisfaction right now." She grinned wider. "Your cookies have painted everyone's mouths crazy colors."

She poked Derek, who lowered his hand and bared his teeth. Too bad Halloween had already passed. All he'd need was sharper canines, and he'd have made a perfect vampire; his mouth looked like he'd been drinking blood.

Sofiya gasped and covered her own mouth with a hand before scurrying off to the bathroom. She came out a few seconds later, her cheeks almost matching Derek's teeth.

"It won't come off with water, and I have a Zoom meeting in ten minutes."

"I have toothpaste," said a small voice behind him.

He turned to see Mackenzie holding up a travel-sized tube of Colgate.

"You're a lifesaver." Sofiya grabbed the toothpaste before retreating to the bathroom once more. Annabelle followed her.

How had this happened? Well, obviously a baker had been too generous with the food coloring. Even he could deduce that. But he'd planned on the cookies being made by a professional so he could avoid disasters like this. He'd gone the extra step to make sure everything would go smoothly, and instead *this* had happened.

Yes, he'd wanted his Christmas efforts to be memorable, but for their success, not their failure.

He closed the lids on the boxes and carried them to his workstation. He'd take them home to Nathan and Natalie. They'd get a kick out of their mouths changing color if the amount of times they stuck out their tongues after eating popsicles was any indication.

He tried to bury himself in his cover design, but the Aquiline Two font treatment on the title didn't have enough power to distract him from the pair of women emerging from the restroom. Sofiya handed Mackenzie her tube of toothpaste with a smile. A regular, white-toothed smile.

At least he hadn't ruined his boss's meeting.

He dragged his focus back to the computer screen. Maybe if he created a light source in the right-hand corner and then cast shadows . . .

Mackenzie rounded the long table and swiveled her chair to sit. Not having individual offices or even cubicles, it was easy to get distracted by the movement and actions of their coworkers. Although he'd never had that particular problem before.

Mackenzie rotated her chair and reached for her headphones. How would she wear them with all her hair on top of her head? She tried to slide the headset on, but it kept snagging on her hair pile. Finally, she set the headphones back down, reached up, and dug around in her hair. A second later, it all came tumbling down her back like a flash flood, stealing Jeremy's breath right out of his chest.

She slid the headphones on and poised her fingers over her keyboard as if she hadn't just done something . . . well, he didn't know what, but she'd certainly done *something*. One minute he'd been obsessing over the stupid cookies, and the next had transported him back to the same thought wave he'd been riding that morning. That he wanted nothing more than for Mackenzie to talk to him. More than two words.

But silently teasing hadn't worked. So, what, then? What would get this beguiling woman to come out from behind her wall of reservation?

Slowly, like a Polaroid being developed, it came to him. And he could have smacked himself on the forehead at how dense he'd been. Mackenzie stepped in when she felt like someone needed her assistance. She wouldn't leave a person stranded if she thought she could help them.

He looked back at his computer screen. He wouldn't even have to fake his distress, as he really could use her insight.

Standing, he walked over to her workspace. With the noise-canceling headphones on, she hadn't heard him approach. He put his hand on her shoulder.

She gasped, whirled around, and clutched the area over her heart. He held his hands up, palms out, an apology on his lips as soon as she removed the headphones to hear it. She did so slowly. Warily.

"I'm sorry. I didn't mean to startle you."

"It's okay."

Like it had the past few times she'd talked to him, her voice made him feel like he'd won a race he hadn't even known he'd been running. The gentle cadence of her soft tones, a trophy.

He slid his fingers into his pants pockets. "I was wondering if you'd look at my current project. Maybe give me some feedback and tips for improvement."

"Me?" She pointed to herself.

"Yeah, you." He kept his smile small. "Everyone knows you've got the best eye for design here. Just look at the tree."

She did, even though his statement was more of a rhetorical device than an actual command. Her expression lost some of its rigidness. She looked like an artist pleased with her work. "It does look nice despite some hiccups."

His hand rose to run through his hair, but he managed to change course at the last second, rubbing the back of his neck instead. He supposed he should apologize again, but what could he say? *I wanted you to talk to me, so I resorted to the grown-up version of pigtail-pulling?*

"So," he said instead, "will you help me?"

She chewed on her bottom lip, enticing his attention. She had nice lips, full and soft. The top dipped in the middle, then curved. He could agree with the design concept of well-formed and flowing lines drawing one's eye. He had a hard time looking away.

Seeming to come to a decision, she released her bottom lip and stood. "Show me what you've got."

He dragged her chair over to his work area, and she leaned forward and studied the design.

"Have you always known you wanted to be a graphic designer?" he asked.

She spared him a glance out of the corner of her eye. She pointed to the keyboard. "May I?"

He rolled his chair over to give her more room to work. She tapped on the keyboard.

So that was it. She would help him with work but ignore his attempts at a conversation. Why was his disappointment so disproportionate? Nothing had really changed, so why did he feel as if he were losing something precious?

"I've always liked art." Her voice filled the space between them.

His middle jolted, and he cleared his throat. "Any specific medium?"

A few clicks of the mouse. "Drawing, mostly. I spent a lot of time with a pencil in my hand, scratching out pictures on blank computer paper." She spoke to him but kept her eyes glued to the screen.

"I'm actually really bad at drawing."

Another quick glance. "How'd you get into graphic design?"

That decision felt like a lifetime ago. "I minored in photography and have always had a penchant for technology. The two sort of merge cohesively as a stable career choice in graphic design."

He watched her work. She hadn't changed any of his elements, but with every click and keystroke, she brought more life to the image, more finesse.

"Is there anything about the job you don't like?" he asked.

When she looked at him next, she searched his face. "Are you trying to find my weakness so you can exploit it and win the promotion?" She sounded serious, but the slight twinkle in her eye gave her away.

He made a show of being hurt and a little offended. "I would never do such a thing."

"You wouldn't sabotage your opponent, then?" One of her brows arched. No doubt she was referring to the ornaments and how he'd kept rearranging them.

"I wasn't sabotaging you," he assured her.

"Then what were you doing?"

Shoot. Time to change the subject. He turned to the screen. Pointed to a random spot. "What's this?"

Her gaze narrowed as she tried to find his imaginary *this*. When she looked back at him, laugh lines crinkled around her eyes. "There's nothing there."

He shrugged. "Weird. I could've sworn I saw something."

She shook her head at him, but the invisible cloak she always seemed to wrap herself in had finally slipped off her shoulders.

I am so confused. And I don't mean the confused you felt as a kid after being spun around the merry-go-round for a solid five minutes by your friend's older brother. You finally step off and you're standing still, but everything else is still spinning. You don't know up from down, left from right, and you only wish everything would just *stop spinning*.

Okay, there is a lot of that going on. I'm definitely merry-go-round disoriented. But I'm talking more the confused when a stranger from another country comes up to you and speaks a foreign language. Not Spanish or French, because there's a slim possibility you might understand a word or two of those languages. I mean you have no earthly idea what's coming out of the other person's mouth. As if they were speaking Silbo Gomero, which doesn't even have verbs or nouns, or any spoken words, for that matter. Just different pitches of whistles to communicate in the mountains of an island off the coast of Spain.

I'm whistling-Silbo-Gomero confused.

A week ago, Jeremy Fletcher was everything I ever wanted in a guy. Confident but not in a cocky way. More self-assured and comfortable in his own skin. Like he knew his place in the world and wouldn't apologize for it. He walked with his chin up and could hold anyone's eyes in a room. His confidence was commanding. Everyone knew they could count on him; a natural-born leader.

He was kind. He always actively listened whenever anyone spoke to him. And I'd never heard him make a single cutting or rude remark. He gave his time and energy. He didn't think he was above other people. I've even seen him help an elderly man cross the intersection a time or two. People seemed to matter to him more than things or ambitions.

He was easy to admire from afar. My favorite way to admire a person. It was easy to let myself dream, let my imagination run wild. In my mind, he always said the perfect things and made me feel warm and mushy inside.

From afar he was . . . well, perfect.

"You look like you're five and someone's just told you Santa isn't real." Keri glances at me from behind the wheel before returning her focus to the road.

She's not wrong. That is a bit how I feel.

"Come on. Tell me what's going through that head of yours."

"I thought you could read my mind or face or whatever." Yes, I'm being a bit sullen, but I'm also trying to reorder my perceptions of the world.

"Unless you want us to wreck, you'd better find the words so I can pay attention to the road and the crazy drivers on it."

I sigh. I know she won't let up. She'll hound me until I finally crack. She always does. But as much as I hate it because she pushes me out of my comfort zone, I also feel better knowing there is someone I can talk to. Even if talking is hard.

"I'm just really confused," I admit out loud.

Keri nods but doesn't say anything.

"I mean, last week I thought Jeremy was this one guy, and this week he turns out to be someone completely different."

Her lips push to the side. "Is he, though?"

I blink. "Is he what?"

"Completely different."

"Yes!" The word explodes from my mouth. "My Jeremy would never have said those hurtful things about me—or anyone, for that matter."

Her gaze flicks to me for a second, and I see her half smile. "*Your* Jeremy?"

"Shut up. You know what I meant," I grumble.

She puts on the blinker to change lanes. "First off, he never should have called you an awkward giraffe that he felt sorry for. That was totally uncalled for, and I would ream him a new one if you'd let me."

"Thanks for reminding me of the exact words." As if I'd ever be able to unhear them and forget. "And for wanting to stick up for me."

"But, Kenz, you've put that man so far up on a pedestal that he had nowhere to go but crashing down. You forgot one very important thing."

"What's that?"

"He's human. Which means he makes mistakes just like the rest of us."

I don't like that she makes sense. It takes the oxygen out of my fire.

"Okay. Fine. Sure." My feelings are still hurt, but I can see that hasn't been his intention. He still shouldn't have said what he did, but like Keri mentioned, everyone makes mistakes. I mean, how many times have I stuck my foot in my mouth without meaning to? Enough to know the appendage leaves a horrible aftertaste.

"It's just, before, I thought I had him figured out, and now . . ." Now I'm not sure if anything I thought I knew about him is real or not.

"Now you're starting to see him as a person with dimensions and layers instead of as an unrealistic ideal."

"Maybe," I admit. "But because of the competition, I'm also

second-guessing everything he does or says. What are his motives? Is he a friend or a foe?"

Keri flashes me a wicked grin. "Why can't he be both?"

I scowl at her.

She laughs. "You know what they say. There's a fine line between love and hate."

My hands tense, so I flex my fingers. "But I don't want him to hate me."

She must hear something in my voice, because she reaches over and squeezes my hand. "No one in their right mind could hate you, Kenzie."

We stop at a red light. The car next to us has their bass turned up to an obnoxious level. Even Keri's rearview mirror rattles. The light changes to green, and the car zooms away.

"Did he seem different to you today?" I ask.

Enough time has lapsed that our conversation could've been considered closed. But I'm still thinking of him. Still trying to puzzle out all the pieces.

"Jeremy?" she asks to clarify.

"Yeah."

"Different how?"

"I don't know. First, he came over while I was decorating the tree to see if I needed any help."

"That was nice of him."

I snort because if that was nice, then it was also only a ruse.

"Uh-oh. What happened?"

"I told him I didn't need help, but he proceeded to 'help'"—I air-quote—"me anyway. The man clumped all the trimmings together in one spot like a three-year-old."

"No." She fake gasps.

I know she's teasing, but the whole thing was super annoying. "When he left, I moved all the ornaments to their rightful places, but when I went back to working on my original area, he came back and moved them all into one spot again."

Keri snickers. "How long did that go on for?"

My fingers drum on my thigh. "He did it at least three times."

"And did you say anything? Ask him to stop?"

I look out the passenger-side window and pretend to be interested in all the different stores and restaurants we pass.

"I thought that's what the outfit was for." She points to the dress and brooch that make me look like a member of the USS *Enterprise* from *Star Trek*. "You pretend to be someone else, and it's the character receiving all the what-if questions or scenarios you worry people are thinking about you."

"It didn't work with him." Although, why, I'm not certain. I was able to converse with all my other coworkers in a way I never had before. Some of them even shared their most cherished childhood holiday memories. I'd gotten the idea that if I had to wring Christmas for all its cheer, then I'd do it in a meaningful way to those around me rather than go off of some generic and contrived premade list.

"Hmm. That's interesting." Keri seems to be contemplating my words. Suddenly, her expression changes from contemplative to impish. She looks like Lucille Ball when she got one of her crazy ideas in *I Love Lucy*. "You know what you should do?" Her grin really does look a bit scary.

"What?" I'm almost afraid to ask.

"You should get Jeremy back for trying to ruin your tree. Muddle up one of his Christmas things, although he's doing a good enough job of that on his own. I'm really glad I didn't eat one of his cookies."

My eyes go wide. "I can't do that."

"Why not?"

"For one, it's not right. I could never stoop to that level to subvert someone else." And the fact that I can never think of subversive things to do means I'd never be an effective saboteur. "For another thing, I'm not sure Jeremy's intention was to ruin the tree. He was being more maddening than destructive."

Keri turns down the street leading to Heritage Hills. "Is that why I saw you fraternizing with the enemy after?"

My cheeks heat. "He's not the enemy."

But I'm even more confused by that *fraternizing*, as Keri put it. Why did Jeremy ask me for help? I mean, his design did need tightening, but he could have asked someone else. If his actions with the tree were cold, then sitting next to each other huddled in front of the computer had been warm. Very warm.

My skin flushes just thinking about it. Not only about his proximity, because I could literally feel the body heat coming off of him, but also because of our conversation. We . . . talked. Like, really talked. More than *hi* or *good morning* or *thank you*. He asked me a personal question and I managed to answer him and then ask him one in return. And I didn't want to shrink and blend in to the wall. It was actually . . . nice.

"I thought you said you didn't know if he was friend or foe?" Keri beams, and I feel a bit like an insect caught in an intricately woven spider web.

I let myself smile for the first time since starting this conversation. "Touché."

Keri pulls into a parking spot and turns her body toward me. "Look, I think Jeremy Fletcher is still the same guy he was last week and last year and every day that you've been pining after him."

I look away. I haven't been pining. More like admiring from a safe distance.

"But he's being forced to fight for a promotion that he wants, and that means things have changed. Just like they've changed for you."

My mouth pulls down.

"You're my best friend, and I love you. I have no doubt you're going to figure all this out." She opens her door and exits the car.

That's it? That's her advice, that I'll figure it out?

Newsflash, people: I feel like I've been thrown into the deep end of the pool without knowing how to swim, and sharks are circling. Yes, sharks. In a pool. The ones I was irrationally afraid of as a child, thinking they came up from the drain at the bottom of the deep end. Call me overly dramatic, but that's how I feel.

Someone show me how to backstroke, please, before I drown in my thoughts, made-up scenarios, and uncharted, confused feelings.

By the time I follow Keri into the lobby of Heritage Hills, she's already found her favorite male nurse and looks to be in a cozy tête-á-tête along the wall. He's looking down at her with a hint of adoration in his eyes, his bronze skin glowing under her pale hand where she touches his forearm. She laughs at something he says, the fingers of her other hand coming up to hover over her lips. Her admirer's eyes follow the movement, his throat bobbing as he swallows.

How do they make it seem so easy? Flirting and talking when there are so many flighty emotions winging around in their chests? Keri looks practically giddy. If it were me standing there with Jeremy so close I could smell his cologne, I wouldn't be able to string two coherent sentences together. I have the elevator experience to prove it.

I avert my eyes and clutch the book I've brought closer to my chest. For the most part, the day and the small step into cosplay has been a success. Though it was tiring, I connected with other people more than normal. It was just my interactions with Jeremy that leave me feeling like I've taken a ride in a front-load washing machine. I don't need Keri's easy manner with the guy she likes to make me feel like I should be hung out to dry as well.

"Mackenzie," Keri calls and waves me over.

I'm a bad friend because my feet are heavy as I walk toward her.

"Alejandro, I want you to meet my best friend and roommate, Mackenzie Graham." She turns to me, her eyes bright and happy. "Mackenzie, this is Alejandro Rodriguez."

"Are you a hugger? I'm a hugger." His dark eyes are kind and his smile nice.

Before I can answer in the negative, I'm wrapped up in his arms, my nose smashed into his scrubs. I'm not sure what to do with my hands, so I awkwardly pat his shoulder three times. I take a step back, thankful to regain a bit of personal space.

"She's just as you described her," he says to Keri. "My friend is a lucky man." He leans down and stage-whispers into her ear. "But not as lucky as I am."

Keri blushes. Maybe not a big deal on most people, but I've never seen her cheeks take on that particular hue before. For a moment, I'm too struck with the sight to register Alejandro's words. But then they catch up with me.

"Excuse me? What friend, and why would he be lucky because of me?"

Alejandro looks confused, and Keri's blush deepens to chagrin. She clears her throat. "Surprise! We're all going out on a double date on Saturday night."

Is she for real? My gaze jumps between hers and Alejandro's before settling on Keri's. Neither of them seems to be hiding a smile that says they're only joking. "No."

A woman in purple scrubs calls for Alejandro.

"I'm sorry, but I have to go." The look he gives Keri is full of regret. "Will you call me later? My shift ends at ten, if that's not too late."

Keri lightly touches his hand. "It's not too late."

She turns back to me as he walks away, and the look on my face erases all the happy feelings Alejandro left her with. This time when she sighs, it's with a hint of exasperation.

"Before you get mad, hear me out," she says.

I can't imagine she'll say anything to make me change my mind and agree to a blind double date, but she can try.

"Wouldn't it be nice to practice dating and flirting and talking to a guy? With a complete stranger you have no feelings for and would never have to see again? And you wouldn't be on your own. Anytime you started to feel too much pressure because the conversation lagged or you were given too much attention, Alejandro and I would be there to step in and say something to ease things along."

Well, cherry cordials, that makes a lot more sense than I want it to.

"Plus," Keri continues, "you'd be doing Alejandro and his friend a favor. Alejandro says he's concerned about his friend because he never goes out. He's too busy worrying and caring about the people in his life. It took a lot of convincing on Alejandro's part to get his friend to agree, and if you back out, Alejandro's afraid he'll never get the guy out of the house again. So, you see, you're his only hope."

I can tell when Keri's speech goes from serious to play. She really does think this date will be good for me, and she isn't above a little teasing manipulation to get her way.

"Your reference is from *Star Wars*. Totally different universe than *Star Trek*."

"My apologies," she says in mock sincerity.

"And I know you're trying to manipulate me into saying yes."

"Is it working?" She grins shamelessly. "Because if not, I'm not above adding a little guilt into the mix." She plants her hands on my shoulders. "I really, *really* like Alejandro and really want to go on a date with him. Saturday is his first day off, and if we don't double date, then he might have to cancel, and I'm not sure when we'd be able to reschedule. Please say you'll go."

I roll my eyes at her pouty lip. "I'll go."

She squeals and hugs me tight. "You won't regret it."

"I kind of already do," I mumble.

She laughs and waves me away. "Go see your mom."

A small sense of dread fills me as I near Mom's door. I hate this feeling, and guilt is a constant companion to it, but I can't seem to suppress either one. Standing in front of my mom's room is a bit like standing in front of a mystery door on a game show. I never know what awaits me on the other side. Will she be having a good day or a bad one? Will we be able to have a conversation, or will she have slipped into the time and space of her own mind? Will she know me, or will my presence only agitate her?

I'm thankful I still have her. That she still has good days that are as sweet as orange blossom marmalade. But I mourn the loss of her as well, even, sometimes, as we sit in the same room.

I prepare myself for the worst but hope for the best as I raise my hand and knock on the door. There's a shuffling of feet on the other side before it swings open.

Mom glares at me, her eyes squinty. "Who are you? What do you want?"

So, not a good day. Her face is lined with irritability, and my heart fissures to see her like this.

"Hi. My name is Mackenzie."

This isn't the first time I've had to introduce myself to the woman who gave me life. Sang me to sleep with the melody of "Hush, Little Baby" while gently rubbing my back. Cheered for me from the sidelines of all my soccer games. Taught me how to drive. Cried at my graduation.

Her face softens. "Mackenzie. I've always liked that name. I want to name my daughter Mackenzie. If I ever have a daughter, that is." Her lips purse as she eyes me. "Do you like football? You can come in and watch with me if you like."

I give her a small smile. "I love football." The fact that she's watching a game on a Tuesday tells me a lot, since no live games are played today in the NFL.

The staff at Heritage Hills have discovered that football has a calming effect on my mom. Well, the Green Bay Packers, specifically. We moved to Wisconsin from Alabama right before I started high school, and Mom became a big cheesehead right away and has been ever since. For some reason, even though her brain occasionally steals her memories of me, her love for the Packers has always stayed intact. She must have become a little difficult earlier in the day, and someone on staff found an older game to replay for her.

"Who's playing?" I ask as I move toward the small settee positioned in front of the TV.

"The Packers versus the Bears."

A rival team. Not ideal if the goal is to calm her. She paces the length of the room—which isn't much space—perturbation making her hands shake.

The television goes from a dog food commercial back to the game. It's the second quarter and the Packers are down seven points, but that just means they need a single touchdown to even the score. The leaderboard wouldn't make her upset. It's still early in the game, and Aaron Rodgers has possession of the ball, the offense going into formation at the line of scrimmage.

Mom is muttering under her breath about idiots and morons and what are they thinking.

The ball is snapped, but one of the Bears' linemen gets around the Packers' right guard, and Aaron Rodgers goes down. Sacked.

An animalistic sound comes from my mom, and she stops pacing. She throws her arm at the TV. "Why is the backup quarterback playing?" she yells at the screen. "Put in Brett Favre!"

It might not be the best time to tell her that Brett Favre retired in 2010 and Aaron Rodgers has been the Packers' starting quarterback since 2008.

She marches to the TV and pokes at it with her finger. Her

nail practically decapitates Matt LaFleur. "Who is this clown?" she demands. "Where is Mike McCarthy?"

I probably also shouldn't tell her that Mike McCarthy coaches the Dallas Cowboys now.

"I gotta pee," she announces and then turns on her heel and stalks away.

I have exactly the length of time it takes someone to empty their bladder to find another Packers vs. Bears game where Brett Favre is quarterback and Mike McCarthy the head coach.

Or maybe Mom will come back out and forget she was even watching football to begin with.

Better not take the chance.

I count it a miracle I'm able to find a game on YouTube from 2005 with the same two teams playing. Will Mom notice the quality difference or the fact that the game is now in Lambeau Field instead of Soldier Field in Chicago?

The toilet flushes, and then the water in the sink runs before the bathroom door opens.

"Who are you? What are you doing in my room?" Mom blinks at me.

I can't tell if she's scared or mad. I don't like either option and hate that I bring those feelings out in her.

"I'm Mackenzie. We're watching football together."

"Oh." She takes three steps closer. "Who's playing?"

I guess I could have found any game and been good. Oh well. "The Packers and the Bears."

She nods. "Who did you say you were?"

My chest pinches. "Mackenzie."

"I like that name." She sits beside me but hugs the armrest like she's afraid to get too close.

I look down at the book in my hands, which I was so excited to share with my mother. When I glance back at her, she's blurry, and I realize it's because I have tears in my eyes. I blink them back.

My mom is in there somewhere, but the disease has taken over for the moment. I doubt it would appreciate an African retelling of Rapunzel as much as my mom would.

I stand. "I'll see you later." I catch myself before saying "Mom" at the end. That would only upset her more.

She looks up at me, her eyes blank. "Who are you?"

This time I don't say my name. I just wave and leave. When I close the door behind me, I swipe at the tear spilling over.

I have a choice. I can dwell on the fact that my mom is slipping away and let myself feel sad and a bit sorry (and some hard days I *do* make this choice), or I can choose to see the positive. There will be more good days. I still have time to be with her and make more memories.

Memories like the ones some of my coworkers shared with me today. The things that brought a smile to their faces as they reminisced about their Christmases as children. What made the holidays special and what things they missed.

Memories are precious things. Not to be taken for granted. They have the power to bring comfort, to make us smile and feel warm inside. Everyone should take the time to cherish the memories they have and be more intentional about making new, good, and lasting ones with those they love.

I can't do much to help my mom regain her memories, but I can do a lot to help those at work relive theirs.

O f course Annabelle's Nana had to make her gingerbread from scratch.

I stare at the mess I've made in the kitchen. Flour on the counters and even some on the floor. Speckles of cinnamon and dustings of ginger. Every surface is covered with cookie sheets, and pre-fab gingerbread walls and roofs ready to be assembled are either cooling or stacked and waiting to be hauled to the construction site—Limitless Designs. I just need to make one more batch of icing to work as mortar, and everything will be ready.

Keri stumbles into the kitchen, blinking against the light. She sniffs, her nose scrunching like a cottontail bunny. "What smells so good?"

I stop whisking my meringue powder, confectioners' sugar, and vanilla extract mixture. "I made gingerbread."

"Men?" She steps closer, and her eyes widen when they take in all the golden-brown rectangles.

"Umm . . . not men."

She grins and lifts her hand for a high five. I'm not sure why we're high-fiving, but I smack her palm with mine anyway.

"I didn't know you had it in you," she says.

To bake enough gingerbread for everyone at work to make a house? Sure, it took a while, but it wasn't *that* difficult.

"To one-up Jeremy like this," she continues. "His bakery-bought cliched cookies ended in disaster, and the next day you're showing up with all the essentials to assemble our own gingerbread houses. With gingerbread you made. From scratch."

"That's not why I—"

"You go, girl."

"Keri." The pride she's directing at me is nice, but I don't like that her perspective is that I deserve it at someone else's expense. "I'm not trying to show my superiority over Jeremy. Even if my baking skills surpass his, that has no bearing on who can perform the duties of the new job better. Sofiya's smart. She knows this."

One of Keri's brows slants up. "As we've already established, Sofiya's judgment gets a little skewed at Christmastime. Whether you meant to or not, this right here"—she sweeps her hand over the kitchen and my three hours of hard work—"will make you look good to Sofiya."

My stomach sinks like it just took a step in fresh snow and didn't realize how deep the drift was.

I think of Annabelle. The wistful, happy look on her face as she told me about going to her Nana's house as a child and making gingerbread houses. How more candy would end up in their stomachs than decorating the roofs and walls.

I hadn't spent all morning baking to impress Sofiya or try to outshine Jeremy. I'd missed precious sleep to bring back a cherished memory for Annabelle.

"I'm going to get ready for work." Keri turns and pads to the bathroom. A couple of minutes later, the shower turns on.

I package up everything I've made, careful not to crack or break any of the baked goods. The candy remains in the grocery bags from the store. I need a shower to wash away the flour and other ingredients pebbling my skin, but I have to wait my turn.

Instead, I walk back to my room and stare at my clothes in the closet.

I've given a lot of thought to which character I should personify today, but I can't make up my mind. It can't be someone too crazy. I thought I was safe yesterday, but I don't think my outfit was subtle enough. In fact, I think Jeremy may have recognized the similarities between my dress and brooch and the Starfleet uniform.

And what must he think of you now? That you're some kind of weirdo playing dress-up?

I shake my head, trying to dislodge the negative questions before they adhere to my brain. The whole point of the cosplay theory is that the character gets hit with the perceived thoughts of others, not me.

But I'm also not going to a convention where everyone dresses up and not doing so will make me stick out. I don't want to be a laughingstock at work, and showing up in a full Wookiee costume would definitely bring unwanted attention. I need something subtle. Something that will make me blend in with everyone else but is different enough that I can look down, see my clothes, and remember that I'm personifying the character. Borrowing her confidence and swagger. Whoever she is.

Maybe Keri will let me borrow pieces from her closet. I know she has a pair of vintage slacks in the style of the forties or fifties. I could pretend to be Agent Carter from *Captain America*. I roll that idea around in my mind, but it doesn't feel right. Who else can I glean a fighter spirit from?

My gaze lands on my light brown faux leather jacket. If I pair it with a plain black V-neck top and my hunter-green dress pants tucked into lace-up boots and then French braid my hair at a diagonal, I can assimilate myself into the character of Katniss Everdeen. She's resourceful and adaptable. Clever and sure of herself. And she sacrifices for her family. All things I want to be.

An hour later, Keri and I ride the elevator up to the ninth floor.

I have the containers of gingerbread in my hands, while the bags of candy are slung over her arm. The elevator doors slide open, and we step out.

"Whatcha got there?" Lincoln looks at all the containers with interest.

Frank stands off to the side, both hands around his coffee cup. He brings the mug up to his lips, but he is unsuccessful at hiding his own interest. Too bad he isn't also looking at the Tupperware housing the gingerbread. No, his gaze trails down my legs and back up. While no part of my skin shows, I still feel exposed. Creep.

By now, more people are crowding around. Keri sets the bags on the break area table, and Derek pokes his hand in and pulls out a bag of mini candy canes. Everyone stares at me, expectation on their faces.

My mouth starts to dry. My breath shallows.

You offer yourself as tribute, Mackenzie. For Annabelle's sake. For Mom's.

I swallow and push back my shoulders, setting the containers on the table. I pop off the lids. Spices billow into the air. Ginger, cinnamon, nutmeg, allspice, and cloves.

"Is that . . . ?" Annabelle looks up at me. Her eyes glisten. "Are we making gingerbread houses?"

"Kind of puts your cookies from yesterday to shame, man." Lincoln elbows Jeremy standing beside him.

My eyes lock with Jeremy's. I hope he doesn't think I chose to bring in baked goods today to make him look bad. Keri thought so. Lincoln seems to think so. I almost want to mouth *I'm sorry* but stop myself. Katniss wouldn't apologize for a holiday tradition with a grandparent, and neither will I.

But I still hope he doesn't think I did it to show him up.

He gives me a small smile, and I exhale.

"Do you think Sofiya will mind if we decorate these now?" Annabelle bounces on her toes.

"What's this? I'm paying you all to stand around and chitchat?" Sofiya exits her office. Her voice is stern, but she gives herself away by the turn of her lips and the twinkle in her eyes.

She stops next to me as she looks over everything I've brought. Her smile grows.

"Did you know that I lived in Asheville, North Carolina, for a few years? They host an annual national gingerbread house competition. It's beyond amazing the works of edible architecture those craftsmen bakers can create."

"My Nana and I used to make houses together every year. It was our tradition," Annabelle tells Sofiya.

Sofiya looks at me. No, she studies me. "And Mackenzie has made it so we can all celebrate that memory with you." I'm not sure what the older woman sees when she looks at me, but she blinks, and the expression on her face changes. "Well, let's get these houses built, shall we?"

The immediate vicinity alights with activity, but instead of bees around a hive, it's adults acting like children around the makings of a home constructed from sugar. Hansel and Gretel would be proud.

Because I know Katniss would do it, I step in and create some order among the chaos. After divvying up all the supplies, I step back and take a deep breath.

Normally after so much time working with others, I need to sneak off and have a few moments by myself to regroup and recharge. Collaborative projects in college were a nightmare. But surprisingly, I don't feel that drained right now. In fact, there's a small hum of energy, a smidgen of satisfaction, and I find I'm actually a teeny tiny bit proud of myself. Especially when I hear Annabelle laugh as she pelts Derek with a green gumdrop.

Clank.

I whirl around and find Jeremy marching up a ladder, lengths of pine branches in his hands. That's right. He was going to *spruce up* the place. What a dad joke. Laughter plays at my lips.

He struggles with the green boughs, the branches tangling with the ladder rungs. A branch falls from his hands when he tries to maneuver it on to a Command Strip. His head tilts back, and I can feel the frustration radiating from him. After a moment, he climbs down, picks up the bough, and mounts the ladder once more.

I press my lips between my teeth, wondering if I should go over and help him but also not wanting to get in his way.

I look back at the construction area. Sofiya has four walls up and is balancing the roof while she pipes frosting along the edge to hold it in place. Lincoln has a square of gingerbread in one hand, bites taken out of it, and an assortment of candy in the other. He clearly decided to skip the assembly part and go straight to the eating part. Annabelle and Derek are huddled close, giving only a fraction more attention to their builds than to each other. Everyone seems to be enjoying themselves and having a good time. I stepped out of my comfort zone, and it wasn't *so* bad. Maybe I could do the same thing with Jeremy, too.

Running my hand over the crisscross pattern of my braid, I remind myself I can be like Katniss, if only a little bit, and stride (maybe with more of a combination of determination and reluctance than confidence) toward Jeremy.

"Do you need a hand?" My voice isn't the strongest, but I manage to project enough volume that he hears me.

He looks down, a shadow hiding half his face. "Sure. Can you hand me that hook right there?"

I grab the plastic hook and hold it up to him. Our fingers brush as he takes it from me.

A jolt of electricity shoots up my arm. Keri's words about my face saying what my mouth doesn't flash back to me. Oh no. Will Jeremy see that I've been harboring a secret crush on him for almost two years? Can he somehow deduce my hidden feelings from the momentary contact of our fingers?

Stop being ridiculous. Neither of you is E.T. with magical glowing fingers that can read the other's thoughts or emotions. Although it's been so long since I've seen the movie, maybe that's not even what E.T's long, creepy extraterrestrial digits did.

"Thanks." Jeremy's voice snaps me back to reality.

He sounds normal. He looks normal. Maybe he isn't aware of my momentary freak-out.

I swallow, wishing I could *be* normal. Noticing he needs another branch, I bend down and grab one from his pile. When he reaches to take it, I see red bumps up and down his forearm. Without thinking, I slide the tops of my fingers along the aggravated skin. Only a small part at the back of my mind registers the corded muscles beneath my touch.

Jeremy jerks in surprise, which makes me snatch my hand back, my face heating like an oven.

"Sorry," we say in unison.

Jeremy smiles, but I duck my head. The rash must bother him. I wonder what it's from.

"Does it itch?" When I look back up, he's scratching his arm.

His smile turns guilty. "I forgot I'm allergic to the resin in pine sap. We've used artificial trees since I was a kid, so it slipped my mind."

"I might have some cream in my purse that could help."

"Your Mary Poppins bag with the toothpaste that saved the day yesterday?" His mouth hitches on one side, pulling his cleft chin and making the feature more pronounced.

I let the noise from everyone else on the other side of the room drag my gaze away. "I wouldn't say it saved the day."

"Don't be modest. You were Sofiya's hero."

I roll my eyes. "That's laying it on a bit thick, don't you think?"

He shakes his head. "You've got to be your loudest cheerleader. Play up your win. Especially to Sofiya."

My head cocks to the side. Why is he telling me this? It won't do him any good for Sofiya to have a bunch of positive thoughts and opinions about me. He shouldn't be giving me tips. Not if he wants to win, and I *know* he wants to win.

"Why are you telling me this?" Wow. A thought actually traveled from my brain to my mouth without any road bumps, stop signs, or detours.

He blinks, his smile falling in confusion. "I don't know." Then he sort of shakes himself, and his cool confidence returns. "Should we practice our trash talk instead?" He puts his face right in front of mine. "You're going down, Mackenzie Graham. Down like the dried fruit in a fruitcake if it's not dusted in a little flour before being added to the batter."

"What?" The word is carried out of my mouth on a laugh.

He grins. "I watched *The Great British Baking Show* with Natalie last night on Netflix." He pokes me with an elbow. "Your turn."

I try to ignore the concentrated heat in my arm from his gentle jab. Trash talk. I've never trash-talked before in my life.

"Umm . . ."

He's totally focused on my face. At one point I would have compared Jeremy to the sun. He brings warmth and light whenever he's around, and he's completely dependable at showing up every day. But you can't look at the sun. Not directly. And I am looking at Jeremy now. Holding his gaze, being drawn in, filling myself with his energy.

His confidence, it seems, has been directed at me. He's looking at me as if he has no doubts at all that I can rise to his challenge. Or any challenge, for that matter. That I am capable and competent, and he's waiting on edge to see what I'll do or say next.

I swallow, the headiness scattering my thoughts. "I'm going to wipe the floor with you, Jeremy Fletcher, like . . . umm . . . a mop?"

His laugh starts low in his chest, but it builds until he can't contain the mirth any longer and the sound erupts from him.

"Hey, keep it down over there. You're ruining my sugar high."

Lincoln tilts his head back and funnels in M&Ms straight from the bag.

"That was awful." Jeremy's brown eyes are still laughing.

"It can't be worse than your comparison to fruit in a fruitcake." He scratches at his arm. "True that."

I look at the red streaks running from his wrist to his elbow. "Come on. Let's see if I have that cream."

I dig through my purse until I find a tube of over-the-counter hydrocortisone cream. I carry the toothpaste with me from years of wearing braces. Old habit. But I have the itching cream because of my dry skin. Winter only makes the dry patches worse.

I squeeze some onto my finger before I realize I should've handed the whole tube to Jeremy so he could rub it on himself. My face flames.

He acts like nothing is amiss as he extends his arm in my direction.

Right. I can do this. No big deal.

With shallow breaths I watch my hand descend. Absorb the heat from his skin into mine. Run my finger along the pronounced vein in his forearm. Feel his pulse. Feel mine.

"It was nice, what you did for Annabelle," he says softly, his breath making the few strands of hair that have come loose from my braid caress my cheek.

He's talking about the gingerbread houses, but I'm having a hard time concentrating on anything other than what's going on beneath my palm.

"When this is all over and we're ushering in the New Year, after Sofiya decides which one of us gets the job . . ."

I glance up, expecting to see him looking at me. But he's not. He's staring at my hand on his arm too, mesmerized by the back-and-forth motion my fingers make as I rub the lotion onto his skin.

He looks up, and I'm caught staring. Caught in his gaze.

"I hope we'll both remember everything we did to win the promotion was only business, not personal."

My hand freezes. Isn't that what the mobsters in *The Godfather* say before they kill people? What Joe Fox says to Kathleen Kelly in *You've Got Mail* before putting her out of business?

Jeremy Fletcher, what are you planning to do to me?

14

Nothing was going according to plan.

Jeremy rubbed a hand down his face, the medical scent of the hydrocortisone cream filling his nostrils. He snorted, both to rid himself of the smell and thus the memory of Mackenzie's soft fingers caressing the sensitive skin of the underside of his forearm, and to scoff at the whole blasted thing.

How had he gotten to this point? All of his plans were failing, every attempt ending in disaster. How could he turn this around?

His instincts told him to stick to what he'd outlined. Strategies were made for a reason, after all.

So where did that leave him in the promotion battle? He had to come up with something to at least even the score, if not put him back on top. Mackenzie didn't *need* the raise, after all. She didn't have two almost-teenagers and their daily expenses. Good grief, Nathan alone ate like he was afraid there'd never be another meal placed in front of him. Not to mention clothes and shoes because neither would heed his pleas to stop growing. They'd be driving in only a few years, so his insurance premiums would skyrocket. Then there was college. Even an in-state school would cripple his current finances.

His gaze washed over the room. The Christmas tree that had made Sofiya so happy. The gingerbread houses that had brought back so many childhood memories for Annabelle. The nativity scene missing Mary, Joseph, and baby Jesus.

Wait. When had a nativity scene been set up? And where were the guests of honor?

Jeremy stood and turned. He took three steps before his feet stumbled to a halt. Hidden behind Derek's computer monitor were Mary and Joseph. Joseph's shepherd's rod looked to be pushing the cords out of the way, while Mary appeared to have tripped over them since she was on her knees.

Why in the world were Mary and Joseph behind the computer, and where was Jesus? Would Jeremy find him in a different obscure location, like on top of the copier? Oh well, better put them with the three wisemen and the shepherds in the nativity set where they belonged.

He picked up the God-appointed parent figurines, and Rosa came flying at him from the other side of the long desk.

"You found them," she declared.

"Yeah, I was just going to set them back in the nativity."

"No, you can't." The ends of her black ponytail smacked her cheeks as she shook her head.

This day kept getting more baffling. "I can't?"

She shook her head some more. "Mackenzie brought the nativity for me."

Of course she had.

"See, when I was a child, all my friends had an Elf on the Shelf. Do you know what that is?"

The little toy elf had been the bane of his holiday one year. Remembering to move it every night and thinking of clever mischief for Santa's helper to get into had sounded like fun, but in reality had ended up using a lot of time and energy. He'd had to scramble to explain why Elfie hadn't moved from the day before the few times he'd forgotten and fallen asleep.

"I wanted one really badly, but my mom is extremely religious and doesn't believe in that stuff. So instead of an Elf on the Shelf, she took the Virgin Mary and her husband, Joseph, from the Nativity set, and every night while I was asleep, she moved them around the house. She said they were on their journey to Bethlehem. As soon as I woke up, I'd search the house for them. On Christmas morning, they'd have arrived in Bethlehem at the stable, and Jesus would be there with them in the manger."

Jeremy set Mary and Joseph back where he'd found them. "That's really sweet."

Mackenzie had struck again.

"I haven't played this game in years. It seems silly, but I almost feel like a kid again." Rosa giggled before making her way to her desk.

Jeremy shook his head. He'd stick with the original plan he'd mapped out. Which meant bringing in a hot chocolate bar and borrowing his dad's record player and vinyls of Bing Crosby, Frank Sinatra, and Nat King Cole.

But just because he was sticking to his Christmas calendar of events didn't mean he couldn't add to it. A plan had to be adaptable to be effective. As he looked out over the space and the touches Mackenzie had brought so far, a common thread wound its way among them all. Mackenzie had found the root of the holiday and was wrapping it up for each person individually. Christmas was, after all, about giving.

What if they could reach outside their office and give to those less fortunate in their community?

He snagged his phone from his desk and retreated to the stairwell. After a few minutes of internet searching, he found a local charity with children and families still in need of sponsors to make their Christmas wishes come true. The deadline to get the gifts to them was tight but doable.

He filled out the information on the website, then sent the list of kids and their needs to the wireless printer in the office. Each name and the three items on their Christmas list were centered in the middle of a snowflake. Already he felt better about playing Secret Santa to these strangers in need than he did about the names drawn from the hat for the office party.

Retrieving the printouts from the machine, Jeremy cut out the individual snowflakes.

"Hey!" He raised his voice to be heard over the clacking of keys and any music being played in earbuds. "I thought it would be nice if we spread the Christmas cheer outside our four walls. So grab a snowflake, adopt a person or two, and let's make their holiday brighter."

He passed out snowflakes to Derek and Annabelle. Rosa asked for two, and Frank begrudgingly took one. Jeremy didn't see Keri or Mackenzie—maybe they had stepped into the stairwell after he vacated it—and Sofiya appeared to be on a phone call. He'd approach them with the snowflakes later.

He turned back to his station, ready to get his work done, but paused at the steaming cup of coffee on his desk. A Post-it had been set next to the mug. Reaching down, he peeled the memo paper off the surface of his desk and read.

You look like you need a hug, and I've heard coffee is a hug in a cup.

The note was unsigned, but he knew it was from Mackenzie. He'd noticed her half print, half cursive style before. The edge of his mouth moved toward his ear in a grin. The note felt bold for her. He couldn't imagine her ever walking up and wrapping her arms around him.

He lifted the mug and drank deeply, managing to singe his tongue. He hissed and set down the cup, staring into the near-black liquid. She'd made the coffee just how he liked it. A spoonful of honey instead of sugar and a splash of half-and-half. How did she know?

The stairwell door opened, and Mackenzie stepped over the threshold. Their gazes met. Her cheeks flushed a becoming pink before she dropped her gaze to the ground. He picked up the snowflakes with a small smile. The perfect excuse to talk to her. That and he had a cup of coffee to thank her for as well.

"Hey, ladies," he said as he approached the duo. "You missed my announcement, but I signed Limitless Designs up to sponsor some kids and families in the community for Christmas. These are who we have left." He handed them the snowflakes.

Keri sifted through them first, reading each name and Christmas list. She chose one and handed the rest to Mackenzie. "This is a great idea," she said almost accusingly as she glared at him.

"Aww. This little boy only listed clothes and shoes." Mackenzie's eyes were round in her face. "What nine-year-old wants only clothes for Christmas?"

Keri looked at her friend, and her face softened. "You're going to buy a whole wardrobe and a toy department for him, aren't you." Her inflection did not imply a question.

"If I could afford to, I would. But a few toys along with clothes and shoes shouldn't break the bank. Plus, it's Christmas."

Keri shook her head, gave Jeremy one last look, then walked away.

Jeremy cleared his throat. "Thank you for the coffee. That was thoughtful of you."

Mackenzie ducked her head, but she couldn't hide the rose pink flushing her skin. He hated to say it, but that particular hue was fast becoming his favorite color.

She looked up at him through her lashes. On another woman, he'd think the move coy. Maybe even flirtatious. With Mackenzie, he saw the action as brave.

"How's Natalie doing?" she asked.

"She's good. Complains about the braces, but that's normal." He leaned his shoulder against the wall.

She nodded. Paused. Should he wait for her to say something or fill the growing silence?

"And your nephew? Sorry, I don't know his name," she finally said.

"Nathan," he supplied. "He's good. Has a hockey game tonight."

"Fun."

Not exactly tantalizing conversation. Nor what he'd call an easy exchange. Every repartee seemed to be fought for instead of coming naturally. And yet, at the moment, there was no one else he'd rather talk to. No one else he'd rather get to know better.

"So," he said as a transition, "you've been recreating some childhoods around here."

"Memories are powerful things." She tucked a strand of hair behind her ear. "What was your favorite thing about Christmas growing up?"

He thought back to his childhood. How he and Heidi would camp out under the Christmas tree on Christmas Eve's eve and look up through the branches, the twinkling lights like stars above their heads. How they'd bundle up in jackets, scarves, and knitted caps to walk around the neighborhood looking at everyone's yard decorations. The Victorian at the end of the street always went all out. The owners must have strung thousands of lights over every surface of their home and yard. As a kid, he'd been awestruck at the display. As an adult, he wondered how they afforded their electric bill for the month.

Mackenzie studied him, waiting for his answer. He grinned and playfully shook his finger at her. "Nope. I'm not going to help you beat me. You're doing a good enough job of that on your own."

"I . . . that's not . . ."

She seemed to have a hard time formulating the response she wanted. He didn't want her to get overwhelmed, so he stepped in. "What about you? Favorite childhood Christmas memory?"

She took a breath. Her face cleared. A small smile followed.

"How do I know you didn't just accuse me of using your childhood memories for nefarious purposes because that's actually what you're going to do?"

He lowered his voice and leaned toward her. "You don't."

She laughed. "I'm glad you understood what I meant. Once I heard it, I realized what I said was a bit confusing."

Jeremy straightened. "I don't think I've ever heard you say anything that wasn't understandable."

A pained expression filled her face, and she averted her gaze to the left. Pretended to be fascinated by something Rosa was doing at her desk.

He knew in his gut she was replaying the MedHealth debacle. While saying *I love you* in a business presentation made for story fodder later that day around a dinner table, it wasn't so outrageous that she should keep beating herself up over it.

He bent at the knees. Tried to intercept her gaze so she'd look him in the eye. If only for a moment. "You shouldn't worry so much about what other people think."

She said something under her breath that he thought sounded an awful lot like *like you,* but her voice had been so quiet, he wasn't sure.

She looked down. Shifted to take a step back.

He was losing her.

"I've got to get back to work," she mumbled before breezing past him and scurrying to her desk to duck behind her computer.

What had just happened? Sure, the conversation had started a bit stilted, but he'd thought they were beginning to find a rhythm. Then it screeched to a halt. What had he done? What had he said? How could he fix it?

Bewildered, he returned to his workstation and opened a file in Photoshop that he'd been working on. He tried to focus on blending the images he was manipulating, but his mind kept wandering back to Mackenzie.

She'd looked . . . hurt. And for some reason, he felt guilty. Talking the matter out face-to-face would be no problem—for him. For Mackenzie, though? Well, nothing indicated she'd appreciate a direct confrontation of the issue. In fact, everything pointed to the opposite. So how would he get to the bottom of the problem? How could he find out if Mackenzie was upset with him and then learn from that mistake and make it right?

The icon at the bottom corner of his monitor caught his attention. Every work computer had an in-office messaging system. He clicked on the app, then Mackenzie's name. He thought for a moment about how to phrase what he wanted to say.

> Hi. I can't help but feel like there's something I need to apologize for. If I made you uncomfortable when we were talking, I'm sorry.

He pressed send, then looked up. His workspace was positioned behind Mackenzie's and at an angle. He could see the moment she read his message. Her back tensed, and she chewed on her nail. After a moment, she started typing. Three dots appeared in the message box on his screen.

> You didn't make me uncomfortable.

He felt better than he probably should.

> I'm glad. But I did do something, didn't I? Please tell me so I can learn to do better in the future.

The ellipses returned. Vanished. Started again. Stopped. What was so bad that she had such a hard time saying it?

> It's nothing.

Jeremy's fingers danced on the keyboard.

> It's not nothing. Especially if I hurt your feelings.

You're not going to let this go, are you?

I don't think I can. Or should.

Fine. But it's not a big deal.

Don't downplay my stupidity.

He hoped his self-deprecation put her at ease. A little joke to cut any tension she might be feeling.

Like I said, no big deal, but I overheard you and Lincoln talking about me after the MedHealth pitch.

With clarity, the exchange came flooding back. How he'd mentioned he felt sorry for her because of her visible social discomfort. He winced, sliding down in his chair.

Sitting back up, he pecked at the keys. She'd let him off the hook, but he didn't deserve to be. He deserved to be flogged. Caned. He'd give her a candy cane to hit him with a dozen times. Not really a penance, but it would probably make her laugh. He hated that instead of a smile and a lighter heart, he'd added to her burdens and made her feel worse about herself.

That's a very big deal, and I can't apologize enough. Mackenzie, I am truly sorry.

It's okay.

No, it's not. What can I do to make it up to you? And don't you dare say it's fine or that it's okay again.

The apology is enough. Thank you.

I'll think of a way to make amends. Watch and see.

15

Coming up with a way to even the score with Mackenzie and make amends for the things he and Lincoln had said was harder than Jeremy expected. He'd ended up texting his partner in crime for ideas for punishment equaling the charges against them. Lincoln hadn't been much help, but Jill all too gleefully came up with a plan that she said was poetic justice. A maniacal laugh might have been thrown in, making his brow break out in a cold sweat.

But Jill was right. He and Lincoln had embarrassed Mackenzie further, adding insult to injury. It was only right that they taste the sourness of embarrassment as well. And Jill's idea to perform a dance set to *The Nutcracker* ballet in front of all of his coworkers would do just that.

Jeremy glanced at the clock on his vehicle's dashboard. For the first time since school started, he was ten minutes early for work. Of course it had to happen on the day he willingly (sort of) planned to make a fool of himself. Although being a little late wouldn't have postponed anything. Except maybe the two hours of anticipatory dread he had in front of him. He couldn't march up there and get the whole thing over with because he had to wait for Jill to show up with costumes for him and Lincoln to wear.

He could only blame himself for that one. After Nate's hockey game and the kids falling asleep, he'd gotten to thinking. He didn't know a plié from a relevé, so he'd done what he always did—a little internet research. He'd by no means learned enough to join a dance group, but he now knew a few basic terms and what they meant. He'd even watched a couple of the dances from *The Nutcracker*. The choreography in every one of those dances was beyond him, except perhaps the little children's roles of tiptoeing mice. That, however, wouldn't make the cut. Even he knew that.

But his small dive into the world of dance had led him to the question of wardrobe. Jill had said *the whole nine yards and nothing less*. His pressed Dockers and oxford button-ups wouldn't work while he attempted to arabesque and chassé around the communal desks.

Was dance a sport? That niggling question sent him to the Dick's Sporting Goods website, which confirmed what he'd suspected—a regular sports store didn't sell ballet equipment. If it was even called equipment.

They did, however, sell men's compression pants, which appeared an awful lot like the tights or leotards or whatever male ballet dancers wore.

Those things looked tight. Hence the name, but seriously, they were like a very thin layer of second skin. They conformed to every line and curve of the model's body. *Every* curve. Jeremy would gladly put on a tutu just for a bit of modesty.

He was about to text Jill that there was no way he'd show that much of himself—yes, everything was covered, but everything was also still on display—when she'd beaten him to the punch and texted that she'd gotten what they needed—music and wardrobe—and she'd bring it by Limitless Designs around ten in the morning.

Was this how Mackenzie had felt before the presentation?

No wonder she'd looked and acted so uncomfortable. Did she have to deal with this feeling all the time? How did she manage?

Minute by minute, he supposed. Which was what he'd have to do. He might as well get upstairs and keep himself busy for the next couple of hours. Maybe that way he could avoid dwelling on what he was about to do, then just do it and get it over with.

His dad's turntable lay heavy in his arms as he rode the elevator up to the ninth floor, a canvas bag of albums slung over his shoulder. He was interested to see what songs and artists his coworkers chose. He'd almost bet money on Keri wanting to listen to Bing Crosby and Old Blue Eyes. Annabelle struck him as a Bublé fan. Derek would probably go for the fun kids' classics like John Denver and the Muppets.

The elevator doors slid open, and he stepped out. As he walked over to the tree to set down the record player, he noticed the Mary and Joseph statues from the Nativity hiding under Rosa's chair. Either they were lost, had taken a detour, or directions didn't matter, because they were farther away from "Bethlehem" than they had been the day before. But he imagined Rosa would be happy simply because of the pleasant memories her family tradition brought her and not even think of the logical fallacy in the direction of movement.

He set up the turntable, plugging it into an outlet. He pulled out a random record from the bag—Handel's *Messiah*—and loaded it onto the player. Orchestra music filled the air. Heads turned in his direction.

"I thought it would be fun to listen to Christmas music. Feel free to peruse the albums and make your own selections."

"What a great idea." Sofiya set down her coffee mug and walked over. "I haven't listened to music on vinyl in ages."

Jeremy left her exclaiming over a Beach Boys album. Go figure.

Lincoln intercepted him on his way to his work area. "My wife had a particularly evil glint in her eye when I left the house this morning."

"Did you see what she expects us to wear?" Jeremy whispered, glancing left then right to make sure no other coworkers were within earshot.

"She slapped my hand when I tried to peek inside her bags."

"I brought basketball shorts. Just in case."

Lincoln's eyes widened. "That's smart. I might have a pair in my trunk from the last time I went to the gym."

"I mean, I'll humiliate myself because we both kind of deserve it, but I draw the line at doing something that will require a talk with HR."

"Word."

Jeremy continued down the line of the back bank of office chairs while Lincoln went to the front. A second later, twin gasps shot through the tenor singing "Comfort Ye, My People."

His workstation had been the victim of a festive TPing. Except instead of toilet paper, green and red crepe paper streamers had been used to wrap, crisscross, swag, and all manner of drape until not an inch of his desk was visible. And his chair. His chair had been wrapped in Buddy the Elf wrapping paper and shackled to the table by layers of streamers. Will Ferrell looked up at him with a crazed expression on his face. Jeremy could almost hear him yelling *I love you* three times in increasing volume and speed.

Lincoln's deep laugh interrupted the violin strains coming from the turntable. "Mackenzie, I can't believe you did this." He took out his cell phone and snapped some pictures of his vandalized desk.

Mackenzie gave a shy smile and shrugged a shoulder. "It was fun. Your whole family sounds as impish as you are."

He laughed again. "You have no idea."

So, the Christmas fairy had struck again. And closer to home.

"You too, Lincoln? I thought we were friends, man. You gave up secrets to the enemy, and now she's used them against me." Jeremy winked at Mackenzie so she'd know he was only messing around. He wasn't really upset about the state of his desk or that

Lincoln had spilled his own holiday memories and she'd used them in their race to the top.

Her cheeks flushed, and she ducked her head. Man, he liked her reactions to him. It made him want to tease and flirt to see just how red he could make her skin flush. Not that he would, but the thought was fun to ponder.

"I honestly don't even know how she found out. I was telling Derek yesterday—" Lincoln cut himself off and swung around to face Mackenzie. "I see you and your superpowers of observation as well as stealth listening skills."

Mackenzie held up her palms in a guilty gesture.

"Anyway." Lincoln turned back to Jeremy. "My parents used to decorate and booby-trap my brother's and my doors on Christmas Eve so that on Christmas morning when we opened them, we'd have to free ourselves before stampeding down the stairs to the presents. One time there was an avalanche of balloons waiting for us when we opened the door. Another time it was a spider web of buffalo-plaid duct tape."

"I guess I should feel privileged to be considered your brother today, since my desk got messed with too?"

Lincoln tapped his chest with a closed fist. "That's an everyday privilege, bro."

Annabelle and Rosa said *awww* in unison. A quintet of blended male voices with a Southern California vibe of decades past broke through the moment.

As Jeremy turned, he caught Mackenzie looking at him. He'd noticed a few of her furtive glances before but had never stopped to wonder what she might think of him. As a principle, he tried not to care too much about others' opinions. If he lived his life with integrity, then he shouldn't worry about outside conclusions of his character.

But he did wonder what she thought. He did care about her opinion. Maybe because he was getting to know Mackenzie as more than just the quiet woman at work who kept to herself. She was opening up little by little, and every small taste of her only made him hungry for more.

Her gaze moved back to her computer screen. Jeremy should follow her example and get to work. He had a social media ad campaign graphic to design. The parameters on some of the platforms only allowed for a small percentage of text, so the graphic really needed to catch the consumer's eye as they scrolled.

A couple of hours later, Jill showed up with a bag in each hand. Jeremy saved his document before intercepting her.

"Please tell me there's nothing too shocking in there."

"Just shocking enough." She winked and handed him and Lincoln each a bag.

Lincoln opened the door to the restroom. "I'm pretty sure this question doesn't need to be asked, but have you ever danced before?"

"If you count swaying side-to-side at middle and high school dances." Jeremy eyed Lincoln. "Don't tell me you've got moves hiding behind that flannel."

"Like Jagger." Lincoln brushed at his shoulder. "You remember the talent show in tenth grade? I crushed it with my hip-hop routine." He jumped and spun on his heels.

"I vaguely recall that the only locking and popping happening was everyone's jaws as they dropped in horror when you attempted a jump split."

Lincoln held his arms out wide and started a wave motion from the tips of his left fingers, up and down his arms to his right fingertips, and back again. "Don't hate because you don't have any rhythm, white boy."

Jeremy patted Lincoln's back. "Sure, let's go with that."

They each entered a stall to change into whatever Jill had packed in the bags. Jeremy reached in and pulled out the first item. Unfolding the article of clothing, he let out a sigh of relief. Instead of something half the diameter of one of his thighs that he'd have to try to shove his legs into like a sausage casing, he held up a pair of joggers. The sweatpants were more on the fitted side, but they were still sweatpants. Everything that needed to stay inconspicuous would remain so.

He quickly changed out of his pants, working so none of the material or his sock-clad feet touched the dirty public restroom floor, and slid his legs into the stone-washed grey athletic wear, tying the drawstring at his waist.

With that done, he reached back into the bag. His hand came out grasping a T-shirt at least two sizes too small for his frame. He guessed this was what Jill had meant by nothing *too* shocking.

"Your wife has a wicked sense of humor. And I don't mean that in a New England way either," Jeremy said as he unbuttoned his shirt.

Lincoln laughed. "You have no idea."

Getting into the white cotton shirt turned out to be a workout of its own. Once Jeremy had finally managed to battle the hem down to meet the waistline of the joggers, he was slightly out of breath.

He looked down at himself and bit back a groan. The point of this whole endeavor was to perform an act of embarrassment. Success already, and nobody had even seen him yet. Besides being too tight, the shirt had a deep V-neck, exposing a large patch of chest hair. He wasn't a prude, but he preferred to look a certain way—professionally attired—while in the workplace.

Jeremy clenched his molars. He was going to do this. And not with his head down like he had something to be ashamed of. No, he was going to *own* this ballet. He'd sashay with his shoulders back and pirouette with his chin in the air. He'd look every single person in the eye and dare them to laugh in his face.

Lincoln's stall door opened at the same time Jeremy opened his. Jill hadn't been more kind to one of them than the other. They wore matching outfits.

"Ready to do this?" Jeremy asked.

Lincoln looked down, taking himself in. "Not really."

Jeremy clapped him on the shoulder. "Come on, Jagger, time to get your moves on."

Jill waited for them at the bathroom entrance. When she saw them, her face broke out into a huge grin. "Wait right here. I'll go put the music on. This is going to be so epic."

She hurried over to the record player and loaded an album. "Can I have everyone's attention?"

Heads peeked up behind computers like groundhogs darting from their underground burrows.

"Jeremy and Lincoln would like to perform for you an original dance set to music from *The Nutcracker*." Jill lowered the needle onto the record.

The opening notes of "Dance of the Sugar Plum Fairy" filled the large industrial space. Jeremy rose onto his tippy-toes and took tiny steps, his arms in an arc over his head. When the bassoon played a lower register, Lincoln followed him out, mimicking his moves.

Jeremy had no idea what he was doing as far as the dance was concerned. An internet crash course on ballet could never replace the years of training and discipline it took for real dancers to master the choreography for the actual Sugar Plum Fairy ballet. But that wasn't his goal. If anything, the more he hammed it up, the closer he'd be to his objectives. Yes, plural, because he found he'd added to his original goal of making things right with Mackenzie. Now he also wanted to see her smile. Hear her laugh. And maybe even imbue her with confidence so that the next time she found herself in a situation where she felt embarrassed, she could snub the thoughts of those around her and keep dancing. Figuratively speaking.

Jeremy kicked his leg out as high as he could, which didn't even make a ninety-degree angle. The muscle in his groin protested. Okay, no more of that. He hopped from one foot to the other, trying to stay in time to the bell-like sounds of the song. He made sweeping motions with his hands. Lincoln spun around him in a tight circle. Giggles and undecipherable murmurings drifted to him from their audience.

Jeremy dropped from his toes to a flat-footed position, his arms in a circle in front of him like he was making a hoop for someone to throw a ball into. Up on his toes, then down again. He had no idea if the move was even a real ballet step, but it allowed him to look out and see everyone. As expected, there was a lot of laughter going on. Jill had her phone out and was recording the whole thing. Jeremy found Mackenzie standing in between Keri and Sofiya. Her hands were up and covering the lower portion of her face so he couldn't tell if she was smiling or not. Her eyes were large, as if she were in a state of shock.

He remembered reading that when ballerinas spun, they found a focal point to stare at and always came back with their eyes to that spot so they wouldn't get dizzy. Jeremy focused on Mackenzie's face and spun. His head whipped around to find her again. The skin around the outside of her eyes crinkled, and her shoulders rose and fell in silent laughter.

Lincoln ran into him, causing him to lose his balance and stumble. Lincoln caught his waist to steady him, but then held on. Jeremy gripped Lincoln's wrists to shove him away, but Lincoln stopped him by saying, "Jump."

Jeremy jumped, scissoring his feet in quick succession. He remembered one of the dancers in the videos he'd watched doing something like that.

"Is this song ever going to end?" Lincoln grumbled in his ear.

Finally, the music started to fade. Jeremy and Lincoln bowed in unison. Sofiya darted over to them.

"That was . . ." She laughed. "Well, it's safe to say I've never seen anything like it before."

Jeremy looked around Sofiya to Mackenzie. He didn't want to be rude to his boss, but he really wanted to talk to Mackenzie and apologize face-to-face.

"You've taken the Christmas spirit to a whole new level."

His neck snapped back around to face his boss. Sofiya thought the dance was for the promotion?

"I like the dedication." She looked him up and down, appraising him. "Keep up the good work."

As soon as she walked away, Jeremy headed toward Mackenzie. Keri saw him first. He was afraid she'd cut him off, but she surprised him by saying something to Mackenzie and then walking away.

Mackenzie faced him, her hands folded in front of her. Her head dipped slightly down, but she didn't stare at the floor like he'd seen her do before.

"I told you I'd think of a way to make amends." He slid his hands into his pockets, thankful yet again for the joggers and not tights.

A breath of a laugh escaped her lips. "You did warn me."

"Hey."

At his single word, she looked up and met his gaze. He couldn't believe how careless he'd been to hurt someone so undeserving of his backhanded comments. He only hoped he'd been able to mend any pieces of her he might have broken and vowed he'd never be so negligent in the future.

Staring down at her, he had an overwhelming urge to reach out and trail a finger down her arm. Maybe push back the curtain of hair that sometimes fell to hide her face. He knew she felt more comfortable at the edge of the crowd. In the shadows. But somehow a spotlight had been turned on her for him. One he wasn't quite sure how to turn off.

She tried to look away, but he ducked his head to maintain eye contact. She needed to see he truly meant it when he said, "I'm sorry, Mackenzie."

She opened her mouth to respond, but no sound emitted. "I—" she finally managed to squeak out. Her breathing quickened. Her gaze darted away. "I've got to go."

She turned on her heel and fled.

16

Why can't my brain work normally like everybody else's? Why does it have to short-circuit all the time? Other people would have been able to look at Jeremy after he apologized, after he performed that wonderfully ridiculous dance number, and come up with something to say. Anything would have worked.

A simple *I accept your apology*, for example.

Or *You and Lincoln should take your show on the road*. Friendly teasing to reassure him I don't hold any hard feelings. How can I, after he pranced around the office like a graceless gazelle, flailing around with such confidence? Never once did he appear as if he'd do anything to escape. He *looked* awkward, but nothing in his countenance said he felt uncomfortable with his inelegance. How was that even possible?

He'd stolen the breath right from my lungs the moment he'd tiptoed center stage. For starters, I've never seen so much of Jeremy before. Glimpses of his forearms when he rolls up his sleeves is the extent of skin he normally shows. Who knew he's been hiding such a toned body beneath all his oxford-style dress shirts? But besides the revelation that I'm even more physically attracted to Jeremy than I originally thought, what really made my heart pinch is the fact that he was there because of me. He made a spectacle of himself . . . for me.

Maybe I should be glad the lines of communication between my brain and mouth were momentarily severed. At least I didn't say something I'd regret. Like: *I'll be thinking about this moment for the rest of my life.* Or: *I could easily fall in love with you.* Or even more horrifying: *I might already be halfway there.*

My pulse quickens just thinking such a thing, and I place my hand on my chest, my heart pounding beneath my palm. My fingers shake, so I close them into a fist.

I hate this feeling. This jittering of nerves that overtakes me. How can I ever tell Jeremy about my growing feelings for him if I can't even respond to his apology when he's standing in front of me?

If only I weren't such a train wreck.

I press my back to the wall and slide down until I'm sitting on the hard concrete floor. Like a coward, I'm hiding in the stairwell. I've descended two levels and am tucked into an alcove between the seventh and sixth floors. If Jeremy or Keri come looking for me, they won't be able to see me here. Hopefully they'll assume I went outside for some fresh air.

I take my phone out of my pocket and open the Bible app even though I have the particular verse I want to read memorized. My screen fills with the words from Philippians.

Do not be anxious about anything,

I close my eyes. Take a deep breath in through my nose. Will the swirling chaotic thoughts in my head to still. My erratic pulse to quiet.

Nothing changes. I open my eyes and continue reading.

but in every situation, by prayer and petition, with thanksgiving, present your request to God. And the peace of God, which transcends all understanding, will guard your hearts and your minds in Christ Jesus.

I close my eyes again. This time in prayer.

Lord, please hear my cry like you did David's. He called to You for help, and You healed him. Heal me from my anxiety around people like You healed the woman You called daughter. I know You can, God. I have faith as she did. I know I have no reason to fear because You're with me and have promised to strengthen, help, and uphold me. I'm asking for that now. Give me the peace You promise so my heart doesn't give way to trouble or fears. I know I can't do it alone or in my own power, so I'm asking, I'm begging, please release me from my anxious thoughts and feelings and make me whole.

I wait a moment and then open my eyes, only slightly disappointed at not feeling any differently than I did before I prayed. I always hope I'll experience a surge of power coursing through my body like the woman with the issue of blood must have. I'm not sure how God measures faith, but He must not think I have enough yet because He hasn't answered this particular prayer of mine. No matter how many times I've prayed it.

A door above me opens and closes. I hold still. Embarrassment clings to me that I ran away. If the person in the stairwell is Jeremy, I don't know what I'll say to him.

The sound of feet on steps gets louder. I look up and breathe a sigh when first Keri's ankle boots come into view, then her full swing skirt.

"There you are," she says.

"Here I am."

She takes a seat beside me. "So, that was a crazy performance up there."

"Sure was."

"Want to talk about it?"

I inspect my fingernails. I can't look at Keri. Her voice has taken on that soft, compassionate quality that always makes a lump form in my throat. "What's there to talk about?"

"Well." She drags out the word. "From my perspective, there are two things that could have you holing up down here. One,

Jeremy's production rivaled your Christmas tree, and you're fretting about losing the promotion and raise. On top of that, you're now worrying about how you'll pay for your mom's care."

Gah, I hadn't even thought of that.

"Or," she continues, "you see Jeremy's performance as a grand gesture on scale with Heath Ledger serenading Julia Stiles in *10 Things I Hate About You*."

I pick at my cuticle. "Why would you think his dance had anything to do with me?"

Her stare burns the side of my head. "Girl, he literally only had eyes for you. Did you not notice how he used you as a focal point when he did those awful pirouettes?" She makes a humming sound as she studies me. "I thought so." After a moment, she asks, "What did you say when he came over to talk to you?"

I give a self-derisive snort. "I said, and I quote, 'I've got to go.' Then I turned and literally ran away."

"Oh, honey." She wraps her arms around me.

I lay my head on her shoulder. "Do you think it's possible for me to get to the point where I'll be able to communicate with a guy the way a healthy relationship requires?"

She smooths the hair from my brow. "I know you will. It'll just take some patience on both of your parts."

"I can't imagine I'd need to exercise much patience with Jeremy."

"He's a man, so yes, you will, but"—she moves so I'll look at her—"I meant you need to be patient with yourself, Kenz." Her blue eyes dart between my own. "Give yourself a break, okay?"

I try to smile, but my lips wobble. "Okay."

"About Saturday night." She sighs. "I'll understand if you don't—"

"I'll go." I surprise us both by interrupting.

"You will?" Her eyebrows rise.

Already my pulse is picking up speed. My mouth floods, and I swallow. My body is sending out its high-alert signals to flee the situation. Instead, I nod. If I'm ever going to get to the point where I can look Jeremy in the eye for longer than three seconds or hold a conversation that lasts past half a dozen exchanges, then I can't avoid every social situation that makes me uncomfortable. I need to strengthen my people-skills muscles. Maybe then, eventually, I'll be able to confess the secret feelings I've been harboring for him. Maybe then some of my daydreams could become a reality.

"And I think we should go shopping tonight. Get presents for the community kids so we can wrap them and turn them in tomorrow, but also maybe pick out a new outfit as well?"

She eyes me up and down. "Who are you thinking of going as?"

"Me," I say. "I think I'll dress as myself this time."

She gives me a squeeze. "I've always liked you best of all."

W hat do you think of this?" I step out of the dressing room and hold my arms to the sides. I have on an emerald-green sweater dress that skims the tops of my knees. The waist is cinched in with a wide black belt that gives the cable-knit material the illusion of shape.

"Gem tones are for sure your color palette." Keri eyes me up and down. "All you need are some black leggings under that and your knee-high boots, and you're all set."

I'm not sure *all set* is the phrase I'd use, since nerves have burrowed into my stomach and decided to make it their permanent home. But I like the dress. It's comfortable and, more importantly, I feel comfortable in it. One less thing to worry about come Saturday night, since I know my headspace is already going to be overcrowded with too many thoughts about trying to keep the conversation flowing instead of acting like a beaver and damming it up with my awkwardness. It's a date with training wheels, so to speak, but if I crash and burn instead of learning to pedal on my own, then I'll never be able to ride the bike I really have my heart set on—Jeremy.

Oh, wow. That's not what I meant at all. Sugar cookies, I need to work on my metaphors. I can*not* say stuff like *that* out loud.

I shut the changing room door behind me and put back on my jeans and Packers hoodie. I wanted to watch the football game with Mom, but after how she was on Tuesday, I thought it might be a good idea to call ahead and see what kind of day she was having. Gabriella told me Mom had been agitated most of the day, and she didn't think it would be a good idea to add any more stimulus to her environment.

I run my hand over the green-and-gold embossed stitching of the football team's name, sending up a prayer for my mom. Tears prick my eyes, but I blink them back.

I suck in a breath and exhale on a tremble, flicking my wrists in an attempt to shake off the anxious energy beginning to travel my spine like an interstate highway. Mom always told me not to borrow tomorrow's trouble, but I can never seem to help myself. The same creative imagination that allows me to design intricate and complex renderings also has a dark side: the ability to think up multiple conclusions to any scenario. And those conclusions aren't always so happy.

Folding the dress, I exit the changing area and then pay for it. Keri is looking at a rack of accessories when I tuck the receipt into the bag.

"Is there anything you want to shop for?" I ask.

"Yes. I'm dying for a Cinnabon."

There aren't any lines when we arrive at the food court, but the majority of the tables are filled. After we order, Keri runs to the restroom, and I assure her I'll grab the cinnamon rolls and find us a seat. I have to serpentine around people and tables but finally find an open spot near the middle of the dining area.

The smell of warm, yeasty, cinnamon-filled dough and melty, gooey cream cheese frosting makes my mouth water. I pinch off a piece with my fingers and stuff it in my mouth. My eyes roll into the back of my head. So good.

Suddenly, a man at the table to my left stands, uses his chair as a step, and climbs on top of the table.

What in the world? People start to notice, and conversations begin to die down.

In a loud voice, he sings out in a rich, smooth tenor, "We wish you a merry Christmas." He holds the last note.

The woman to my right follows his moves, and soon she's on her table, adding her voice to his. "We wish you a merry Christmas."

Stomping of feet in front and behind. Two more people on top of tables. I am literally surrounded by a quartet towering over me, drawing the attention of everyone in the vicinity. I slouch farther down in my seat, but I can feel them. I can feel all the eyes of everyone watching. My skin flushes.

"We wish you a merry Christmas and a happy New Year."

A flash mob.

I'm stuck smack in the middle of a food court flash mob. My throat goes dry. I know I'm physically safe, but I feel as if I'm being circled by sharks. Like I'm in the center of a tornado swirling all around me. A sharknado.

I look for a way to escape, to slide unnoticed from the spotlight these singers are creating. I stand, but I'm not the only one. As if choreographed, a few others around me also rise.

In perfect harmony, voices blend. "Joy to the world, the Lord is come."

The man behind me lays down a beat using only his vocals. A soprano beside me sings out in a ringing tone, "Let Earth receive her king."

This is not the rendition sung for decades in church or by those caroling door-to-door. The lyrics are the same, but the beat is new, fresh, and much quicker than the old hymn. The singers begin to sway their bodies.

I take two steps to the left, but my escape closes as a man steps off his table and turns to the crowd gathering and growing larger by the second. People along the periphery hold up cell phones to record the spontaneous spectacle, in which I'm stuck as an unwilling participant. I spin around, hoping to slip through the other side, but the a cappella flash mob pins me in. My head whips to the other side. Back again. I'm getting dizzy.

"Let every heart prepare him room."

My heart feels like there is less and less room in it. Each beat comes quicker. Louder. It could be a back-up to the beatbox guy.

The group moves as one, and then individually they spin and repeat, "Let heaven and nature sing" until they all join their voices together again.

I'm like Dick Van Dyke in *Chitty Chitty Bang Bang*, caught up in a song-and-dance number, the old bamboos blocking every means of exit. Except, unlike Dick Van Dyke, I don't magically learn the lyrics or the steps of the dance and then steal the show in the end.

In fact, the only thing being stolen is my breath. Why is it so hard to fill my lungs right now? I can't seem to take in enough oxygen. I need to slow my breathing, slow my pulse, but both have run away from me.

My fingers begin to tingle, then shake. Again, I whip my head around, but all I see is faces. A sea of faces. Laughing, pointing, cell phones recording. The room spins, a carousel of people pulsating the air around me. I can see lips moving, but the chatter is a hum beneath the concert I can't escape from. The static in my ears swells.

Panic is clawing its way up my breastbone while control slips from my fingertips.

I *know* I'm not in any real danger.

I *know* nothing horrible is waiting in the wings to pounce on me.

I *know* I'm overreacting.

But I can't shut off my brain.

I can't rein in my body.

I need it to stop.

God, please make it stop.

"Joy to the world!" The song ends on a staccato, and the silence is immediately followed by applause. The man to my left shifts forward, creating a gap. Somehow, I manage to grab my packages, jacket, and the cinnamon rolls before I dart through the opening.

I need to get out of here. The thought replays in my mind on repeat. Nothing else matters but getting someplace else. Anywhere else.

The automatic doors slide open to the outside.

"Mackenzie!"

I hear Keri call, but I don't stop. The cold air burns my throat as I take in quick gulps through my mouth. My forehead is colder along my hairline, and I realize I've been sweating.

A warm hand touches my back. "Hey. Are you okay?"

Tears spring to my eyes for no real reason. Maybe all the adrenaline that flushed my system decides to hang ten through my tear ducts. I don't know. I've never understood why I react the way I do in what I know are benign situations.

I force myself to smile even though it comes out wobbly and my vision is swimming. "I'm fine."

Keri pulls me over to a bench. The cold seeps through my jeans when I sit, but it feels good against my flushed skin. Tiny snowflakes fall, only visible under the yellow glow of the streetlights illuminating the parking lot.

People exit the mall, excited chatter about the impromptu serenade hovering in the air with their breath. Everywhere around me, things move. People. Cars. Snow. I shut my eyes and search for some stillness. Some peace.

Where is Your peace, God?

"Want to talk about what just happened?" Keri asks.

I open my eyes.

She takes the rolls and packages from me and sets them on

the other side of her. My jacket is wrapped around my shoulders. I pull the down coat closed at my middle and fold my body, hunching my shoulders.

Keri retrieves the cinnamon rolls and hands me mine. "Take a bite," she commands. "The sugar might help."

Dutifully, I comply. My teeth sink into the baked treat, sugar and spice playing on my tongue.

"Better?" she asks after I've eaten almost half of my roll.

I nod, though I curl into myself more.

"Good. Now talk." She's turned into an interrogating bad cop, and I know I'm not going to be allowed to leave without some sort of explanation. She has the keys to the car, after all.

I shrug, hoping she'll deescalate from her bloodhound stance. "I just got a little overwhelmed is all."

One sculpted brow rises in a pointed manner. "A little over-whelmed? Honey, even I could tell you were having a panic attack."

I shrug again.

Keri sighs. Looks away. Looks back at me. "I'm guessing this isn't the first time this has happened. Have you seen anyone about it? Talked to anyone?"

"I'm talking to you," I offer.

Her lips thin.

I sigh. "I talk to God in prayer about it all the time." The white huff of breath my words travel on barely leaves my mouth before dissipating.

"Good. That's good." She nods, and I think that's it.

I'm wrong.

"What about a professional?" she presses.

I slide my arms into the sleeves of my coat, then zip it up. "I just need to have more faith. God can take away my anxiety."

She blinks at me like I'm back in my Star Trek outfit, speaking Klingon, so I try again.

"'If you have faith as small as a mustard seed, you can say

to this mountain, "Move from here to there," and it will move. Nothing will be impossible for you,'" I quote from the book of Matthew. "Three times Jesus told those He'd healed that it was their faith that made them whole. See? I just need to have more faith." My eyes warm with a rush of fresh tears. I widen them, hoping the cold air will dry them out. I don't want to cry anymore.

"Mackenzie." Keri says my name in a way that pleads with me to look at her.

Slowly I turn my head and raise my gaze. Her nose is pink. I'd think the cold air the culprit if not for the telltale sheen making her own eyes glisten.

She takes my hand and holds it between hers. "If I were to slip on black ice right now and land so hard that I either sprained my ankle or broke it, and we didn't know which, what would you do?"

I cock my head, trying to figure out where she's going with this question. "I'd take you to the emergency room to get an x-ray."

"To a professional," she reiterates. "Because something is wrong, and it needs to be checked out by a doctor so it can heal properly."

She lets her statement hang so it can seep in. I hear what she's saying. I do. But there isn't anything physically wrong with me. This is different.

"Your brain is a part of your body, Kenz," she says as if she's read my mind yet again. "If you'd see a doctor for your ankle or when you're sick, then what's the difference about seeking professional help for your mental health? Would you leave an infection to fester and eventually kill you when you could get antibiotics, even though God could heal you of the infection? And He could. I won't argue that He isn't all-powerful. But He also created us with brains. Scientific brains that led to the discovery and creation of antibiotics and other medicines to help heal us of all kinds of things." She squeezes my hand. "Even mental health things."

"So," I say slowly, "you're saying some healings come from prayer and faith and others modern medicine?"

"Not really. I'm saying all healing comes from prayer and faith but that God uses doctors and medicine as His hands to perform the healing." She waves a hand in the air. "Or something like that. You know I'm not one to philosophize. I just think the stigma of mental health needs to end." She bumps me with her shoulder. "And I think you need to talk with someone about your social anxiety."

God uses people. Why haven't I ever considered such a thing before? Even in the Bible, after Jesus ascended into heaven, the apostles healed in Jesus's name.

Keri stands and blows air into her cupped hands. "Let's find warmth before we turn into popsicles. Come on, it's freezing out here."

She's right yet again.

18

Snow must have fallen steadily all night because the ground has been covered in a blanket of white. The sun has yet to rise from its nighttime slumber, but the streetlights cast a warm glow on the holiday postcard picture.

Things seem extra still and calm after a snowfall. Why is that? Maybe the pristine white makes everything feel dreamlike and magical, like endless possibilities wait within reach, and it's up to us what type of tracks we want to leave in our wake.

I breathe in snow's familiar and distinct scent. I've never been able to describe it, but I could recognize that scent anywhere. I fill my lungs, breathe in all the possibilities, and thank God for a new day. A new beginning. A fresh start. As fresh as the undisturbed first snowfall of the season.

Last night I made an appointment to speak to a therapist. I didn't even have to pick up a phone or dial a number. They had the appointment forms on their website. It sounds silly, but not having to call is a huge relief, and the fact that things were accessible online makes me feel like the therapist will understand me a bit better. I'm still nervous, though. It's still talking to a stranger face-to-face, after all. That always makes me uneasy.

But I'm also hopeful. Maybe I won't be miraculously healed, but perhaps I'll learn more about God, myself, my brain, and how to better process and cope with the world around me.

Basically, I'm hoping not to be quite such a hot mess.

"I'm going to drop this stuff off upstairs." I indicate the bags of things we bought for our Christmas children. Jeremy is collecting them all today to deliver later. "Then I'll meet you in the empty lot next door." We decided not to let the fresh blanket of snow go to waste. What is holiday cheer without building our own Frosty?

Keri agrees, and I hurry upstairs, thankful that Sofiya always arrives early so I can get into the office. She's typing away on her computer. I don't want to disturb her. I also don't want to get pulled into a conversation when Keri is waiting for me, so I slink through the office and gently set down the bags so I don't make any noise.

My gaze snags on miniature Mary and Joseph where I left them yesterday on their journey to Bethlehem. Taking a figurine in each hand, I move them to the top of the refrigerator. My placements of them have been quite random, but they are steadily getting closer to the manger and nativity.

I push the button for the elevator, then listen to the gears grinding on the other side of the stainless-steel doors. The conveyance settles, and the doors open. Jeremy stands on the other side, his hands full with a Crock-Pot and grocery bags hanging from his arms.

"What are you doing here?" The words jump out of my mouth before I can reel them back in.

He smiles, the corners of his eyes crinkling. "Good morning to you, too."

I step out of his way so he can exit the elevator. "Sorry. I didn't mean that. I meant, good morning, you're here early."

He sets the Crock-Pot on the counter. "I could say the same

thing about you. Is the Christmas fairy out sprinkling her magic, impressing bosses and scoring more points?"

I search his words and tone for any bite, but they seem innocuous. Maybe even a bit endearing. Then again, that's probably just my wishful thinking.

I don't know why I suspect an undertone of anything other than friendly mock feuding. When Sofiya first told us we were pitted against each other for the job, I worried things would get gloves-off heated. At least on Jeremy's side, since I'm the type to run from confrontation, not go at it head-on. I mean, I didn't *want* to think he'd turn into someone who'd do anything to win, but I also knew he really wanted the job. Then when I found out about Nathan and Natalie, I knew he really *needed* the job.

So perhaps I've been waiting for that no-holds-barred moment. For the sweet man I've observed from a distance to change. But being thrust into Jeremy's path, each of us forced to allow space for the other in our lives, hasn't changed the way I see him at all. The things I admired about him from a distance have only magnified upon closer inspection. My feelings have only deepened. Our story hasn't gone from wallflower to enemies to more. If anything, it has the potential to grow from secret crush to unrequited love.

Leaning around him, I peer into the Crock-Pot. "What's in here?"

He lifts the lid. A plume of sweet, creamy, chocolaty goodness rises to my face. "Homemade hot chocolate."

I tilt my chin so I can look at him but also still inhale the mouth-watering aroma.

My thoughts must be written on my face again, because he laughs. "I learned from the bakery mistake. Although I can't take full credit for the hot chocolate because it's my mom's recipe." He puts the lid back on, then starts unloading the grocery bags. Mini marshmallows. Candy canes. Whipped cream. Caramel sauce.

Cayenne pepper. Any add-in you can think of for hot chocolate is lined up on the counter.

"I never wanted to be your rival," I blurt out.

He turns, his light-brown eyes steady on me. My face heats and my skin tingles. This is where I normally turn away. Retreat. Instead, I force my tongue to cooperate.

"I know Sofiya chooses who to promote based on who has the most Christmas spirit. Everyone knows. But I wasn't going to play along."

His head tilts just a fraction. I've seen him do this before. Usually when he's considering a new idea. "You weren't?"

I shake my head. "I hoped you wouldn't jump through her hoops either and we'd force her to decide on merit alone."

His smile is crooked. "That would've been smart."

We get caught up in each other's gazes, and for the first time, Jeremy is the one to look away first. He clears his throat. "Then I brought the pomander balls."

I remember smelling the citrus and spice on him when Keri deserted me and forced me to ride the elevator with him alone. Glorious torture, if ever there was such a thing. Orange and cloves may forever be my new favorite scent combination.

"Even after you laid down the gauntlet . . ." My brows do a sort of lift thing of their own accord.

Oh my goodness. Did I just attempt to flirt? My cheeks get even hotter. My internal temperature is set to broil.

I try again. "Even after that, I . . . What I'm trying to say is . . . um . . ."

Shoot! I was doing so well there for half a second, too.

"We both have our reasons for wanting this promotion." He pauses. Watches me.

Mom. I have to get the raise so Mom can receive the care she needs. The actual job—the client-relations and leadership parts—scares me out of my wits. But for Mom, I'll do anything.

"Let's make a promise. No matter who Sofiya appoints, there

won't be any hard feelings on either side." He holds out his hand. "Deal?"

I slide my palm against his. In a weird sort of reverse, it's not my hand in his that tingles. It's the skin not being touched that responds like a starving street beggar holding up his bowl. My arms are on their proverbial knees, imploring for just a caress from his fingertips. My neck whispers a plea to feel his warm breath against it. My face longs to be cradled between his hands. My lips—oh, my lips ache with the need to feel weight upon them. The weight of Jeremy's kiss.

He holds on to my hand longer than necessary for a simple shake. I risk a look into his face, afraid he can feel my pulse pounding through my fingertips or see my thoughts in my eyes.

His head is tilted again, his clear eyes cloudy as if he's confused about something. His gaze drops from my eyes to . . . my mouth? His grip tightens a fraction, pulling me toward him, but then immediately releases my hand.

He takes a step back and runs his fingers through his hair. "Good. I'm glad we got that settled."

I barely register his words as I'm staring at the top of his head. Jeremy never runs his fingers through his hair. He's raised his hand as if he's meant to a few times, but he always stops himself before his fingers touch a single strand. What does it mean that he didn't stop himself this time?

My cell vibrates in my pocket. It's Keri, wondering what's taking me so long. I hook a thumb over my shoulder. "I've got to . . ." I walk backward a few steps before turning around.

One thing's for certain: touching Jeremy was a bad idea. Like the key to Pandora's box twisting and opening the lid. How am I supposed to keep all these feelings stuffed inside now?

19

Stick to the plan. Jeremy had told himself those exact words no less than a dozen times as laughter climbed the air and slipped through the walls of the brick building, taunting him as he plucked away at his keyboard. He'd undone more than he'd accomplished on his design, but he refused to budge from his seat even though everyone else in the office was in the empty lot next door, making snowmen and hitting one another with snowballs in a massive winter war.

Sofiya was normally a stickler for productive hours at work, but today she'd smiled like a benevolent queen and declared a late start to the workday so everyone could play in the fresh snow. Only in December would Sofiya cast her normal standards aside in favor of fun and frivolity.

Another chorus of laughter echoed through the empty room, making Jeremy clench his teeth and fumble his fingers.

Another wrong keystroke. Delete. Delete.

It wasn't that he didn't know how to have a good time or was a workaholic. Those weren't the reasons he refused to go outside and join the others. He didn't trust himself. For the first time in a long time, he didn't trust himself to stick to the plan.

When he'd held Mackenzie's hand, a shockwave had traveled up his arm. Like an earthquake shaking the ground, something in him had cracked open, dislodging blinders that had been covering his eyes. He didn't know how else to describe it. How could he look at someone he'd seen almost every day for years and suddenly see her so differently?

But maybe it had been more gradual than he'd realized. Bit by bit as he'd gotten to know her better. So slow that the knowing had snuck up on him unawares until, boom, he couldn't look away. Step away. Let her go.

Stick to the plan.

He pulled out his wallet and opened the trifold. With cell phone picture galleries, no one really carried around printed photos anymore, but he'd always been a little old-fashioned when it came to sentimentalities. The frayed corner of the wallet-sized photo protruded from a side panel, and he tugged it loose.

Heidi lay in a hospital bed, a newborn on each arm, with Jack grinning like a fool beside her. Nate and Nat were so tiny. He remembered the first time he held them, the first time they wrapped their little fingers around his. He'd been a goner in seconds.

When Heidi died, they'd been so little. He'd had no idea what he was doing. Being a fun uncle was worlds different from being a single caregiver. More days than he'd like to admit, he'd fallen into bed too exhausted even to shower or take off his shoes before he started snoring.

The twins were older now. They didn't need him physically quite as much, but he knew the teen years were going to bring their own reasons for exhaustion. His niece and nephew still needed him as much now as they did then. And he'd made a promise and commitment to them and to Heidi. It wouldn't be fair to deviate from his plan or let his focus, time, or attention shift in any way.

Which was why he'd added a clause to his work plan—keep his distance from Mackenzie.

It shouldn't be that hard. Before the promotion announcement, they'd hardly spoken to each other. He'd just have to return to the old status quo.

And ignore any ideas of hanging mistletoe around the office to catch her under. He remembered the way her lips looked earlier as they shook on their deal not to harbor any hard feelings no matter who got the promotion. They had parted slightly, almost in invitation, and he'd felt himself tilting forward. It would have been so easy to pull on her hand so she stumbled against his chest. He'd hold her close. Dip his head. Taste. Test. See if the earth would shake again the moment his mouth covered hers.

He raked his fingers through his hair, his mind catching up with his movements a second later. He held his palm out in front of his face and stared at the guilty culprit. He'd broken himself of that habit of frustration years ago. Now he'd mussed his hair twice in one morning. Control was literally slipping through his fingers.

The elevator opened its doors. Keri, Mackenzie, Frank, and Lincoln exited amid animated chatter. Their noses were red, attesting to the cold outdoors.

Jeremy met them near the kitchenette. "You guys want some hot chocolate to warm you up?"

Keri tugged at her gloves. "Do you have whipped cream to go on top?"

Like a game show announcer, he swung his arm to reveal all the toppings lined up. "I have everything I could think of that a person might want in their hot chocolate."

Mackenzie unwrapped a scarf from around her neck. "He even has candy canes. If you mix the hot chocolate with some coffee and let a candy cane dissolve inside, I bet it would taste like a peppermint mocha."

Keri's eyes widened. "You're a genius."

Mackenzie hung her jacket on the coat rack while Frank hovered nearby, tugging on the sleeve of his own coat. "I've been meaning to ask you," he said to Mackenzie as he freed an arm. "You've been recreating all these childhood memories for everyone else. When is it going to be ole Frank's turn?"

Mackenzie pivoted to face him, a tight smile on her face. "What are some of your fondest memories of the holidays, Frank?"

Jeremy grabbed a mug from the cabinet. He wasn't intentionally eavesdropping, but he couldn't help overhearing their conversation either.

Frank rubbed his chin. "Well, it's not a memory exactly. More something I've always dreamed of doing."

"What's that?" Mackenzie asked somewhat warily.

"I've always wanted to dress up as Santa Claus. Maybe for the office party. Then all you lovely ladies can sit on my lap. That would make Santa really jolly." He hung up his coat, putting him even closer to Mackenzie.

Frank's suggestive tone made Jeremy slam his mug on the counter. Four pairs of eyes stared at him. "My bad." But he wasn't sorry in the least.

Mackenzie continued to look at him long after everyone else. He read the gratitude in her eyes, and his insides warmed even without the hot beverage.

She returned her attention to Frank. "I'm sorry, but that won't be possible. Did you have a favorite Christmas treat growing up? Reindeer chow or peppermint bark or chocolate fudge, maybe? I can make you something like that."

Frank considered her. "Can you make a caramel slice? My grandmother used to make them every year, and I haven't had one since she passed."

Mackenzie's face softened. "I'm sure I can. I'll just need to find a recipe."

Keri sidled up to Jeremy. "I'm surprised he didn't ask her to put up mistletoe and then manage to steal a kiss from every woman in the office." Disgust dripped from her words.

Jeremy hid his face behind his mug. Keri was astute enough to read the guilt there if she looked. His own thoughts of mistletoe rang in his head.

She peered up at him, cast her gaze toward Mackenzie, then looked at him again. Her lips curled. "Then again, maybe a small, discreet mistletoe bundle, one that only a few people knew the location of, wouldn't be such a bad thing."

Jeremy choked on a sip of chocolate.

Keri patted his arm. "Easy there, tiger. Someone might suspect you're flustered for some reason."

Jeremy swallowed, then licked his lips. "And what reason would that be?" He met her challenging gaze with one of his own.

She shrugged before looking back over at Mackenzie. "Maybe time will tell." She lifted her cup. "Thanks for the drink."

Everyone seemed to love the hot chocolate bar, especially Sofiya. She put a little of everything in her cup, and Jeremy had to press a hand on his stomach to keep it from rolling. Even so, his Christmas activity for the day was a success.

He'd celebrate, but he'd lost his enthusiasm for keeping score. Otherwise, he'd add another tally mark to his side of the leaderboard. He had a sinking suspicion, though, that no matter which of them won, they'd both also have lost.

"Hey, Jeremy." Rosa walked over to him later that day after lunch. "I have the gift for my Christmas child. Did you bring wrapping paper?"

He snapped his fingers. "I left it in the car. Let me go grab all the supplies."

He took the elevator down to the parking lot, quickly retrieved the rolls of wrapping paper, tape, scissors, and gift bags from the back of his SUV, then returned upstairs.

"Oh, good," Mackenzie said as she walked over to him. "I need to wrap my gifts, too."

The space in front of the Christmas tree turned into Santa's little workshop. Ribbons lined the floor. Bows were scattered in a semicircle. Rolls of wrapping paper leaned haphazardly against the wall. Mackenzie selected a red-and-white-striped bow, but instead of sticking it on her gift, she placed the swirled ribbon on her head, holding her arms out wide as she said something to Rosa that caused the other woman to laugh.

As he was realizing more each day, Mackenzie had been keeping the different sides of herself hidden. At work, she'd always tended to be quiet and shy, but watching her now, she obviously had a fun and playful side as well.

But no matter how tempting she looked as a gift that could quite possibly be perfect for him, he couldn't allow himself to discover just how fun she could be.

The weekend was just around the corner. He had that blind date Alejandro had set him up on the next day. A reminder that his social life had already been planned out. As in, to not have one. Although he knew that hadn't been his friend's intention.

Jeremy watched Mackenzie throw her head back and laugh in almost carefree abandon. His chest swelled.

What if he gave himself one day? A few hours to forget that he didn't have room in his life for a relationship and give in to his growing attraction to Mackenzie. Letting his guard down and enjoying her presence would by no means get her out of his system, but maybe it would be the bolster of strength he'd need to resist her in the future. Plus, he'd have all weekend to gather his resolve and shore up his determination.

Before his thoughts even had time to settle, his feet took him in her direction. She looked up at him from her position on the floor, her smile at what she'd been laughing at still on her lips.

Jeremy leaned down and reached around her, his hand on her shoulder in the guise of needing her to help him keep his balance. She inhaled a sharp breath as he let his thumb trail the wing of her shoulder blade as he stood back up.

He looked at the long roll of wrapping paper in his hand.

Bears with Christmas sweaters and festive hats marched along the parchment with the words *Beary Christmas*.

"When I was a kid . . ." he began.

Mackenzie perked up. He knew those words would get her attention. She seemed to love all things relating to family holiday traditions.

He moved the roll to his other hand. "My sister and I would pretend we were pirates, the presents our treasure, and sword fight each other to see who got to discover what the hidden treasure was first." He looked at Mackenzie and Rosa and winked. "Meaning whoever won got to open the first gift."

"How'd you determine the winner?" Rosa asked.

"Well, we used empty wrapping paper rolls, so whoever's broke first lost."

Mackenzie reached for a roll of wrapping paper. She rose slowly, never taking her eyes from Jeremy's. When she gained her feet, she went into a fencing position, the cardboard tube held out in front of her like a rapier and her other arm curled up behind her head.

"Hello, my name is Mackenzie Graham. You're trying to take my job. Prepare to lose."

Her Spanish accent and Inigo Montoya impersonation were so bad, and yet she was so cute doing them. Jeremy had a hard time keeping a straight face. The first thing that popped into his head was to respond with a bow and the iconic line from the movie, "As you wish." But everyone who'd ever seen *The Princess Bride* knew those three words represented another, more meaningful trio—"I love you." Better to respond with something that had no hidden meanings at all. That kept this thing between them light and fun.

Only today, he reminded himself.

He screwed up his lips and held himself with an air of self-importance. "The thing that bwings us togeder todaaay is Chwissmas."

Mackenzie's lips twitched as she tried to keep from laughing. Rosa, on the other hand, had no such restraint, her high-pitched gales following a pig-like snort. Both Jeremy and Mackenzie swung their gazes toward Rosa, which caused her to snort again, then cover her mouth with her hand.

Laughter bubbled in Jeremy's chest, getting harder to contain by the second. He made the mistake of glancing at Mackenzie. Their eyes locked, and they both erupted.

It took a few moments for both of them to catch their breath, but then Mackenzie raised her tube back into a fighting position, her brows following the motion in challenge.

He lifted his own weapon. "En garde."

The attacks were slow and exaggerated to start, easily blocked by both of them. In his peripheral vision, Jeremy noticed they had a crowd gathering to watch their antics. Mackenzie didn't seem to note the extra pairs of eyes on them and swung her wrapping paper roll at his head.

He ducked and grinned at her. "Trying to give me a haircut?"

"Why would I mess with perfection?" Her roll wobbled as soon as the last syllable left her lips. Her eyes widened. "I didn't mean—"

Jeremy chuckled. "Perfection, huh?"

She sealed her mouth, her lips disappearing she pressed them together so tightly. Probably afraid to let any other words slip out. Too bad. Jeremy wouldn't have minded hearing what else she thought of him besides how much she liked his hair. If he was only going to allow himself this one day, he might as well make it count.

With that thought humming in his ears, he advanced his pursuit, pushing her back with the thrusts of his cardboard tube. Her back hit a wall. Their swords crossed under Mackenzie's chin.

He was so close now that his shoes butted up against hers. He could smell the peppermint on her breath from when she must have brushed her teeth after lunch. "Now I have you where I want you."

Her chest rose and fell in quick succession. A product of their proximity or from their play sword fight?

"My back against a wall?" she asked breathlessly.

He let his gaze roam her face. He'd never have another opportunity like this. Never let himself get this close again. "In my sights with no obstacles in the way."

Her owl-like eyes looked up at him in wonder. He felt the same sentiment ballooning behind his sternum. Wonder. Amazement. Christmas might come every year, but a woman like Mackenzie only came along once in a lifetime.

20

Jeremy was not looking forward to this date. He'd much rather lounge around the house in a pair of sweatpants and get caught up on episodes of *The Mandalorian*. When he'd said as much to his mom, she'd patted his cheeks and told him that was part of the problem.

Of course, everyone thought his lack of participation in the dating scene was a problem. He didn't see it that way. Except for recently, he'd been completely satisfied with how he filled his days. Work. Hockey practice and games for Nathan. Violin lessons for Natalie plus community theater camps throughout the year. Orthodontist appointments. Parent-teacher conferences. Church.

His life was filled. Which no one argued, but they always replied, was it *fulfilling*?

He wasn't as sure on that point as he had been. His growing awareness of Mackenzie had awakened a longing within him he hadn't even known he'd buried. Letting his guard down the day before had been like hydroplaning in a car. He'd momentarily lost his grip on the steering wheel of his life, and he was having a hard time forcing it back onto the road it needed to travel.

But he would. He had the rest of the night and all of tomorrow to get his head back on straight. Then, when he saw Mackenzie at work on Monday, he could ignore whatever feelings she brought to the surface in him.

In the meantime, he'd put on his best manners, a convincing smile, and be a wingman for one of his best friends.

Jeremy pulled into the Italian restaurant Alejandro had chosen. As soon as he stepped inside, he was welcomed by the warmth of air and atmosphere. Amber Edison bulbs hung from beams in the ceiling, and a textured plaster coated the walls, bringing the Mediterranean feel more than stenciled grapes ever could. The scent of rich, tangy tomato sauce mingled with the bite of garlic in the air. Jeremy's stomach rumbled. Even if the woman Alejandro had set him up with turned out to be awful—and secretly he hoped she would so his friends never got the idea to set him up again—at least he'd get a good meal out of the deal.

The hostess at the podium smiled at him. "Do you have a reservation?"

Alejandro stood from a table draped in white linen and raised his hand. Jeremy nodded at him. "My friend is right there," he told the hostess.

She looked back, then stepped out of his way. "Have a nice meal."

Jeremy thanked her and made his way past others enjoying various types of pasta.

"Glad you could make it." Alejandro slapped Jeremy on the back before both men took their seats.

Jeremy looked around. "I take it the ladies aren't here yet?"

Alejandro shook his head, his fingers drumming on the table. "Not yet."

Jeremy zeroed in on his friend's hands. Alejandro noticed his pointed gaze and stopped tapping. But then the table linen started shaking around him.

Jeremy smirked. "Nervous?"

Alejandro stilled his bouncing leg. "Is it that noticeable?"

"Relax, man." Jeremy leaned back in his chair. "You're a great guy. If this woman can't see that, then she doesn't deserve you."

Alejandro exhaled. "Thanks."

"Tell me about her," Jeremy said, hoping talking would distract his friend. "You met her at work, right? What's she like?"

Alejandro's face lit up like the Christmas tree at Rockefeller Center. "I have never met another woman like her. I know that's cliché, but it's true."

Jeremy nodded. "What makes her so special?"

Alejandro thought a moment. "She is a walking contradiction, but then again, not."

"How's that possible?"

He held up his hands. "I don't know. She looks one way but then talks and acts another. She dresses like an actress from a show on Nick at Nite but then talks like she learned at the feet of Ruth Bader Ginsburg."

Funny. That sounded an awful lot like—

Alejandro shot up like a rocket, the backs of his knees knocking into his chair. "Here she comes."

Jeremy stood, then turned. All the moisture in his mouth dried at the sight of the woman making her way toward the table, another following in her shadow.

Keri blinked at him before a grin played at her lips. She shifted her gaze to Alejandro, and her features softened. It looked like the interest between the two went both ways. Jeremy relaxed slightly. At least he didn't need to worry on that front.

Keri still stood in front of the mystery woman. All he could make out was the long sleeve of a green knitted sweater and a pair of brown leather boots. Was Mackenzie his date for the evening? Did he want her to be?

His brain said no. He needed the whole weekend to get himself back in line. If Mackenzie stepped out from behind Keri, it'd be much more difficult to remain committed to his long-term plan.

His heart told his brain to shove it.

Keri whispered something to Alejandro, then shifted to the side. Standing there, looking more beautiful than should be legal, was Mackenzie. Her eyes widened when she saw Jeremy, surprise then a flash of fear streaking across her face. She shot a look at Keri before her lips wobbled into a smile.

"Seems like everyone already knows one another." Alejandro pulled out a chair for Keri.

"Small world." Keri smiled as if she couldn't imagine the night getting any better.

Mackenzie, on the other hand, seemed paralyzed. Compassion overrode Jeremy's own sense of self-preservation. He stepped toward her and placed one hand on the small of her back as he pulled out a chair for her with the other. "Breathe," he whispered in her ear as she stepped in front of him to lower herself into the seat.

She picked up the menu and studied the options like she'd be tested on the contents at the end of the night. More than likely, she was attempting to hide behind the thick cardstock paper.

Jeremy put a hand over the menu so she'd look at him. He didn't want her to be scared or nervous. Not around him. "Do you think we could get them to give us two dry spaghetti noodles? You could challenge me to a rematch."

She giggled, tension leaving on the breathy sound. "I'm pretty sure dueling was outlawed in the seventeenth century."

He mock gasped. "Does that mean we're fugitives now?" He grabbed her hand and gave it a playful tug. "We've got to hurry if we don't want the po-pos to catch us."

She grinned, the last of the tightness leaving her body, and relaxed against the back of the chair. "Po-pos?"

Jeremy matched her grin. "That's what Nathan used to call the police."

Mackenzie looked as if she was about to say something in response, but Keri interrupted. "Have you guys eaten here before? What's good?" Her eyes scanned the menu.

Jeremy leaned closer to Mackenzie so only she could hear him. "If the police show up, I'll cause a diversion so you can make a clean getaway."

Her smile hinted at secrets. More than the quiet exchange they'd shared.

Jeremy's throat thickened. He reached for his water glass and took a sip. The cool liquid did little to ease the lump lodged there.

"What are you going to get?" Mackenzie asked him, looking back at her menu.

He let his gaze wander over the entrée options. Everything sounded good. "I'm not sure. You?"

Uneasiness seemed to crawl up her spine. He could feel the disquiet reach out and take ahold of him as if it were a tangible thing. "I think I might try the truffle mac and cheese? I've never had truffles before."

Why did her statement sound like a question? And why did she look at him like so much rode on his response?

"Oh, the truffle mac and cheese does sound delicious." Keri nodded at Mackenzie, which made her shoulders relax.

The server came and took their orders, refilling waters and dropping off a bread basket with some dipping oil and herbs.

Alejandro offered the basket to Keri first but addressed Mackenzie. "I want to thank you, from the bottom of my heart, for coming tonight."

Mackenzie gathered her long hair and draped it over her shoulder. "It's no problem." Color rose up her neck.

Keri passed the bread back to Alejandro, who held the basket out to Mackenzie. She selected a crusted slice of baguette and set it on her white porcelain plate.

"Without you, this guy would probably be microwaving leftovers and wasting away in front of the TV."

Mackenzie shifted in her seat. Her gaze darted to Jeremy then away.

"Yes," Jeremy drawled. "Thank you for having mercy on my poor, miserable soul. For truly, without you, I'd have to listen to this guy's heartsick complaining over missing the opportunity to see if Keri is the woman he's always waited for."

Alejandro laughed as he turned toward Keri. "It's true. You make my heart beat at a rhythm it's never felt before."

Keri rolled her eyes, but the glow about her belied the expression of exasperation. She knew Alejandro exaggerated and at the same time fell under the spell of his charm. Their bodies faced each other, their conversation dropping in volume, their worlds shrinking for the moment to a population of two.

Mackenzie mumbled something, but the only word Jeremy could decipher was *rescue*.

"What's that?" he asked, hoping she'd repeat herself.

She looked away, guilt framing her eyes. "Oh, nothing."

"Tell me," he urged. "I heard you say rescue?" He adopted his bad medieval knight impersonation. "If milady doth need rescuing, pray, let thy humble servant attend thee."

She snickered but shook her head. "It's nothing. Really."

"Please." He didn't know why he pressed except he could see capitulation behind her eyes.

She sighed and smoothed an invisible wrinkle in the table linen. "If you hadn't noticed, I'm not the most, shall we say, *gifted* person when it comes to conversations."

He did his mock gasp again. "Say it isn't so."

Her lips quirked. "Shut up," she said without any bite.

He grinned back at her.

She moved her hair away from her face. Jeremy tracked the movement, wishing the next time that strand of hair fell to the corner of her eye that he could be the one to tuck it behind her ear.

"Anyway," she continued, "Keri assured me she'd step in and rescue me if my awkwardness became too palpable."

Jeremy tilted his head and looked at her. He wanted to reassure her that he'd be her rescuer if she'd let him, but even as he considered that thought, he rejected it.

Tentatively, he reached his hand across the table and let his fingers trace her knuckles. He didn't want her to just hear the words he was about to say. He wanted her to feel them. All the way down to her core.

"You are not awkward, Mackenzie Graham." His hand stilled, and he waited until she looked into his eyes before continuing. "You, milady, are unescapably endearing."

Her grin went lopsided. "As endearing as a baby giraffe?"

He leaned forward, gaze intent. "Didn't you know? Giraffes are my favorite animal of all time."

She tucked her chin, but not before he noticed her smile. She licked her lips, then pulled her hand down into her lap. Her head lifted to look at him. "I have to say, never in a million years would I have guessed you'd be here tonight."

Jeremy leaned his forearm on the table. "Oh yeah? And why is that?"

Her big brown eyes twinkled. "Keri led me to believe I was doing this mystery guy a huge favor. Like he was a charity case or something, and if I didn't show up, then he would be doomed to become a full-fledged hermit."

He dipped his bread in the oil and took a bite. "So you're here out of pity. I see how it is."

Mackenzie tore off a small piece of her baguette and popped it into her mouth. "More like Keri knows how to manipulate me into doing things I don't want to do." She dashed the crumbs off her fingers. "Okay, now you know how I ended up here tonight. What's your real story? No way do I believe you need your friend to set you up on a blind date."

Jeremy reached for another slice of bread. "Coercion, same as you." He chewed, then lifted his water glass to his lips. "Actually, Alejandro said he met someone at work who came with her friend who—" He stilled, pieces sliding into places. "You have a loved one at the memory center."

Mackenzie ran her finger over the stitching of her cloth napkin. "My mother."

He studied her, almost seeing her in a new light. He didn't know the actual price care like that cost, but he knew it didn't come cheap, and insurance rarely covered all the expenses. Which meant . . .

Mackenzie nodded as if confirming his sudden epiphany. She wasn't competing for the promotion for the status the new job brought or even because she wanted the change. The driving force shoving her outside her comfort zone had everything to do with taking care of her mother.

Jeremy's spine crashed against the back of his chair with the impact of a head-on collision. Which was kind of how he felt. Disoriented. Shocked. Wondering what he should do next.

Thankfully, he was saved by the server arriving with their main courses. She set steaming plates of fresh pasta down in front of them, asked if they needed anything, then wished them a good meal before checking on other diners.

Alejandro offered to pray, and they all bowed their heads. After a quiet *amen*, the sound of silverware bumping together prologued Keri leaning forward and jumping back into conversation.

"Alejandro told me there's an ice-skating rink next door. Are you guys up for that after dinner?"

She looked at Mackenzie, silent communication traveling between them. Anyone could decipher the message, though. Keri's eyes were practically begging, while Mackenzie seemed hesitant.

Alejandro caught Jeremy's gaze, raising his brows with his own question. This night had already made Jeremy's resolve to stick to his objective so much more difficult. Not only would he have to grapple with his growing attraction and appreciation for Mackenzie, but he'd have to untangle the mess brought by knowing of her need for the promotion to pay for her mother's care.

He turned to Mackenzie. "Do you want to go?"

She searched his eyes. "It could be fun?"

"Okay, then. Let's do it."

Fun and torture. He had a feeling tonight the two went hand in hand.

21

I finish tying the laces, the length of which surpassed the obnoxious level a long time ago, and tuck the ends into the top of the tan skates. My ankles wobble as I try to stand on blades the width of kitchen knives. My arms flap, my balance pitching me to the side. I'm about to yell *timber* in warning when a strong pair of hands wraps around my waist and steadies me.

"I've got you." Jeremy looks down, his breath warm on my face.

Now that you've got me, never let me go.

Christmas magic really does exist, because I successfully keep that thought to myself instead of blurting it out.

"Thank you," I manage to say.

Slowly his hands fall away to settle at his sides. I want to believe the delay in letting me go is due to reluctance. A truer explanation is that he probably wanted to make sure I was steady on my feet.

I still can't believe he's even here. This whole night was supposed to be a practice run with someone I had no feelings for and would never see again. All to prepare me for the man standing in front of me.

He snaps the clips of his hockey-style skates to his feet, then unfolds and stands tall. "Ready?" He holds out his hand to me.

I want to take it. I want to cling to him and rely on his strength to hold me up. But I want to walk on my own two feet too. Figuratively more than literally, because there is a 99.8% chance I'm going to bruise my backside by falling before the night is through.

"I can do it," I say, more of a pep talk to myself than anything.

Jeremy moves so he's not in my way but stays close in case I need him. I can picture him doing the same with his niece and nephew. Quietly offering support but giving enough space for them to step out on their own, even if they end up falling on their faces.

I hold my arms out like I'm on a tight rope. My ankles start to fold outward, so I press my thighs together. If I can just make it to the wall . . .

I take tiny baby steps, shuffling forward. At this rate, it will take all night to get to the ice.

Jeremy chuckles, but when I look at him, he's managed to swallow his smile.

"What are you laughing at?" I fake scowl.

He holds up his hands, all innocence. "I'm not laughing."

"Uh-huh."

"I do love your penguin impersonation, though." Even though his lips are in a straight line, his eyes are laughing.

I plant my hands on my hips. I don't know what's come over me. Maybe it's the way Jeremy has put me at ease time and again tonight, but I feel . . . different. I don't know what adjective to use to describe the energy coursing through my veins like they've become electrical wires. Daring? Flirty? How does a person name something they've never experienced before? All I know is I want to vocalize things I would normally keep locked inside my head.

But Jeremy's made me feel safe all night. A small measure of courage has managed to break free of the doubts and *what ifs* in my brain to make me wonder what would happen if I let out a little of the dialogue I keep to myself. How would he respond?

I tilt my chin up, purse my lips. "I've at least made it three feet. You're still standing where you started."

His mouth quirks to the side, humor alight in the amber flecks in his eyes. In one step, he moves farther than my ten got me.

"Hey, are you two ever getting on the ice?" Keri's on the other side of the half wall, her cheeks and nose red.

Jeremy shakes his head but offers me his hand a second time. "What do you say? Ready to join them?"

Am I ready? The unknown of what accepting his hand means scares me, but I don't want to be frozen by my own inhibitions any longer. Isn't that why I made an appointment with a counselor in the first place?

I slide my hand into his and hold on. Peeking up at him, I give a small grin.

Jeremy wears an odd expression on his face. I want to ask him about it, but whatever courage I possessed was only fleeting and has vanished faster than a white rabbit in a magic act.

He helps me to the door in the half wall, then opens it so I can step over the lip and onto the shiny ice on the other side. Using the wall for support, I plant my feet on the frozen water. Stiff-legged, I pull myself forward hand-over-hand along the wall. A little girl who looks no older than five breezes past me. I pitch forward. Back. Throw myself at the wall.

This was a bad idea. If I don't get off the ice, the night is going to end with me in the emergency room.

Jeremy glides past, then spins so he's facing me, skating backward.

"Show-off."

"Practice. I played hockey growing up."

"Nice." I rotate my body. I'll be a salmon swimming upstream, but I'm determined to get back to that door and off this dangerous ice.

Jeremy skates around me and blocks my escape route. I can't go around him because there's no way I'm letting go of the wall keeping me upright. That would be my death sentence for sure.

He frowns. "Where are you going?"

"This was a bad idea. I don't know how to skate."

"You'll never learn if you don't try. Come on. I'll teach you." His body is leaning toward me, his hand resting right beside mine. His gaze is intent. Invested. As if me trying this seemingly insignificant thing means more than the act of gliding across the ice.

"Okay." I say yes because I'm unable to give any other answer. Not when Jeremy is looking at me the way he is now.

His shoulders relax, and his face softens. "Good." He skates in a half circle around me, and I turn so I'm facing the flow of traffic again. "The first thing you have to do is let go of the wall."

My fingers tighten on reflex. "I don't think I can."

"Trust me." His voice is low, reaching deep inside me to touch a hidden chord. "You won't be able to move forward if you're clinging to what's keeping you rooted in place. If you feel like you need to hold on to something . . ." He peels my hands away from the top of the rail and grips them firmly. "Hold on to me."

Slowly he starts to skate backward, pulling me along. My gaze drops to my feet, and I begin to lose my balance.

"Look at me, Mackenzie," Jeremy instructs, his voice steady. "Focus on my eyes."

I raise my gaze and hold on to him tighter as I falter.

"That's it. Good job," he croons as my legs steady. "Just keep looking at me."

I don't think I can look away if I try. All the other skaters have melted into the background. It's just me and Jeremy on the ice, our gazes connecting us even more than our clasped hands. Each second our eyes are locked, he's lacing another strand on the rope binding us together. Maybe this is why I never let myself look into Jeremy's eyes for too long before. Somehow I knew if I did, my heart would become irrevocably tied to his.

The toe of my skate catches the ice. I pitch forward, my hands leaving Jeremy's as my arms windmill to try to regain my balance. Visions of my face meeting the cold, hard ice dance in my head. I close my eyes. Brace myself.

And am immediately wrapped in a pair of strong arms, my face pressed against the wall of a chest that smells faintly of citrus but feels like the comfort of coming home. My breathing catches and my pulse begins to race. Two anomalies I'm miserably familiar with, but this time the reactions are different. Instead of pain and panic, they bring with them anticipation and desire. They bring me to life, awaken me, instead of making me want to shut down and run away.

My arms are prisoners, locked between Jeremy's body and mine. I expect his arms to fall away. For him to glide backward on his skates and put a little space between us. But he doesn't. If anything, his arms tighten. Draw me closer. Or is that my imagination?

"Mackenzie." The way he says my name is a caress.

I tilt my chin up. He's looking down at me, his eyes a riot of emotions. Our lips are only inches apart. If I weren't wearing skates, I could push up on my toes and press my mouth against his. Put my wonderings to rest and *know* what it's like to kiss the man I've been longing for, who holds a piece of me and is collecting more each day.

His eyes vacillate between mine. His gaze drops to my mouth. The whole world stills.

"Mackenzie!"

Keri's voice shatters the sphere that encompassed Jeremy and me like a snow globe. Jeremy blinks, his eyes clearing. His hands move from my back to my arms, and cold air fills the space he occupied only a moment before.

Keri and Alejandro slow to a stop beside us. "Do you have your cell phone on you?" she asks. "I want a picture of everyone together."

I dig my phone out of my coat pocket. The screen lights up, showing I have a missed call from Heritage Hills. My heart plummets to my toes.

"What's wrong?" Jeremy moves closer to my side.

I take comfort in his warmth as I tap first the phone icon and then the voicemail. Keri's brows fold in concern.

"Heritage Hills called," I say as I wait for the message to start playing.

"Hello, Mackenzie. This is Gabriella from Heritage Hills. I'm calling to let you know your mother has been taken to Mercy Memorial Hospital. The doctors there can tell you more about her condition, but feel free to call me here if you have any questions, and I'll do my best to answer them. You have the number. Just know we're praying for you and for Caroline. Good night."

Mom's in the hospital. A dozen scenarios roll through my mind, each one worse than the last, until the weight of them all threatens to bury me in an avalanche. Black spots dance in my vision. A high-pitched ringing sounds in my ears. Somewhere in my mind, I register voices talking, but they're muffled, and I can't make out what they're saying.

A shadow falls over me. Fingers lift my chin. I'm looking up into Jeremy's concerned face.

"Take a deep breath, Mackenzie." He draws in a large breath of his own, his chest expanding as his lungs fill with oxygen, then lets the air out slowly.

Now that I have something to focus on, my tunnel vision widens. This time when he inhales, I pull in a lungful of oxygen as well. As I slowly exhale, the static between my ears begins to clear. By the third breath, I've calmed enough to think rationally.

I shift my gaze to Keri, who's standing beside Jeremy. "My mom was taken to the hospital. I don't want to cut your date short, so I'll take a rideshare—"

"You certainly will not!" she exclaims at the same time Jeremy says, "I'll take you."

Jeremy and Keri stare at each other.

"I'll take her," Jeremy repeats.

Keri looks at Alejandro, an apology written on her face before she turns to me. "Kenz—"

I cut her off with a shake of my head. I know what she's going to say. The fact that she'd choose to sit with me in a hospital is enough. "On top of worrying about my mom, I'd be worrying about making you leave your date. Please stay and have a good time. Don't let me ruin this night for you."

She bites her lip, and I turn away so she can't argue with me any longer. Jeremy takes my hand and guides me off the ice. He keeps me steady as I make my way to the bench my shoes are tucked under. My fingers shake as I try to untie the laces. The moisture in my eyes making my vision swim isn't helping any.

I've lost count of how many times Jeremy has taken my hands tonight, but he does so again, gently moving them to the side. He unties my laces and, with a warm palm to my calf, guides my foot out of the skates. Without a word, he collects the rented footwear and returns them to the rink's window. When I stand, he's in front of me, holding out my purse.

"Which hospital?" he asks when we're in his SUV.

"Mercy Memorial." I'm trying not to let my imagination think of horrible reasons Mom could be in the hospital, but it's hard to quiet my internal narrator.

Jeremy plugs the address into his phone. The computerized voice tells him to make a right on Church Street. "Tell me about your mom."

"What?" I'm having a hard time focusing.

"Your mom," he says again. "Tell me one of the Christmas traditions she made special when you were a kid."

I gather all the thoughts in my head and make them line up single file like a teacher with elementary students. I remember back to Christmases past. I didn't think it would be possible to smile in this moment, but the sides of my mouth curve upward. "My mom loves Christmas. It's always been her favorite holiday."

"What about the season is so special to her?"

So many things, but what she loved the most . . . "She says people are nicer at Christmas. More kind and generous."

"Your mom must not be the cynical sort." He merges onto the highway. "I have a grumpy uncle who'd argue with her that people are more selfish and greedier at Christmas. Commercialism and all that."

"There are people like that," I concede. "But my mom always maintained the belief that people thought of others more around the holidays."

"So was that your tradition growing up? Being generous to strangers?"

"Yes and no. I mean, she always emptied the spare change out of her purse every time we saw a Salvation Army bell ringer. But my mom used Christmas to broaden my worldview and respect for people from other countries and cultures, and she often invited people to come celebrate those cultural traditions with us."

Jeremy glances at me. The GPS tells him to get off at exit fifty-four in two miles. "How did she do that?"

"Every year she'd pick a country, and we'd learn about and celebrate that country's holiday traditions. She's always believed that the more we know and understand people from their perspectives and backgrounds, the more common ground and respect we can have for one another."

He makes a left turn. "I really like that. What are some things other countries do to celebrate Christmas?"

I think back to some of the things Mom and I did when I was growing up. "In Finland, families make a porridge out of rice and milk sprinkled with cinnamon. They place a single almond inside one of the dishes, and whoever finds the almond is the winner. Later, they warm up in a sauna together."

Jeremy chuckles. "I can get behind the idea of a sauna on a blizzardy winter day."

"One year, we made our own *paróls*, which are paper lanterns shaped like the star of Bethlehem. If you think people in the US start celebrating Christmas too early by not waiting until after Thanksgiving, in the Philippines, the Christmas countdown begins on September first. That year, we ate our Christmas dinner at midnight, *Noche Buena*."

"I have a friend whose family is from Mexico. They eat a late dinner as well. Usually around ten, I think. Then open presents around midnight."

I nod. "A lot of Latin American countries do that."

"Tell me one of the strangest things you did in these celebrations," he says. "Or strange for someone from the United States, at least."

I don't really have to consider this one. "We kept a live fish in the bathtub one year."

His head rears back. "Seriously?"

I nod. "In a lot of central European countries like Poland and Slovakia, they keep a live carp in their bathtub for a couple of days before Christmas. Then it becomes the main course in a twelve-course feast, one course for each of the twelve apostles."

The sign for the hospital is bright against the moonless sky. As Jeremy turns into the entrance, I realize what he's done. He's distracted me and kept me talking during the whole drive so I wouldn't get worked up again and make myself sick with worry.

How did he know what I needed when I didn't even know myself?

Now that I see the hospital, though, everything comes rushing back. I pray things aren't dire. That I'm not too late. That my mom will be okay.

"You can drop me off here," I say, not wanting to be any more of a burden. "I'll call Keri to pick me up later or just sleep here tonight in her room if I'm allowed."

Jeremy ignores me and continues driving toward the parking area. "I'm not leaving you to face this alone." He turns off the ignition. "And you won't have to call Keri because she's been following us the entire time."

"What?"

He nods behind me. I turn to see another car pull up beside us. Alejandro is behind the steering wheel, Keri in the passenger seat.

"They left right after we did. We're all here for you, Mackenzie."

My nose and the back of my eyes burn. I blink, trying to keep the well of tears from rising to the surface. If I give in to them now, I won't be able to stop crying, and I need to be strong to face what's going on with my mom and what's in store for me.

I'm surrounded as we make our way inside the hospital. Keri breaks away and walks ahead.

"We're looking for Caroline Graham," she tells the lady behind the desk.

"Are you family?" she asks.

I step forward. "I'm her daughter."

She types on her keyboard, looking at her computer screen. "Your mother is in room 202."

"Thank you."

There's a bank of elevators to the left. We ride up to the second floor and look at the numbers on the doors to find the right one.

Finally. 202.

I reach for the handle just as the door opens. A doctor in blue scrubs startles when he sees us standing there.

"Oh, hello. Are you here to see Caroline Graham?" He peeks down at the tablet in his hands.

"I'm her daughter," I offer before he can ask. "How is she? What happened?"

"Miss Graham, your mother is going to be fine." He lowers the tablet to his side. "She's sleeping now, but the condition was caught in the early stages. She's now receiving effective treatment."

"I'm sorry, what condition?" Did condition mean cancer? Some other disease? Would my mom have yet another long fight ahead of her?

"My apologies." He takes a step so he can shut the door behind him. "Your mother came in with an increased heart rate, low blood pressure, and mental confusion."

I shifted my weight. "She has Alzheimer's. She's often confused."

"Which is why it took a little longer for the staff at the memory care facility to recognize the symptoms. Your mother has sepsis stemming from a urinary tract infection."

I gasp. People die from septic shock.

"As I said," the doctor reassures me, "she's receiving effective treatment for both the sepsis and the active infection. I have every confidence that she will make a full recovery from this episode."

I swallow. "Can I see her?"

He takes a step to the side so he's no longer blocking the door. "Of course. But like I said, she's resting now."

I thank him, and he continues down the hall.

"Do you want to go in alone, or do you want us to come with you?" Keri asks.

She's holding Alejandro's hand, their fingers intertwined. It's sweet that they came to be with me and offer their support, but they don't need to sit on uncomfortable hospital furniture in a dark room and watch a lady they have no connection to rest in a medicine-induced sleep.

"Why don't you guys see if the cafeteria is open and split a Jell-O cup? You never got dessert at the restaurant." I try to smile to reassure Keri that I'll be fine.

"You sure?" She's searching my face for any signs of hesitancy.

"I'm sure."

Alejandro cajoles her down the hall while Jeremy holds out a torn piece of paper. "My number. Call or text, and we'll be here in a heartbeat."

I stuff the paper into my jacket pocket. "Thanks."

"I'll be praying." He pivots to follow the other two.

I take a deep breath and push open the door. I predicted I'd end up in the hospital before the night was through. Who knew I'd be so right and yet so very wrong? If given the choice, I'd happily trade places with Mom.

I f I ignore the IV port in the back of her hand and the hospital gown visible beneath the thin blanket, and imagine we're in a regular bedroom instead of inside the sterile walls of a hospital, I can almost pretend there's nothing wrong with my mom. That an infection isn't raging in her body and that her mind is as quick and sharp as it was before Alzheimer's invaded like a terrorist and began massacring her brain cells. I can almost pretend she's just sleeping. That in a few moments her eyes will flutter open, crystal clear, settle on me, and she'll smile.

Almost.

I tug a chair from the corner and position it next to Mom's bed. Sitting, I lay my hand on her forearm and take in a shaky breath as I wrestle the reins of my thoughts away from the bad things and point them toward the positive.

- Mom is still here. We still have time together.
- The doctor is confident she will recover from the sepsis and UTI.
- I'm not going through this alone. I have Keri and Jeremy.

I mean, I don't *have* Jeremy. But maybe I do? A little bit? He did insist on driving me, after all. Even if he did it to be nice and give Alejandro more time with Keri and not because he has any romantic feelings for me. I'm still counting it.

I lay my head on the bed, my crown resting against the fleshy part of Mom's bicep. The physical contact is soothing. Connection without the need for words. I close my eyes. Allow myself to be in the present instead of running ahead to the future and the problems that may or may not await me there.

The next thing I know, the click of the door handle jerks me upright. I blink and look at the clock. The minute hand has traveled halfway around the face. I must have dozed without meaning to.

Jeremy stands in the doorway, a bag in his hands. He shifts his weight, his expression unsure. "Sorry to intrude. I brought your mom something. I hope that's okay."

"That's really sweet, but you didn't have to." I motion for him to come in.

"I wanted to." He holds the package out to me. "Besides, it's not much. Just a little something."

I take the bag and peek inside. All I can see is the top of a white box. I reach in and pull out the box. It's a vintage ceramic tabletop Christmas tree with multicolored lights.

"I didn't know if she'd get to go home before Christmas or not, and hospital rooms can be a little stark." He clasps his hands behind his back. "Everyone needs a tree for Christmas. Especially someone who loves the holiday as much as your mom does."

When she wakes up, she probably won't even know what year it is, much less what month. But bigger than that is the gesture I hold in my hands. My mom always talked about the spirit of Christmas, and now I'm holding it. Emotion clogs my throat. I'm overwhelmed. But in the best way possible.

He opens the top of the box as it rests in my lap, then pulls out the white Styrofoam housing the ceramic tree. Slicing the tape holding the two Styrofoam pieces together with a pocketknife, he frees the tree.

"How about over here?" He juts his chin toward a side table. "The lamp should be safe to unplug so we can use the outlet."

"Good idea."

He plugs in the cord, then flips the small switch. The lights on the tree go bright. It looks exactly like I remember from my childhood. My heart clenches with a bittersweet twist. Jeremy's thoughtfulness; my mother's health. Feeling both emotionally high and low simultaneously leaves my head spinning.

"I love it," I manage to force out. He says the gift is for my mom, but I can't help but think it's for me as well.

He gives me one of those soft looks I noticed earlier in the evening. "Good." He clears his throat and shoves his hands into his pockets. "I assume you're staying here tonight?"

I nod. "There are extra linens in the closet, and the couch pulls out into a bed."

"I guess I'll say good night, then." He takes a step toward the door.

I stand. "Thank you," I repeat. At least I think I recall thanking him multiple times tonight. "For everything."

His hands fall from his pockets. "Mackenzie, I—" He shakes his head.

Before I know it, his arms are wrapped around me and my face is pressed against his chest. My hands rise of their own accord and fist his jacket at his back.

I'm not a hugger. People in my personal space? That's a hard no from me. But as I'm encased in Jeremy's embrace, breathing in his scent and absorbing his heat, I relax instead of stiffen. I hope it doesn't end instead of counting the seconds until I can pull back and create space between us. I lean into him, not away. I somehow feel safe and secure and could build myself a little nest right here. I tuck my chin to my chest and cuddle closer.

He doesn't seem in any hurry to let me go either. His cheek

rests on top of my head. I can hear his heartbeat against my ear. It's steady and sure. Just like Jeremy.

He squeezes and then takes a step back. "Good night, Mackenzie," he says before walking out of the room and leaving me alone.

W hy do teachers give tests right before Christmas break?" Nathan slumped on the couch, looking as though someone had stolen all his bones and left him a skincasing of sullenness.

Jeremy looked up from the prep questions sheet he held in his hands. "Would you rather have the test when you get back after the New Year?"

Nathan's eyes were the only thing that moved, and even that he made look exhausting. "I'd rather not take a test at all."

"Sorry, bud, not gonna happen." Jeremy read the next question on the list. "What are three contributions the Sumerians gave to civilization?"

Nate's head lolled to the side. "Tell me the truth, Uncle Jeremy. Am I ever going to use this knowledge of ancient cultures in real life?"

"If you want to be an anthropologist or—"

"No."

"Okay, even if the facts you learn don't pertain to your career field, yes, you will use everything you learn in school in the real world."

"How?" Nathan's mouth turned down in skepticism.

"Because you are learning about applying yourself to a task. Doing something simply because someone above you said to even if it doesn't make sense to you. You are learning time management, study skills, being respectful to others, and a myriad of other character traits that will stay with you into adulthood and the workforce."

Nathan blinked at him. Finally, he sighed. "The wheel, written language, and the number system."

It took Jeremy a second to realize Nate's response was in answer to the history question. "Correct. Next one. What is the *Epic of Gilgamesh*, and how was it written?"

Natalie walked into the living room with a bag of Doritos. "Oldest surviving piece of literature, and it was written in cuneiform," she said around the crunching of a chip.

Jeremy turned the page. "Correct, but that was your brother's question."

She shrugged. "I can't help it if I'm so smart I know all the answers."

Nathan contorted his face. "Mee mee mee mee." He mimicked his sister's inflection and cadence but sounded like Beaker from the Muppets doing it.

She stuck her tongue out at him. He mirrored her.

Jeremy shook his head. No one had warned him that preteens were basically toddlers in larger bodies. He really thought the twins would have learned to coexist without saying things like "he started it" by now.

"Natalie, I already went over these questions with you. It's your brother's turn."

She rolled her eyes as she sucked on her red-coated thumb. "Fine."

"Thank you." Jeremy looked down at the next question. "Nathan, what modern countries were once part of ancient Mesopotamia?"

The doorbell rang before Nate could answer.

Jeremy stood and dropped the study sheet on his nephew's lap. "Keep studying."

He walked to the front of the house and opened the door. Lincoln, Jill, and Alejandro stood on his porch.

"This is eerily like déjà-vu," he said. "I feel like I should ask why you're here before letting you in so I don't get blindsided or blackmailed again."

Lincoln pushed his way past Jeremy to enter the house. "Bro, you should be thanking us. And we didn't blackmail you. We gave you an incentive to make a deal."

"Same thing," Jeremy called over his shoulder. "I guess you guys can come in too." He stepped back to let Jill and Alejandro enter.

"Such a warm welcome," Jill teased.

"I do what I can."

Alejandro shrugged out of his coat and hung it on the coat rack while Jill kept hers on. Jeremy wasn't sure she ever took her jacket off for the months spanning October to April.

"Uncle Jeremy, can I go play Xbox in my room since I can't study anymore with your friends here?"

"Sure."

If Nate got a bad grade on his test, that was just a natural consequence, right? At some point he'd have to start taking responsibility for his studies anyway. Although more than likely, Jeremy would spend the morning while the kids ate breakfast and got dressed for school quizzing them both again.

Nathan's feet pounded up the stairs as he bolted for his room and his controller. Natalie followed, yelling that it was her turn to be a zombie instead of a plant.

"So?" Jill barely waited until the door slammed upstairs before she launched in. "How did it go last night? Have you called her today? When are you two going out again?"

Jeremy stared at her, not sure what to answer first. Actually, he had a question of his own. He turned to Alejandro. The inquiry must have been written on his face, because Alejandro answered without Jeremy saying anything.

"I got a text from Keri this morning," he said. "Mackenzie's mom is awake and responding well to the medication. She even had a long duration of lucidity in which she made a big fuss about your ceramic tree." He paused. "Oh, and I'm supposed to tell you that Keri says you're Luke Macfarlane to Mackenzie's Lacey Chabert. Whatever that means."

Jeremy shrugged and shook his head as Alejandro waited for him to decipher the message. "I have no idea what she's talking about."

Jill groaned. "You guys are hopeless." She tapped Lincoln on the arm with the back of her hand. "Tell them, sweetie."

Lincoln scratched the back of his head. "I'd rather not."

Jill clucked her tongue. "Luke Macfarlane and Lacey Chabert are made-for-TV movie royalty. Luke usually plays characters who are sensible, responsible, and even-tempered, while Lacey specializes in sweet but highly stressed heroines looking to find their voice in the world. They've portrayed falling in love at Christmas at least a dozen times."

"So she's saying they're a predictable cliché?" Alejandro dodged Jill's swatting hand.

"No," she stated emphatically. "She's saying they're what millions of people all over the world are looking for—someone to fall in love with."

Jeremy rocked backward. "No one said anything about love."

"Not yet anyway." Jill's eyes gleamed.

"Not ever." Jeremy needed his friends, especially Jill, to drop the idea that he should advance directly to GO and collect $200— or a wife, in this case. He still had to travel all the way around the board—see Nate and Nat graduate—before he'd be at that stage in the game.

"You can't say not ever," Jill argued.

"I just did."

Her lips thinned.

Lincoln leaned toward Jeremy. "Abort. Abort," he whispered out of the side of his mouth.

"Why are you being so stubborn about this?" She folded her arms over her chest.

"About my own personal life?" Jeremy gave her a patient look. It was *his* life. The only people his decision affected were himself and the twins, and he'd been thinking of Nate and Nat when he devised his dating timeline to begin with.

"Love, specifically," she pressed, ignoring his subtle jab that she should stay out of his business. "I've seen you adjust your life plans before, but when it comes to being open to the possibility of love, you're a steel door."

"I make exceptions for small things. A change in the menu or what present I'm going to buy someone. Not things that affect the twins' futures."

"Why?" She was a dog with a tug-of-war toy. She refused to let go and clamped her jaws tighter.

"Jill." Lincoln tried to intervene.

"No." She shook off his hand. "I want to know why." She pinned Jeremy with a look. "Why do you insist on making and sticking to all these plans that you have? Don't you think it would be better to accept the gifts that come along rather than reject them simply because they aren't a part of your blueprint?"

Alejandro studied Jeremy. "Does this have anything to do with your sister and brother-in-law's sudden deaths?"

Jeremy had forgotten how much Alejandro sat back to listen and observe. He was like Mackenzie in that respect.

Just thinking about her brought an instant ache to his chest. Seeing her every day at work and keeping his distance—not folding her into his arms, breathing in her scent, tasting her lips— would be agony. But one that he'd have to endure.

Maybe when she got the promotion, their paths wouldn't cross as much. And she would get it if he had any say in the matter. He couldn't keep competing. Not when the reason she'd been pushing herself so hard was to afford her mother's healthcare. But maybe then the attraction and connection between them would slowly dissipate until things went back to the way they had been before.

That thought was its own kind of torture.

But he had his plans. *Some warm company they bring*, he thought with no small amount of sarcasm. Still, they were there for a reason.

"Jeremy?"

Alejandro's voice brought him back to the conversation at hand. "Heidi didn't have any plans in place in case the worst happened," he said succinctly. No need to go into details of how much of a mess not having a will created. How hard he'd fought to give the twins a safe and loving home. "I won't let that happen again." A second blanket statement, but his friends knew how wide a net he'd cast with each.

The air grew thick with the heaviness of their discussion.

"What about God's plans?" Jill asked, her voice much softer than it had been a minute before.

"What about them?"

"Are you leaving room in your strictly ordered life for God's plans to unfold as well?"

The room was so silent Jeremy could hear the music from the video game upstairs.

Had he organized his present and future so much that he hadn't allowed for God showing up with blessings? Even worse, had he shoved those blessings away because they didn't line up with his own ideas of how his life should go?

""For I know the plans I have for you," declares the Lord,'" Jill recited from Jeremiah 29:11. ""Plans to prosper you and not to harm you, plans to give you hope and a future."'"

"I told you to abort." Lincoln attempted to lighten the mood.

Jill ignored him. "Just—" She paused, searching for the right way to phrase what she wanted to say. "Just be open enough to accept that Someone greater than you might know better. Be willing to follow His plan instead of your own."

24

Jeremy lay awake in his bed, staring at the ceiling. The yellow glow of a streetlamp snuck through the top of his curtain and crawled across the textured drywall above him. At first, he'd thought the light's outline resembled a craggy mountain, but he'd changed his mind. After staring at it for this long, he could now make out the image of a wolf howling at the moon.

He rubbed his eyes, his vision going dark. Blank. The way he wished his mind would. Then he'd be asleep, which was what he should be at—he tapped the screen of his cell phone on the bedside table—2:17 in the morning. But he couldn't turn his thoughts off.

Was Jill correct? Had he become so rigid in doing what he thought was right and best for the twins that he'd inadvertently and unconsciously told God that he knew better?

Jeremy massaged his temples. No matter how many times he asked himself or how he framed the question, he always came to the same conclusion.

That was exactly what he'd done.

Forgive me, Lord.

While he'd likely never adopt the ideology of *YOLO* or *carpe diem*, he could become more lenient with how he envisioned the future. Less strict with managing every aspect of his life to fit within the parameters he'd determined would achieve the greatest outcome.

Which meant . . .

His heart skipped a beat.

Mackenzie.

He'd never really allowed himself to see her in the scope of anything outside of work. But now . . .

Like a bird who'd had his wings clipped all his life but was now given permission to fly, he soared with the freedom of being unrestrained.

His mind jumped to a year from then. They could be celebrating their first Christmas together. Maybe Mackenzie could teach the twins the different ways people celebrated around the world. They could share their own traditions, like camping out under the tree the night before Christmas Eve, watching movies and playing board games in their pajamas.

In five years, Natalie would be attending school dances like winter formal. She'd need a woman's touch and influence to help her pick out dresses and to teach her about makeup and hair styles. How to navigate the waters of dating and relationships with female friends. (He'd seen *Mean Girls*. He was unequipped to handle the social structure of teenage girls.) Why hadn't he thought of that before? Having Mackenzie in their lives wouldn't only be good for him. It would be good for Nat and Nate as well.

In ten years—

You're doing it again.

Jeremy wiped a hand down his face. It was so easy to fall back into old habits. He'd have to be on alert just to allow things to unfold naturally and not organize his life to such extreme measures.

But still the question remained. What was he going to do about Mackenzie? Because now that nothing stood in his way, he very much wanted to *do* something.

The last time he'd seen her, sitting beside her mother's hospital bed, filled his mind's eye. Mother and daughter shared similar features. The roundness of their eyes. The delicate upturn at the tips of their noses. The soft curve of their chins. He knew the devastation of losing a loved one. He wasn't sure which was worse, not getting to say good-bye or watching the person who held a piece of your heart slowly fade away over time, leaving only a shell behind.

Was that why Mackenzie had focused on recreating everyone's childhood memories?

Was that something he could do for her?

He reached for his phone and unlocked the screen, the idea of a possibility erasing all thoughts of sleep from his mind. Beneath the surface, he buzzed.

Mackenzie had spent so much time and effort reviving the cherished childhood traditions of her coworkers. Why couldn't everyone at Limitless Designs return the favor and do the same thing for her?

He looked at his calendar app. The office holiday party was in two days. Not a lot of time to plan and put things into action, but not impossible either.

He called Lincoln. His friend's granny was originally from Jamaica, and Jeremy recalled a bright red, slightly sour drink she made around the holidays.

He was about to give up and end the call when the ringing stopped.

"Someone had better be dead for you to call so late." Sleep thickened Lincoln's voice.

Jeremy winced. He'd forgotten the time. "We're all very much alive. Sorry to disappoint."

"That's a status that can easily be changed." The sound of covers rustling filtered in through the background. "If not an emergency, what's so important that you had to call at—" He paused, his voice muffled. "For crying out loud, it's a quarter to three, Jer."

Oops. "Well, you're up now, and this will only take a minute."

"What is it?" Lincoln asked on an exhale of exasperation.

"What's that red drink your granny makes for the holidays?"

"Sorrel?" Lincoln sounded incredulous. "You woke me up in the middle of the night to ask me about sorrel?"

Jeremy tapped his thigh with his fingertip. "Do you know how to make it?"

A softer, fainter voice mumbled something in the background.

"It's Jeremy." Lincoln had turned his head away from the phone to talk to someone else. Jeremy winced again. He'd woken Jill as well. "I know it's almost three, but the man has lost his mind and is talking about Granny's sorrel." Rustling magnified over the speaker. "Jill wants to talk to you," Lincoln said straight into the receiver.

"What's going on, Jeremy?" Jill had a smidge more patience in her voice than her husband had.

Part of him wanted to apologize and tell them to go back to sleep. The other part of him figured they were already awake and on the phone. The damage had been done, so he might as well ask his questions.

He remembered something. "Hey, didn't your brother marry a woman from Nigeria?"

Silence hung on the line. Jeremy checked the phone. They were still connected.

"I'm trying to make sense of why you're asking about a holiday drink and my sister-in-law, but you're going to have to connect those dots for me."

He really didn't want Jill to make a big deal out of his idea of the global Christmas party, but he couldn't think of a way around telling her.

"Mackenzie has been making everyone else's Christmases special. I thought it would be nice if we gave back to her by celebrating the way she and her mom did growing up. A little holiday world tour without leaving the office."

Jill didn't respond. Jeremy thought she'd squeal or gush or go on about how it was about time he saw the carrot for his nose. She didn't do any of those things.

"My sister-in-law makes the most delicious coconut jollof rice at Christmas. I'll ask her for the recipe."

"Thank you."

"And Lincoln's granny's sorrel as well."

"I appreciate it."

Jill yawned. "And Jeremy?"

"Yes?"

"I'm glad you finally came to your senses."

He chuckled. "Me too. Good night."

"Good night." The phone clicked, ending the call.

He'd have to talk to everyone else from work tomorrow. Especially Sofiya. He didn't think she'd hesitate to change plans for the office party, but he needed to bow out of being considered for the promotion as well. While the job description fit him like a glove and he could use the money for the twins' college fund, he didn't feel right running against Mackenzie any longer. Because of his personal feelings and the revelation as to why she needed the raise. He couldn't do that to her.

He closed his eyes and drifted off to sleep as thoughts of mistletoe and new beginnings danced in his head.

How was he going to organize an office party that required everyone's cooperation in a single day's time while keeping it a secret from Mackenzie? What he needed was a reason for her to leave the office. Then he could call a meeting and share what he wanted to do and how everyone could help.

He could enlist Keri for backup. Yes, that would work. Keri could take Mackenzie out for lunch, and he could get everyone on board to surprise her for Christmas.

Jeremy stepped out of the way of a mother pushing a stroller, then opened the door to the office building. He rode the elevator up, mentally going over the list of things he'd need to purchase or organize to make the party perfect.

He'd already ordered a few large paról lanterns the night before and had paid extra for one-day shipping. He hoped the design was similar to the one Mackenzie and her mother had made together. As far as table decorations, he'd ordered some wreaths with candles like those worn on girls' heads in Norway, and Christmas crackers that people in England loved to pop at their holiday feasts. After work, he planned to pick up a number of poinsettia plants. He'd learned they were used to decorate nativities in Mexico because of a legend of a brother and sister who were poor and set a bouquet of weeds at a nativity on Christmas Eve. Miraculously, the leaves of the weeds turned a vibrant red, just like the poinsettia plant.

Did Mackenzie know that legend? He only had the memories she'd recounted to him in the car on the way to the hospital to go on, but even if he didn't get every detail correct about places and traditions she and her mother had celebrated in the past, he thought it would be all right.

The elevator settled, and the doors opened. Jeremy looked around the office. He didn't see Mackenzie or Keri. It was the perfect time to talk to Sofiya about his plans for the party. He walked to her office and knocked on the door.

"Come in," she said. She raised her head as Jeremy entered. "What can I do for you?"

"I wanted to speak to you about the Christmas party."

He laid out all he had planned and why he thought it would be a good idea to hijack the event and turn it into something special for Mackenzie.

Sofiya's eyes sparkled. "I love this idea. I will bring *bulochki*, which is a yeast roll, and pryaniki, my favorite cookie. I cannot cook, but there is an excellent bakery that makes these."

"There's something else I want to discuss with you. It's the promotion." Jeremy folded his hands in front of him.

A knock sounded on the door before it opened and Mackenzie poked her head in. "Oh, sorry. I didn't mean to interrupt."

Sofiya waved her in. "You're not interrupting. Jeremy was just about to say something about the promotion."

He'd planned to bow out in private, but now that he'd decided not to live by his filed blueprints, more of them seemed to be falling to the wayside.

Mackenzie stepped more fully into the office and settled beside him.

"How's your mother?" he asked softly.

She looked up at him. "They said if she keeps improving, she could be released tomorrow."

His gaze traced her face. How could he have been so blind the last couple of years? Working beside her every day but never truly seeing her? Well, he saw her now. And he couldn't seem to make himself look away.

Sofiya cleared her throat. When Jeremy shifted his focus to his boss, he found a small, secret smile tugging at her lips. "The promotion," she prompted.

Right. "I decline the honor of being considered."

Mackenzie gasped. "You can't do that."

He tilted his head toward her. "Why not?"

"Because that's what I came in here to say." She faced Sofiya. "Jeremy is clearly the better candidate for a supervisory role as well as client liaison. He should get the job."

"She can't give me the job," he argued. "I've already declined."

Mackenzie pursed her lips. "Well, I decline too."

They stared at each other.

Sofiya's hand slapped her desk. "I am the boss. I will decide. Now go. Get back to work before I give the job to Frank."

An empty threat, but it did its job. Jeremy and Mackenzie filed out of the office.

"You'd be better at the job and you know it," Mackenzie said as soon as he'd closed Sofiya's door.

"You're a better designer and *you* know it," he countered.

Their eyes locked in a standoff, but then she gave a short laugh and shook her head. "As long as it doesn't go to Frank."

Jeremy grinned. "Agreed."

She twisted the ends of her hair in her fingers. "I guess I better . . ." She pointed toward her desk.

"Right." He stepped to the side. "I'll get out of your way."

She offered him one of her soft, shy smiles as she glided past him. He couldn't help but watch her walk away.

A tap on his arm startled him. He turned to find Keri grinning at him in a knowing way.

"You're just the person I was looking for," he said.

Her brows rose in teasing speculation. "Oh, really? Because from where I'm standing, it seems like you were looking at someone else." Her eyes glinted in silent amusement.

He chuckled under his breath. "You and Alejandro really are a pair."

Her grin widened. "Why, Jeremy, I do believe that's the nicest thing you've ever said to me."

"I need to ask you a favor." He cut to the chase. "Can you take Mackenzie out of the office for lunch today?"

She cocked her hip and anchored her hand on the jutted curve. "I'm sure she'd rather go to lunch with you if you asked her."

"While the idea is tempting, it'll have to wait for another day."

Keri dropped her hand. "Why do you need her out of the office?"

Jeremy laid out his plan.

"It's about time," Keri exclaimed once he finished. "The two of you give a whole new meaning to the term *slow burn*. I've been trying to fan these flames for years."

"So you'll do it?"

"Count me in."

Jeremy must have checked the clock a dozen times. The minute hand moved as quickly as a tortoise with a sprained ankle. Sloughing through a mud pit. Carrying an elephant on his shell. Finally, Keri and Mackenzie grabbed their bags and made their way to the elevator.

He stood and clapped his hands to get his coworkers' attention. "Emergency meeting in the conference room." He passed confused faces and whispered murmurings as he strode across the large space and opened the door to the conference room.

"What's going on?" Rosa asked as she stopped in the doorway.

He flicked his chin toward the long table in the center of the room. "Take a seat, and I'll fill everyone in at once."

After everyone had arrived, he marched to the head of the table and swept his gaze over his coworkers. From mildly harassing Frank to sweet-as-sugar Rosa. He'd need each of them to come together to make this a Christmas Mackenzie would never forget.

"There's been a change of plans with the office party tomorrow."

"Is it canceled?" Rosa asked, her tone making Jeremy wonder if she hoped that were the case or if she'd be disappointed.

"No, it's not canceled. But, with Sofiya's permission, I have taken it over, and I need your help."

"Our help with what?" Annabelle leaned forward.

"To make Mackenzie Graham's Christmas just as special and memorable as she has made all of ours. She's given us our childhood holiday memories back in living color. I say we do the same for her in return."

Derek and Annabelle shared a look. "We're in," they said in unison.

"Me too." Rosa smiled. "I'd forgotten how searching for Mary and Joseph every day leading up to Christmas made me feel as a child. I'd lost some of the Christmas magic, and Mackenzie found it for me again."

"Can I wear a Santa suit?" Frank asked.

"No," half a dozen voices chorused.

He held up his hands. "I was just asking. Sheesh."

"What do you need us to do?" Rosa asked.

Jeremy shared about Mackenzie and her mother's Christmas tradition of exploring the world and the people in it without ever leaving home.

"I've already bought the ingredients for *bibingka* and *puto bumbong*," Rosa offered.

"What's that?" Frank's upper lip curled.

Rosa turned toward him. "They're both rice cakes served near churches in the Philippines during *Simbang Gabi*. They're delicious, but you don't have to eat them if you're going to look at them like that."

To his credit, Frank tried to hide the disgust twisting the lower half of his face.

Derek raised his hand. "I'm from the heartland of America. The only Christmas foods I know are honey-glazed ham and mashed potatoes." He looked unsure.

"That's fine." Jeremy pointed. "You can be in charge of bringing Christmas in Japan to life."

Panic crept into Derek's face. "But I just said—"

"Do you know where over three million people in Japan get their holiday meal from?"

Derek's head oscillated on his neck. "No."

Jeremy grinned. "Kentucky Fried Chicken. Colonel Sanders will cook for you."

"Really?" Derek's jaw slackened. "That's so cool."

Jeremy finished assigning food and decorations. His mom always said the best gifts weren't ones that came from the store but ones that came from the heart. Hopefully Mackenzie would agree.

I have some hummus and carrot sticks in the refrigerator at work. I would have been happy to share." In fact, the veggies and dip were the saving grace I'd fallen back on when I'd finally left Mom's hospital room last night, too exhausted to even think of stopping by the grocery store like I'd originally planned.

"Next," the employee at the register calls, and the line shuffles forward.

"I know." Keri looks up at the menu on the wall behind the order counter. "But it's freezing, and I'm in the mood for some soup."

It is rather cold. I bury my hands in the sleeves of my sweater. I wish it would snow again. It sounds weird, but it feels warmer to me on snow days.

"Next."

We move to the front of the line. "I'll have the creamy potato soup in a bread bowl, please," Keri orders, then steps aside for me.

"And I'll take the half soup and salad. Minestrone and Caesar, please."

The person working the register rings us up, then gives us our drinks as well as a number to set on the table, telling us someone will bring our food out when it's ready. I follow Keri to a booth in the corner, then slide onto the bench seat across from her.

"So." I unwrap a straw and stick it into the glass of water in front of me. "Did you finally settle on a present to give Frank for Secret Santa?"

Keri screws up her lips. "I'm a nice person, so he's getting the generic but acceptable gift of a pen set."

I take a drink of the ice water, a shiver running through my body. The hot soup was a good idea.

"Speaking of guys from work." Keri makes her eyebrows jump up and down like they're hurdle runners on a track-and-field team.

The heat racing toward my cheeks chases the chill of the ice water away.

"What are you going to do with Jeremy?" she asks.

I look around the restaurant, pretending to be fascinated by the people slurping soup from spoons and talking around mouthfuls of sourdough. "I don't know what you mean."

"I *mean* you've had a crush on him for as long as you've known him. I *mean* you went out with him two days ago. On a date. I *mean* when are you going to tell him how you feel?"

I move my glass closer and wipe away the condensation puddled on the table. "I don't know," I admit on a breath.

While I'd like to claim that going out with Jeremy, holding his hands ice-skating, and feeling the security of his comforting arms around me in Mom's hospital room miraculously knocked down all the walls of timidity that imprison me, that isn't the case. My chest still tightens when I envision doing something daring. Like walking up to Jeremy and confessing that I've been falling in love with him for years. I can't even get through the made-up conversation in my own mind before my heart gallops away from me.

Keri reaches across the table and covers my hand with her own. "I haven't gotten to ask you yet. How did your first session go with the counselor yesterday?"

An aproned employee approaches our table. "Soup and salad?" The plate bearing my lunch hovers over the table.

I point a finger in the air, and she sets the plate down in front of me.

"Have a good meal," she says after presenting Keri with her steaming bread bowl full of white, creamy soup.

We each say a silent prayer before picking up our silverware. The minestrone is perfectly seasoned. The noodles not over-cooked.

"So?" Keri brings the conversation back around.

I swallow and wipe my mouth with a napkin. I haven't decided on an adjective to describe how the meeting with the counselor went. "It was . . . good," I settle on for lack of anything better. "Different than I expected."

"What did you expect?"

I shrug. "My expectations come from television, so I kind of thought I'd be lying on a sofa, forced to come up with deep thoughts to say, and the therapist would hum and respond with something like, 'Tell me more.'"

Keri snickers. "You mean things on TV aren't reality?"

That pulls a half smile out of me. "Hardly."

She takes a bite of her lunch. "Okay, so if you didn't reenact a scene from a movie, what did happen?"

I share with Keri some of the things the counselor said about social anxiety. About the way the brain functions and reacts. About some of the work I'll need to do to retrain my neural pathways.

Keri nods while she chews, her eyes distant like she's deep in thought. She takes a sip of her water. "What about when you have to be in an environment with other people, like at work? Did she give you any tools to use when you start to feel over-whelmed and panicky?"

Somewhere in the restaurant a cell phone rings, the sound cutting through dozens of conversations.

"She gave me some breathing techniques that will help in the moment to reset that fight-or-flight instinct." I stab a cherry tomato with my fork. "But the hard work she warned me about is something called systematic desensitization or exposure therapy."

Keri's nose wrinkles. "What's that?"

I grimace. "Slowly putting myself in situations of increasing anxiety levels. I'm also supposed to practice shifting my focus off myself and what my brain is telling me and back onto the person I'm interacting with so I can pay more attention to the way they're actually responding and not how I'm telling myself they're perceiving me."

Keri's mouth falls open. "Wow. That's a lot."

My sentiments exactly.

We eat in silence for a few minutes, but I can tell Keri's still thinking over everything I've said. Finally, she puts down her spoon and pushes her food to the side. She leans forward. "I'm sorry. I can't stop thinking about you and Jeremy together. Why don't you use him as part of your exposure therapy? Talk to him as one of your social experiments."

I'm shaking my head even before she's done speaking. "I have to learn cognitive restructuring first. Besides, the social exposure experiments are supposed to start with things that are really low risk." Telling Jeremy I'm secretly in love with him is off the charts on the risk-factor scale. Not only because I'd be risking embarrassment, what he'd think of me, and rejection, but also because I'd be risking my heart.

Keri leans even closer. "Believe me, telling Jeremy how you feel is almost no risk at all for you."

My hand pauses as I reach for my water glass. "What do you mean?"

She looks away, the debate in her head only visible in the jumping muscle of her jaw. Eventually, she turns back to me. "Try the attention training thing with him. Where you focus on the other person's reactions to you instead of what's going on in your own head. That's all I ask."

Why? What does Keri think I'll see?

I want to parse her every word. Examine each of them for a different meaning. Does she know something I don't? Why won't she just tell me? I'm about to jump down that rabbit hole like Alice when I stop myself. I need to get out of my head more, not curl up there.

I need a change in subject.

"We've talked enough about me. I want to hear about you and Alejandro. Will there be a second date?"

Like a match to a candle, Keri's eyes light. "I'm going over to his place tonight to wrap presents and watch our favorite holiday movies. *White Christmas* for me and *Planes, Trains, and Automobiles* for him."

"That sounds very homey," I tease.

"I know it's only our second date, but it feels like we've been together for years already." Keri's sigh has a dreamy quality. "Like we skipped over the awkward bits and the wondering what the other was thinking and arrived at the best, most comfortable part. The secure part." She sighs again. "It's wonderful."

I'm happy for Keri. She deserves all the good things life can bring, and Alejandro seems like the best kind of man for her. But I can't help feeling a little jealous. There will be no skipping the awkward to revel in the comfortable for me.

Jeremy's arms were pretty comfortable.

That's true. They were. So . . . maybe?

Maybe . . .

I'll leave that thought right there. Let it keep every ounce of possibility it can feasibly hold. Who knows, right?

Maybe . . .

W hat if I just skip the office Christmas party? Yes, Sofiya is supposed to make her announcement of who is getting the promotion, but I don't even want the job anymore, so maybe if I'm not there, she'll automatically name Jeremy as the winner.

Besides, now that the raise won't be coming to me, I need to spend some time brainstorming ideas to earn extra money to pay for Mom's care. I can take on a few more freelance clients, but that income isn't reliable. More like feast or famine. I need an income I can depend on.

I wonder how much a kidney goes for these days on the black market.

The sound of cereal being poured into a bowl filters through the thin walls of the apartment. I push my feet into a pair of fuzzy slippers and pad out of my bedroom and into the main living area.

"Morning." Milk drips from the corner of Keri's lips. She wipes at it with her thumb.

"Can you take my Secret Santa gift with you when you go to the party?" I shift my weight to the other foot.

Her spoon stills. "Aren't you coming?"

"My mom is being discharged today." My fingers brush against my flannel pajama bottoms, and I pinch the excess material between my thumb and index finger and rub them back and forth. "I'm going to hire a rideshare over to the hospital and see if I can take her back to Heritage Hills. Maybe even take her to one of her favorite restaurants."

"Oh, sweetie. I wish you could." She taps her phone, which lies beside her bowl. "Alejandro texted. He's already on his way to pick up Caroline and take her back."

I run my finger along the seam of my pants. "Then I'll meet her there and spend the day making sure she feels comfortable in her room again."

"Kenz." Keri's jaw is set, but her eyes are soft. "Alejandro says days like this are often hard. There's a lot of change, and your mom may begin to feel unsettled. I know you want to be a familiar face for her. I hate to say this, but sometimes your presence has the opposite effect. I think that even on the days where she's her most confused, a part of her recognizes that she should know you, and the fact she doesn't makes her even more upset."

My eyes sting. I want to argue with Keri, but I can't. Everything she said is painfully true.

"Come to the party," she coaxes. "It'll help take your mind off things. Alejandro will tell us when your mom is settled and what kind of day she's having, and then I promise I'll drive you over to see her."

A sigh deflates my chest. "Fine."

I trudge back to my bedroom and change into a pair of jeans, a black-and-white-striped long-sleeve shirt, and a mustard-colored chunky cardigan that pools at my wrists and grazes the middle of my thighs. If I have to go to this stupid party, I'm at least going to be dressed comfortably.

Twenty minutes later, I'm sitting in the passenger seat with two wrapped presents in my lap—my Time-Turner necklace for

Rosa and Keri's pen set for Frank. Sofiya has the party catered every year, so at least I can count on some good food.

A fresh dusting of snow looks like a baker sprinkled confectioners' sugar all over the ground. It crunches beneath our boots as we walk to the building from the parking lot. Keri reaches the doors and pulls one open, letting me inside first. Warmth seeps through the knit of my sweater, my skin a welcoming recipient. The elevator already rests on the ground floor, so we don't have to wait. Mannheim Steamroller plays over the speakers as the steel cable pulls us up. The elevator settles, and the doors open. I step out.

And immediately stop. My mind can't wrap around what my eyes are taking in.

The office has been turned into a global bazaar. Sights, sounds, and smells compete for my attention. On one wall is a backdrop of Mount Fuji. The volcanic mountain is resplendent with its white-capped top and the pink cherry blossoms in the foreground. A table has been set up like a booth with origami Christmas trees alongside what appears to be Valentine's Day decorations. Large white-and-red buckets with Colonel Sanders's face on them overflow with crispy fried chicken.

Derek drapes an arm across Annabelle's shoulders. "Did you know Christmas in Japan is a romantic holiday for couples?"

The way he grins then winks down at Annabelle pulls a laugh out of me. I whirl around, my gaze trying to take in everything at once but snagging on the paróls hanging from the ceiling by Sofiya's office, the vibrant red poinsettias flanking a two-foot-tall nativity scene with a banner declaring *Feliz Navidad* in bold colors behind, and the sandbox in the shape of a lobster with a free-standing electric grill beside it and a smorgasbord of seafood cooking on the wire racks.

"What is all this?" I breathe as I turn back around, expecting to see Keri. I can't believe she's done this.

Keri isn't behind me. In fact, I can't see her at all. Instead,

Jeremy stands off to the side, his hands shoved into his pockets. He looks uncertain. Almost as if he's waiting for something. So different from his usual confident and calm demeanor.

"You've made it your mission the last couple of weeks to bring back all of our best memories of the holidays." He clears his throat. "We wanted to make your Christmas just as special."

My whole body shakes. I press the palm of my hand against my thigh to still the movement, but it's no use. Tremors run up and down my spine like my backbone is a fault line. "You did this?"

He tilts his head. Man, I love when he does that.

"We all did." His lips form the words, but I can see the truth behind them. The idea, his. The initiative, his. The heart . . . his.

I rarely know what to say, but this is different. The words aren't refusing to form because my brain isn't cooperating or because fear and panic have stolen them. They aren't coming because my heart is so full there isn't any room left for words.

Jeremy holds his hand out to me. "Let me be your tour guide as we travel around the world in eighty minutes." He winks.

The light tease is enough to break me of my trance. My muscles cooperate again, and I close my fingers around his. He tugs me closer, and I have to keep myself from leaning all the way into his side.

"The first stop on our trek across the globe is none other than Australia." He leads me to the right.

A wireless speaker is set on a table. It blends in with coconut shells on top of a cloth printed in tropical leaves. A fake palm tree no more than two feet tall is lit up with multicolored lights and has a Santa hat on top. A version of "Jingle Bells" plays, but instead of dashing through snow in a horse-drawn sleigh, the lyrics sing of going through the bush and kicking up dust in their rusty Jute.

Frank grins. I'm not sure which is more surprising—seeing him in a Magnum P.I.–style shirt with Santas on a beach drinking out of pineapples, or the fact that he seems to be extremely comfortable in such attire.

"G'day." Frank's greeting doesn't sound like an American doing a poor Australian accent. He sounds good. *That* might be the most surprising. "Can I interest you in some prawns?" He indicates the large shrimp cooking on the grill.

Jeremy looks at me, brows raised in question.

I feel bad, since so much thought has been put into each destination. "I'm allergic to shellfish."

"No worries." Frank doesn't seem to be put out at all. He sidesteps away from the grill to stand behind a white-domed confection spilling over with decadent-looking berries of red, green, and blue. "How about a slice of one of Aussie's favorite desserts?"

My mouth waters just looking at the treat fit for a bakery window. "What is it?"

Frank beams. "Pavlova. It's a meringue with a crisp crust and a light, chewy center topped with strawberries, kiwi, passionfruit, blueberries, and fresh whipped cream."

My eyes widen with each descriptor. "That sounds heavenly."

He plates the pavlova, then leads us to two lawn chairs opened beside the sandbox. After we sit, he hands us our desserts, then pulls out his phone. The sound of ocean waves crashing on the shore adds to the ambience. He sets down the phone and grins. "One more thing."

As he walks away, I wonder what else he could possibly have up his sleeve. I already feel transported to the beach. Sand, the sound of the ocean, a Christmas palm tree. What more could there be?

Frank wheels out a large lamp and positions it directly over my head. In seconds, I feel like the sun is beating down on me.

I smile up at Frank in gratitude. Honestly, I never would've thought he had this level of selflessness and kindness in him. It just shows that people are always more layered than we give them credit for. "Thank you, Frank."

He smiles and backs away.

"Did you and your mom ever 'travel' to Australia for any of your Christmases?" Jeremy asks as he spears a kiwi slice with his fork.

I shake my head. "We never made it south of the equator. It's funny, I haven't given much thought to half the world celebrating Christmas in the summer. While we're bundled up around the fireplace, watching the snow fall, they could be at the beach, picnicking and barbequing."

I make sure to get a little of everything on my fork—meringue, fruit, and cream—then take a bite. The meringue is sweet but balances with the tart tang of the fruit and the smooth creaminess of the whipped cream. I take three more bites in quick succession before I slow down enough to focus on anything else.

When I look up, Jeremy is grinning at me. "Safe to assume you like it?"

"It's divine," I say around the last strawberry.

"Ready for the next stop on your tour?"

Jeremy takes my plate from me, and I extricate myself from the beach chair. His hand is warm on my lower back as he steers me to the next country. I measure my steps to feel the pressure increase along my spine. Maybe to slow time as well. This must be how Cinderella felt dancing with the prince. Wanting the night to last forever.

Rosa is backlit by two large paróls hanging behind her. A white five-point star shines from the middle, each point touching the circle surrounding it wrapped in a shimmering garland of red and gold, thick strands of ribbon hanging like tassels off the bottom. On her table sits the small nativity scene that has decorated the office for the last couple of weeks. Mary and Joseph now stare lovingly down at baby Jesus lying in the manger.

"They finally found their way to Bethlehem," Rosa says, noting my line of vision.

I look up at her and smile. "They sure did."

"My mother and I made this especially for you. It's our favorite Christmas treat."

"What is it?"

"It is a baked rice cake called bibingka." She cuts a slice and hands it to me on a small plate. "Try it."

There is a faint sweet smell as I hold the cake to my mouth. My teeth sink into the soft confection. The texture is slightly chewy, but I especially love the hints of coconut I'm picking up on my tongue.

"This is delicious," I say before I go in for a second bite.

Rosa grins. "After the nine-day Simbang Gabi masses, we would stop at the vendors outside the church selling bibingka and puto bumbong. They would warm our hands as we walked home, and then my mother would open the curtains to let in the dawn light, and we would eat our cakes."

I take another bite. "That sounds like a wonderful memory."

Rosa nods. Her eyes glisten.

Jeremy gently leads me away from my small taste of Christmas in the Philippines and guides me to the next booth. The smell of the red chili sauce in the tamales mixed with the floral and fruity notes of the *ponche navideño* is familiar. The year we celebrated the traditions in Mexico, Mom's coworker who was originally from Oaxaca invited us into her home and family and taught us how to make tortillas by hand.

Out of all our Christmases and all the different traditions we learned and experienced, I always suspected that year was Mom's favorite. I think because Christmas, at its heart, is a celebration with family, and that year we felt as if we'd been adopted into one bigger than just the two of us.

I breathe in deep. Hold the smells wafting up from the two steaming pots, one housing tamales and the other ponche. Embrace the memories, both the sweet of Christmases past as well as the bitter of Christmases in the future. When Mom will be gone, the only family I've ever had.

A tear spills out of the corner of my eye, but it's caught on my upturned lips. Crying and smiling. How appropriate.

Jeremy squeezes my shoulder. "Are you okay?"

I blink back a second tear trying to form, which leaves just the smile on my face as I tilt my head up to him. "Just thinking how much my mom would love this." There's more inside me. Deep, unexplored places. But that's enough to touch the surface.

His shoulders round. "I wanted to surprise you both. Alejandro was going to bring her here before taking her back to Heritage Hills. All of this was for both of you, really. But—"

His hand lifts toward his scalp, and I map its trajectory. This time he's not stopping his fingers before they run over the top of his head. The motion fills me. Breaks me. A sign that Jeremy Fletcher has lost his firm grasp of control.

For me.

I snatch his hand out of the air before his fingertips graze the signature swirl of his gelled hair. Before I know what I'm doing, I'm tugging him toward the elevator, punching the button to open the doors, and dragging him inside. Once the doors shut, I hit the emergency stop switch.

Jeremy looks down at me, his face a mixture of confusion and amusement. He doesn't say anything. Just waits for me to explain why I've manhandled him into a suspended box and locked him inside.

Try attention training with Jeremy. Focus on his reactions to you instead of what's going on in your own head. Keri's advice echoes around my chest cavity. Now that I'm here, standing in front of Jeremy in the privacy of the elevator, I don't know what to say. Or, rather, how to say it. Whatever boldness took me over to get to this place has fled.

I bite my bottom lip. I have a choice. I can flip the emergency stop switch and open the doors, pretend this never happened while slowly dying of embarrassment. Or I can push myself out of my comfort zone. Open myself up to Jeremy and see how he reacts instead of telling myself how I think he will.

I push my chin up. Force myself to look into Jeremy's amber-flecked eyes instead of finding a spot over his shoulder to focus on. He looks down at me. The pinch between his brows releases. A small smile softens his lips.

"I . . . I've never been good at putting thoughts or feelings into words," I admit.

He takes a step closer, and I have to tilt my head back to maintain eye contact.

"The truth is—" I swallow. If I tell him the truth, that I've been falling in love with him from afar for years, there's no going back. No laughing the confession off as a joke. Every time I see him, I'll know that he knows. I'm not sure I can take the rejection. How am I supposed to act around him after that? How can I ignore the pity in his eyes or the knowing glances of everyone else in the office? How—

His warm hand cups my cheek. Like a fish on a line, he reels me back in with his steady gaze. "What's the truth, Mackenzie?"

Focus on his reaction to you.

The tips of his fingers curl into my skin with insistent pressure. His chest rises and falls in quick succession. His eyes have a singular focus—me. Could this really mean . . . could he actually . . . ?

The truth is right in front of you. My heart beats a staccato on each word. A light turns on, chasing away the shadows that hover in the form of negative self-talk.

I grip his shirt at his waist to anchor myself. "I . . ." My voice wobbles. "I love you."

I still. Wait on bated breath for his reaction. *No turning back.*

His smile spreads like royal icing on a sugar cookie. Joy pulses in his gaze. "What you said earlier about not knowing how to put your feelings into words? You were wrong." His thumb caresses my cheekbone. "That was the best thing I've ever heard in my life."

His gaze drops to my mouth. The delight slides from his brown eyes, replaced with something more intense. His lashes lift as he pins me with a look so acute with longing, I feel it in the core of my being.

"May I kiss you? Please."

I barely nod before his mouth descends. It's a good thing I'm holding on to his shirt, or my knees would have given out on me, washed away on the wave of feelings surging through me. Love, desire, joy, passion, contentedness, belonging.

His arm wraps around my back to support me further. My lips have taken on the vocation of cartographer. I map each ridge and crest of his lips. Record the way he moves above me. The push and pull. Give and take. I'm sure I could explore his kiss for the rest of my life and still learn new things each time. A challenge I willingly and ardently accept.

I can feel his mouth pulling away from mine, but I'm not finished cataloguing the security of his arms around me or the way his teeth deliciously but gently scrape across my bottom lip. I chase him as he pulls back. He chuckles and rewards me with another kiss.

Click. Swish.

The elevator doors slide open.

Applause erupts from the office. Someone whistles. Jeremy grins against my mouth. Slowly, he lifts his head and shifts his body to shield me from our spectators.

I'm a deer caught in headlights. Waiting. Frozen.

Jeremy kisses the corner of my mouth. My jaw. The lobe of my ear.

Like butter on warm toast, I melt.

"Your choice," he says for my ears only. "Face them now or later? I'm with you either way."

With me.

Jeremy is with me. While I know he's not a magic pill that will cure me of every and all social anxiety from here until eternity, having him beside me does buoy me with strength.

213

"There you two are." Sofiya places one foot in the elevator and keeps the other in the office, blocking the doors from closing. "It's time to make my announcement."

She ushers us into the center of the room, effectively stealing the choice Jeremy had given me moments before. He squeezes my hand as he smiles down at me. He's telling me everything will be all right.

He's right. It will be all right. Because Sofiya can't take away the choice we've both already made today.

Each other.

28

Sofiya is ignoring me. I'm staring at the back of her head like my eyes have the power of touch, and she has yet to turn around. She continues to have a conversation with Derek and Annabelle, a fried chicken drumstick in her hand. I've already told her I won't take the promotion if she offers it to me, but she didn't seem to take me seriously. I need to tell her again. Preferably before she gets everyone's attention and makes her announcement. I don't want to make a scene.

Jeremy's hand moves from my back to my waist. His fingers curl around my hip to draw me closer to his side. He hasn't stopped touching me since we were caught making out in the elevator. Little touches. Connections, really. Pinkies hooked together. A light graze of our arms. Every caress and surreptitious smile is a reality check. This isn't one of my daydreams. I'm not going to blink and find I've imagined the whole thing.

"I'm not taking the promotion." He says it for my ears only, but he's lifting his hand in greeting to Lincoln and his wife, who have just arrived.

"You have to," I say around my forced smile as I wave as well.

215

"It's not happening." His face is placid and pleasant. No hint that we're having a disagreement.

I want to stamp my foot. "Yes, it is."

Keri strides up with a cup of ponche in her hand. The drink is bright red from the hibiscus flowers, a variety of fresh fruits floating in the cup. "Congratulations." She envelopes me in a hug. "Attention training?" she whispers in my ear. "I shouldn't say I told you so, but I did." She pulls back. Looks between me and Jeremy. Her brows pucker. "There's tension here, and not the kind I was expecting. What's up?"

"Nothing," Jeremy and I both mumble.

Keri's brows jump. A grin blooms on her lips. "Are you guys having your first fight as a couple?"

I don't look at Jeremy to see his reaction, but if it's similar to mine, he's grinding his teeth.

Keri laughs. "This is perfect."

All the tightness in me shatters in surprise. "Pardon?"

"Kenz. You're the epitome of a people-pleaser. You don't argue with anyone. Ever. The fact that you're disagreeing with Jeremy about whatever it is . . . hon, that's huge."

Jeremy's fingers tighten. I look up at him. He's staring down at me like he understands exactly what Keri is saying and is happy I'm not agreeing with him.

Sofiya claps to get everyone's attention. "Before we move on to the Secret Santa gifts, I want to thank each of you for making this Christmas party the best Limitless Designs has ever seen. Coming to the United States opened up a new world of traditions and customs for me, and I feel closer to each of you for having shared in a small part of your own family celebrations." She lifts her hand to indicate Jeremy. "A special thanks to Jeremy Fletcher for organizing the event. I don't know about you, but I'm happy to see my little holiday matchmaking scheme was a success." Her smile could light the Griswold family decorations for years to come.

A buzz travels the room like the wave at a sporting event. "What's she talking about?" I ask Jeremy. But he seems just as confused as I am.

Sofiya turns so she's facing us. "I never got to have children of my own, a family of my own, so this company became like a husband to me and all my employees like my children. Or brothers, if they're old fogies like me." She shoots Frank a wink. He chuckles in response.

"I knew some of my children would find their way on their own." She smiles at Derek and Annabelle. Derek's arm is around Annabelle's shoulders, hers around his waist.

Sofiya turns back to Jeremy and me. "But others would need a nudge. Either to give love a chance to grow." She looks at Jeremy. "Or to find the courage to let the heart lead." Her gaze is warm as it falls on me. "So I devised a plan that would force you both to overcome the obstacles that stood in your way." Her smile turns satisfied. "I must say, the outcome is even better than I could've imagined."

Jeremy presses a kiss to the top of my head. I lean against his arm and rest my temple on his shoulder. I can't even be mad at Sofiya for overstepping and meddling in my life. If she hadn't, I'd probably still be stealing glances at Jeremy from across the room, too nervous to say three words to him.

"Now on to my announcement. I'm retiring."

"What?" The question darts from so many people it's hard to pinpoint who said it first.

She tries to quiet the ruckus by patting the air with her hands. "Don't worry. I won't leave you all work orphans." The joke does little to erase the worried looks on our faces.

"Is that what the competition was about? The ultimate promotion of taking over the firm?" Lincoln's voice can be heard over the low din of whispers.

Sofiya cocks her head. "Competition? What competition?"

Keri clears her throat. "You, uh, have a history of promoting the person with the most Christmas cheer. The Clark Griswold of the office, if you will."

Sofiya's already thin eyebrows nearly disappear in surprise. "I do?"

A number of heads nod.

She looks at me. "Is that why you brought in the tree? And organized building snowmen and gingerbread houses? The traveling Mary and Joseph?"

I nod, shake my head, and shrug all at the same time. It's too complicated to paint an accurate picture.

Jeremy's hand slides down my arm. He interlocks his fingers with mine. "No. Mackenzie did all those things because they were meaningful memories for each individual here. However, my desire to win was the motivation behind the pomander balls, the hot chocolate bar, and the Christmas cookies."

Sofiya regards us both. "I see."

Is this when she decides neither of us deserves the promotion? Which we are both being too stubborn to accept anyway. And what *is* the promotion exactly, now that she's stepping down? The new head of the company?

"I've decided no one is going to take over Limitless Designs," Sofiya announces.

"So you're not leaving after all?" Rosa asks.

"I didn't say that." Sofiya holds up a finger. "I said no *one* is taking over." She raises another finger. "Instead, I'll be passing the reins to two people."

My heart skips a beat. Jeremy tenses beside me.

Laughter rings from the lines creasing the corners of Sofiya's eyes. She's enjoying her theatrical display. Meanwhile, I think I've had at least three mini-heart attacks in the last ten minutes.

"You two are great individuals." She holds her hands out to us. "But I've known for a while now that you'd make an even better team. In both your personal and professional lives." She squeezes my hand. "Mackenzie will be the head of design. She will continue her excellent work behind the scenes with her creative eye and exquisite touch. Meanwhile, Jeremy will be the face and voice of the company to our customers. The liaison between our product and our clients. A beautiful *partnership.*" She stresses the word in an over-obvious hint. "Don't you agree?"

Keri starts clapping, followed by Lincoln and Jill. Soon everyone is giving us applause.

Have I mentioned how much I hate being the center of attention? My body temperature has spiked so high that if I step outside, I could melt a snowbank in seconds.

Jeremy says something to Sofiya that I can't hear over the noise. Sofiya glances at me in a motherly way. She lets go of my hand and holds her arms up to quiet the room. "Now that that's taken care of, let's open some presents." She leads the way to the tree and the wrapped gifts underneath.

Jeremy catches my eye and nods toward the stairwell.

How did he know I need to escape and catch my breath?

He opens the door for me. The air in the stairwell is colder than the office. I fill my lungs and exhale slowly. I can hear my coworkers on the other side of the door, but their noise is a low rumble. The relative quiet is like a suffocating blanket being lifted from my head.

"Better?" Jeremy asks.

I nod. "How'd you know?"

His smile chases away the chill. "You aren't the only observant one in this relationship."

My heart stills, then races away from me. I lick my lips. I hate that I'm still nervous about speaking what's in my heart and mind. Maybe a recipe of time, patience, practice, and love will result in me being more comfortable with myself and others. Until then, or at least right now, I'm not going to let the nervousness win.

"Is that what we're in?" I force myself to push past my mental wall and meet his eyes. "A relationship?"

The tip of his finger traces my hairline, my jaw. His gaze roams my face. "I would be extremely honored if you would call me yours."

Our foreheads rest against each other. Our noses nuzzle. "You are mine." Who would have thought such a phrase would pass my lips? I lift my lashes and peer into Jeremy's eyes. "And I am yours."

It turns out the stairwell is an even better place to steal kisses than the elevator.

Jeremy stood in front of Mackenzie and Keri's apartment door. A festive wreath with sparkly green and red letters spelling out *Ho-Ho-Ho* framed the peephole in the center. He glanced down at himself one last time to make sure all zippers were zipped and all buttons were buttoned.

He wouldn't have said he was nervous. No butterflies winged around his stomach. While this was the first time he'd found himself standing in front of Mackenzie's door to pick her up for a date, they were so far beyond the usual first-date starting point. In a way, they had entered their relationship at a midpoint, and he found himself working backward, at least in regard to certain milestones. Although, considering they were headed to Heritage Hills so he could officially meet her mother, who knew where on the dating timeline they were.

But who really cared? All that mattered to him was being with Mackenzie, and the only thing currently in his way of that objective was the door in front of him.

He raised his fist and knocked. Seconds later, the clicking of a lock sounded and the door pulled open.

Jeremy sucked in his breath. He'd always found Mackenzie

attractive, no matter how small she'd tried to make herself or how hard she'd tried to hide. But she wasn't chasing shadows now, ducking her head and darting away. She stood fully before him, her shoulders pushed farther back than he'd ever seen, looking at him. Smiling at him. Blushing at him.

He could look at her all day and never get bored. Memorize every fine line of her face. Study each of her expressions so he'd always know what she was thinking even when she had trouble vocalizing those thoughts.

"You look beautiful," he finally said. She had on a winter knit hat, her hair spilling out in silky strands to frame first her face and then the curves of her body as the ends stopped at the hourglass center of her waist.

Her blush deepened, and when she didn't avert her gaze, he couldn't help but kiss her upturned nose and then her lips.

Jill had been right. Since all good gifts came from God, there was no denying that He had brought Mackenzie into Jeremy's life—the best gift of all. Thankfully, he'd finally released his death grip on his own plans to allow room for God's more abundant blessings.

"Give Caroline my love!" Keri called from a room on the other side of the apartment.

Mackenzie broke their kiss. "I will!" To Jeremy, she said, "Let me grab my coat and a few other things, and I'll be all set."

She shrugged into a grey wool peacoat, then grabbed a couple of wrapped packages and a rectangular plastic kitchen container.

"Need help?"

"I think I've got it."

Jeremy took the container and presents out of her hands anyway.

She rewarded him with a grateful smile and buttoned her coat. "Thank you."

When they reached the bottom floor and exited the building, he put a hand to her elbow to steady her in case of any ice. She'd been wobbly enough when she'd had on skates; if she stepped on ice with regular shoes, her feet were liable to fly out from under her.

"What are you grinning about?" she asked.

Was he? "Just remembering you on the ice rink."

She groaned. "Not my most graceful moment."

"Which worked in my favor." His grin turned into a full smile.

"How so?"

"Because then I had an excuse to hold your hands." He winked.

Her mittened fingers covered her cheeks. "I wonder if I'll ever stop blushing around you."

"I hope not," he nearly growled.

"Really?"

They reached his SUV. He had to let go of her elbow to open the door for her. "Your blush has become my favorite color." He chuckled as she scooted past him to get into the passenger's seat. He wouldn't tease or flirt with her if it truly made her uncomfortable, but the opposite seemed to be true. She'd shake her head, give that shy smile of hers, and let her body relax to take a full breath.

He hurried around the vehicle, careful of where he placed his feet so he wouldn't eat asphalt. When he slid into the driver's seat, he handed her packages back to her.

Twenty minutes later, they pulled into the Heritage Hills parking lot and were greeted as soon as they crossed the threshold of the entrance.

"Mackenzie, I'm so glad to see you. Your mother is in the common room. A group has come to sing Christmas carols with the residents, and she's in there, adding her voice to theirs."

"Thank you, Gabriella." Mackenzie handed the nurse the kitchen container. "I made the staff some cookies. Merry Christmas."

Gabriella lifted the lid, revealing an assortment of holiday treats nestled together. She picked out a red-and-white-striped cookie in the shape of a candy cane and took a bite. "Mmm. This is so good. Thank you." She turned and stopped another nurse passing by, telling her she had to try one.

"Let's drop the presents off in my mom's room, then find her with the carolers," Mackenzie suggested.

Jeremy followed her down a labyrinth of hallways. He was glad Mackenzie knew where she was going, because he'd have a hard time finding his way back if left to his own devices. She slowed at a door he assumed belonged to her mom and was about to turn the handle when a woman called out her name.

Mackenzie turned, and Jeremy followed.

Caroline Graham smiled as she gripped Alejandro's arm. She patted his elbow as she beamed at Mackenzie. "This is my daughter that I was telling you about. Wasn't I right? Isn't she pretty?"

Alejandro mouthed *sorry* to Jeremy. "Very pretty, Mrs. Graham. And my friend Jeremy here quite agrees."

Her clear eyes moved to take Jeremy's measure. She looked back at Alejandro. "Are you friends?"

"Yes, ma'am."

She stared at Mackenzie. "Are *you* friends?"

Mackenzie balanced her presents in one arm and took Jeremy's hand. "More than friends."

A telltale sheen caused Caroline's hazel eyes to twinkle. "And I get to meet him on a day my mind has decided to show up for work. Praise Jesus." She pulled Mackenzie into a hug. "My Christmas wish came true."

"You wished that your daughter got a boyfriend for Christmas?" Alejandro smirked.

"No." Caroline Graham's laugh sounded like a missing note in a bell choir. "All I want for Christmas is my mem-or-y," she sang. "And I have it, for now at least." She turned to Jeremy and ushered him into her room. "Come and tell me all about yourself. And don't hold it against me if I forget everything you say. I have a good excuse, you know."

Jeremy followed in her wake, pausing to whisper to Mackenzie as he passed, "I like your mom." He dutifully sat where he was instructed, and Mackenzie shut the door and sat beside him on the loveseat.

"So." Caroline placed her elbows on her knees and leaned forward. "How did you two meet?"

Jeremy looked at Mackenzie. "Do you want to tell the story?"

"Where do I begin? Two years ago when you started working at Limitless Designs, or when Sofiya decided to move us around like pawns in her own production of holiday office matchmaker?"

"Who's Sofiya?" Caroline asked.

"Two years ago?" Jeremy sat up straighter. "I mean, I knew I'd probably wasted a lot of time by not being open to a relationship, but are you saying the possibility of happiness with you started two years ago?"

Mackenzie shrugged, but Jeremy thought that was more because she didn't want to make him feel bad rather than not knowing the answer.

"I'm an idiot." He sat back against the loveseat cushion.

"Not that you've told me *any* of the story," Caroline tsked, "but the important thing is you came to your senses and you're with the best girl in the world now."

Jeremy draped his arm across Mackenzie's shoulders. "She is that."

"Okay. Short version." Caroline snapped her fingers. "Before my brain decides to leave on a lunch break and not come back for the rest of the day."

Mackenzie popped off the loveseat. "How about you open your presents, Mom?" She strode to the table holding the gifts.

"Am I really not going to get to hear the story at all?" Caroline pouted.

Jeremy scooted forward as if he were imparting a secret. "The ending is the best part of any story, and you're seeing it with your own eyes."

She pursed her lips. "I'll ignore you calling this the ending when it's only the beginning on one condition."

"What's that?"

"Is this ending of yours a happily-ever-after kind?"

Jeremy's gaze tracked Mackenzie as she gathered the gifts. "Forever and always."

I hold a gift for Jeremy's family in my hands. It's rather silly, and doubts have been plaguing me all day. I almost begged Keri to drive me to the store earlier so I could find something better. But I didn't. Instead, every time a negative thought enters my mind—*This is stupid. They're going to think you're just as dumb if you actually give them this.*—I engage the little traffic cop in my brain. I imagine he holds up a stop sign to halt the thought from traveling the neural pathway all the way to its destination and instead direct the thought to turn down a detour. Then I force myself to say something positive—*You're sharing a fun tradition that brought you a lot of joy. They'll appreciate the sentiment behind the gift, if nothing else.* This time I imagine a little construction worker paving a new road in my brain.

Even before I have a chance to knock, the front door opens. Jeremy stands on the other side in a flannel shirt that immediately brings to mind lumberjacks, chopping wood, snuggling by a cozy fire, and maybe even getting snowed in, just the two of us.

"She's here, Albert," a voice announces somewhere in the house.

Okay, not just the two of us. But I can still daydream about

Jeremy even though we're officially together, can't I? I hope so, because I'm really not sure I'm capable of stopping.

Jeremy glances behind him, then steps outside and shuts the door. His quick movement has brought him flush against me. His arm snakes around my back to keep me in place. As if I'd go anywhere. Silly man. He brings his lips to mine and gives me a long, slow kiss that makes my head spin. I'm dizzy and blink against the stars in my eyes when he pulls back and grins down at me.

"I wanted to do that before we have an audience."

The door opens, and a boy I can only assume is Jeremy's nephew, Nathan, scowls at us. "What are you guys doing out here?"

Jeremy chuckles and grabs my hand. "Don't worry. We were just coming in."

The house is warm and festive. Evergreen boughs with little red bows wrap around the banister leading up to the second floor. A fire crackles beneath a chunky rustic mantel. Monogrammed stockings hang on hooks with nutcrackers standing sentry. A tall Christmas tree trimmed in glass ornaments and a bright star shining on top stands grand beside the fireplace. The smells coming from the kitchen make my mouth water. I feel as if I've been transported into a Norman Rockwell painting.

"Mackenzie, this is Nathan. Contrary to popular belief, I have taught him manners." Jeremy pulls a reluctant Nathan under his arm and jostles him in a male sort of bonding move.

I give Nathan a warm smile. "Nice to meet you."

He pushes the hair that's fallen into his face out of his eyes. "You too."

Natalie bounds down the stairs. She looks up from her phone and her face brightens. "Mackenzie, you're here. Do you think you can show me how to French braid again? I still can't get it."

"Sure."

A couple emerges from the other side of the wall the fireplace is on. He's balding on top, and she has an elf apron tied around an ample waist. They both have open and welcoming faces that help me lay aside at least some of my nervousness.

"I'm Tracie, and this is my husband, Albert." Jeremy's mom hooks her arm through his dad's. "Welcome to our home. I hope you're hungry."

"Thank you for having me, Mrs. Fletcher. You have a lovely home."

She waves her hand in the air like she's swatting away a pesky fly. "None of that *Mrs. Fletcher* nonsense. I'm Tracie, and that's Albert."

"Is the food ready yet, Grandma?" Nathan asks. "I'm starving."

"Can I help with anything?" I offer. Having a job to do and keeping my hands busy helps me not feel awkward. Especially when the alternative is sitting around a table as a part of the inner circle instead of just outside. Whether the expectation for me to join in conversation is there or not, I still feel the pressure. Maybe something I should bring up with my therapist next time I see her.

"Can you bring in that tray of rolls?" Tracie leads me into the kitchen and indicates a platter of rolls arranged to look like a Christmas tree. Parmesan is sprinkled on top as well as fresh green herbs. The smell of yeast and cheese fills my nostrils and makes my belly growl.

I carry the tray to the table and place it on the cream table runner with gold reindeer. The candles standing amid the woodland berry centerpiece flicker and add to the warm family ambience. There's roasted red potatoes, a shredded brussels sprout and pomegranate salad, and thick slices of perfectly cooked prime rib roast.

"Everything looks delicious," I say as I take a seat next to Jeremy.

"Thank you." Tracie looks pleased with herself. She turns to her husband. "Albert, will you bless the food for us, please?"

He not only prays for the food but says a blessing over each person at the table, including me. Jeremy reaches over and squeezes my knee.

"Amen," we all chorus. Dishes are passed. Plates are filled. Laughter and merriment flow like molasses at a gingerbread factory.

"Is it time to open presents now?" Nathan asks after the last bite of peppermint bark has been eaten and the last sip of eggnog has been drunk.

"I, um," I start. Then stop. Then start again. "I'd like to give you all my present first, if that's all right. It's something small and kind of silly. A game, really, that originated in Germany, but my mom and I played it every year." I look around at the faces watching me. "If that's okay?" I end weakly.

"A game sounds like fun." Tracie rubs her hands together.

Nathan groans.

"Now you've done it." The words sound negative, but Albert's shoulders shake in amusement, and he's smiling.

I look to Jeremy, hoping to get a read on if I said something wrong or not.

He's grinning. "My mom is super competitive."

"How do you play the game?" Natalie asks.

I look at everyone again to make sure no one is really upset before I continue. "How you play is literally in the name of the game—Hide the Pickle. Although instead of a real pickle, I brought a pickle ornament. I'll hide it in the Christmas tree, and whoever finds it gets a special present."

"That sounds like fun," Albert says.

Tracie gives him a mock glower. "You couldn't find something if it jumped up and yelled, 'I'm right here!'"

Natalie giggles.

"Oh, we'll see about that." Albert rises to the challenge.

I stand. "I'll go hide it, then call you when it's ready."

Jeremy stands too. "I'll go with you." He follows me to the living room. "I love that we're blending our families' holiday traditions," he says as I take the green metal pickle out of the box.

"You do?"

He stands behind me, his chest warm at my back. I lean into him as his arms rise to pull me against him. He rests his chin on top of my head. "I do."

I could stand here forever, but his family is waiting for us, so I take a step forward, and his arms fall away. "What do you think? Closer to the top or the bottom?"

"Bottom."

We find a spot hidden by thick branches and hook the ribbon over a knob covered by spiky needles. "We're ready," Jeremy calls.

Feet patter amid laughter and good-natured ribbing. Albert holds Tracie back, and she makes a show of trying to break free while Nathan and Natalie surge forward.

Jeremy takes my hand, drawing my focus away from the game to his entreating eyes. He takes small steps backward, pulling me forward.

"Where are we going?" I whisper. I'm not about to object. I'll follow him anywhere.

He lifts a finger to his lips. "You'll see."

"What about your family?" I only sort of care what they'll think of me if I disappear in the middle of the game. Although, the more Jeremy looks at me the way he is, awestruck and amazed, the less I care.

Until I don't care at all.

He leads me outside, and our breath puffs in white clouds in front of our faces. We didn't stop for coats, which makes me wonder if Jeremy planned this little adventure. I think not. I think my organized, strategic man has let spontaneity take over.

Our feet crunch on the frozen ground until we stop near the edge of the backyard where the lawn gives way to towering trees and the underbrush of northern woods.

The warmth that had hugged me inside the house has been

chased away by the bullying cold. I try to suppress the shiver that travels from my head to my toes, but I'm unsuccessful.

Jeremy laughs. Not at me, but himself. "Guess I didn't think this through. We can go back inside if you're cold."

My little brain police officer waves his stop sign at my agreement. Acquiescing is my reflex, but I don't want to go inside. I want to be here with Jeremy.

I take his hands and pull them until they are behind me, then I place them on my back. His body heat envelops me, his proximity instantly warming my blood. I peer up at him. "Or you can keep me warm."

His lips tilt as his head dips. "Even better."

I think he's going to kiss me, but he doesn't. He just stares at me as if he's memorizing the moment.

"Do you realize how much Christmas we've packed into the last couple of weeks?" His voice is whisper soft. A caress like a gentle wind upon the skin. "Snowmen, gingerbread houses, decorating, music, games, presents, food. But there's one Christmas tradition going back almost three hundred years that I've never participated in before, and I want to right that wrong now. With you."

I frown up at him in confusion. "What are you talking about?"

His eyes take on a glow. His lips twitch as if he knows a secret and he can't wait to share it with me. "Look up."

Hanging from a branch above our heads is a gathering of mistletoe.

Understanding immediately dawns, bringing with it a swell of happiness. We said we didn't need excuses to kiss each other anymore, but I'm not upset if he still finds them anyway.

"I've received the best gift of all this Christmas." Emotion thickens his words. Pulls my line of sight from the mistletoe above us to settle in his love-filled gaze. "You."

He rests his forehead against mine. His eyes only an inch away. Before, this much contact would've made me itch to run away. Now all I want to do is run into Jeremy's arms.

"I love you, Mackenzie."

I breathe in his declaration, his love. Breathe out my own. "You have my heart, Jeremy."

Some will say it wasn't fair or right, Sofiya playing matchmaker and turning Jeremy and me into holiday workplace rivals in hopes of a romantic outcome. But as we kiss under the mistletoe, I think to myself, all's fair in love and Christmas.

ACKNOWLEDGMENTS

This book will always be special to me because it came in a time when I wasn't sure if I had any creativity left. 2020 was a hard year for everyone, and I wasn't special in any way to be left untouched. The navy moved us from one state to another, the pandemic hit, my oldest son started having health problems that doctors couldn't figure out, I decided to homeschool for the first time, and then my husband left for his first military deployment. Needless to say, I didn't have any energy left in me, creative or otherwise. I set aside writing, not sure if I would ever pick it up again. But then, gradually, the dizzying spinning plate I felt myself on began to slow. My husband came home, school ended for the summer, and doctors realized my son's physical ailments stemmed from his mental health, and he began to get the help he needed. Slowly I began to feel the push of story inside me again. But I needed something fun and hopeful. What could be more fun or hopeful than a Christmas story? Especially one where two people are trying to out-Christmas the other? I sat down with a fresh notebook and a pencil and let the story flow through me.

I have to thank my critique partners, Toni Shiloh and Janet Ferguson. They were with me at each chapter, giving me much-needed encouragement when doubt came calling, and helping me hone the story along the way.

Although I have never been formally diagnosed with social anxiety disorder (a reader did diagnose me in a review once), I have a long history of extreme discomfort in any type of social setting, an inability to make even the smallest of small talk, and multiple near-panic attacks when forced to be up front for any sort of reason, among other things. This awkwardness and stammering, the disconnect from brain to mouth, displayed itself in all its painful glory when I pitched this story to Rachel McMillian, a literary agent. When she asked me what the book was about, my response was something like, "It's umm . . . well, it's about . . . uh . . ." It really is a miracle that she offered me representation after that. Rachel, I thank you for looking past my inability to coherently put words into a verbal sentence.

I knew a Christmas book would be a hard sell among traditional publishing houses, so a special thank-you to Jessica Sharpe and everyone at Bethany House for taking a chance on me as an author who has previously been independently published and on this little holiday romantic comedy. I hope neither of us let you down.

Thank you to my mom, who has believed in me and my stories since I first started writing them in kindergarten. My husband, who makes fun of the voices in my head but works hard to provide for our family so I have the time and opportunity to write. To my children, who are proud of me. I love you even if your bragging to your teachers that I'm an author inevitably puts me in a spotlight I find uncomfortable. Thank you for wanting me to shine despite myself.

And finally, my biggest thanks of all goes to the supreme Author of all our stories. I am but a humble steward and will remain thus until you tell me it's time to lay down my pen for good.

A Carol Award finalist and Selah Award winner, **Sarah Monzon** is a stay-at-home mom who makes up imaginary friends to have adult conversations with (otherwise known as writing novels). As a navy chaplain's wife, she resides wherever the military happens to station her family and enjoys exploring the beauty of the world around her. You can follow her at sarahmonzonwrites.com.

If you enjoyed
All's Fair in Love and Christmas,
read on for an excerpt from

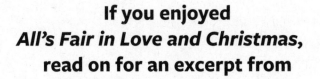

You Make It Feel like Christmas

by Toni Shiloh

AVAILABLE NOW
WHEREVER BOOKS ARE SOLD

1

THANKSGIVING DAY
WASHINGTON, DC

S tarr Lewis hated to return home a failure, but at least she had the cover of the holiday season to hide her embarrassment.

The wind whipped through her as she stepped off the train. She shuddered and drew her coat closed at the neck, then followed her fellow passengers up the escalator to the main building. The man in front of her held the door open, and she trailed in behind him. Warmth caressed her face in a greeting, chasing the chill away.

She sighed and took a moment to admire the arched ceiling over Union Station. People hurried around her as she made her way toward the front doors. Her brother Gabe was picking her up, which meant she'd have thirty minutes to kill until he showed up. Gabe was always late. *Always.*

Starr tightened her grip on the handle of her fuchsia carry-on and headed for Jamba Juice. A mix of passion fruit, mango, and strawberry would be just the thing to freeze out the hot shame of returning home jobless.

Who cared if she'd had a smoothie before leaving New York City? One could never have too many. Besides, she needed the liquid goodness to chase away reminders of being laid off and forced to live in her childhood bedroom for who knew how long. Out of the five Lewis children, Starr was the only one who no longer held an illustrious career.

Shake it off. You're not a failure. This is just a setback.

Of epic proportions. Not only did she have to move back home, but her demise lined up perfectly with her sister Angel's Christmas Eve wedding. To Starr's ex-boyfriend. *Ugh. God, please help me. I'm not sure how I'll make it through the wedding without wanting to gag.*

The hits just kept on coming. She'd better order a large smoothie.

Kelly Clarkson's rendition of "I'll Be Home for Christmas" crooned through the speakers. Starr shook her head at the unnecessary reminder and slowed as she got in line at Jamba Juice. Her cell buzzed in her coat pocket. She moved off to the side, pulling out the pink-encased iPhone and checking the caller ID. "Where are you?"

"Calm down. I'm on Union Station Drive with all the taxis and tourists. Should I park around back, or can you come out front?"

Her bottom lip poked out as dreams of smoothie bliss evaporated. "I'll be out front in a sec."

"Don't sound so enthused."

"I'm just a little hungry."

"You mean hangry? Well, grab some food, then. But keep in mind I'm taking up space, and security might be giving me the side-eye—"

"All right, I get it," she snapped. The moment Gabe had said he was at the front entrance, she'd started walking that way.

Starr exited through the double doors and searched the cars lined up in front of her. "Are you in your car?"

"Dad's. My car died last week."

She sighed in relief when she spotted the familiar black Mercedes. "I see you." She headed his way, dragging her carry-on behind her.

"I see you too." Gabe popped out of the driver's door and came around the passenger side as he pocketed his phone. "Sis!" He picked her up, twirling her around.

She chuckled at his exuberance. "Put me down." Her head spun, but she soon caught her bearings. As she peered into Gabe's familiar features a pang twinged in her chest. Gabe was probably her favorite sibling. Her older brother also had the smoothest skin she'd ever seen. Probably beat out women who held a daily regimen of wrinkle-free cream and exfoliation. He definitely fit into the pretty-boy category.

"Did you miss me?" He waggled his eyebrows, then grabbed her suitcase.

"Maybe." Her lips twitched.

"Yeah, you did." He winked at her and closed the trunk. "Don't stand there all day. Mom and Dad are holding Thanksgiving dinner just for you."

Thank goodness. She was starved. She slid onto the passenger seat and buckled her seat belt. "That explains why I didn't have to wait too long."

"Ha." He shrugged. "What can I say? Life is meant to be enjoyed, not hurried."

"No one says you have to rush for everything. Just be on time for what's important."

"Like picking up my little sister?" He tossed an amused expression her way before turning to look at the road.

"Exactly." She slid her frozen hands under her thighs. "It's so cold here. It wasn't even this cold in New York."

"Oh, look at me," Gabe said in a high-pitched voice. "I just came from New York, and like"—he flipped his imaginary long hair—"I'm such a cosmopolitan now. DC is beneath me and all that I know."

She smacked his arm. "I'm just making a weather observation."

"For now."

Same ol' Gabe. She rolled her eyes. "How's everyone?"

"The same. Noel is going to work himself into an early grave. Eve is following in his footsteps, and Angel is Angel." He shrugged as he navigated through DC traffic.

Wreaths hung about the city streetlights as they had every Christmas since Starr could remember. She couldn't help the smile that tilted her lips. "It's good everything's the same."

"Is it?"

"Sure." Well, maybe the physical things. She didn't want to walk in the house and have everyone treat her like the baby just because she was the youngest Lewis sibling. She wanted to be taken seriously, but losing her job wouldn't add points in that direction.

"I'm surprised your boss gave you such a long break. Mom said you don't have to go back until the day after New Year's. Is that right?"

"Yep. Nice, huh?" Though it wasn't a vacation but her being handed a severance package and two letters of recommendation.

But that tidbit was her secret.

Starr had packed her household goods into a storage unit before leaving the city and returning to DC. If she was smart with her money, she could pay for the unit for four months. Obviously, she'd have to come clean to her parents well before then. If she was still here in the springtime, there was no way her folks would believe she'd been given that long of a vacation. Then again, maybe telling them she was working remotely would help her save face.

That's lying.

She tensed. Hopefully by the end of the month, she'd find another job, and they'd be none the wiser.

"Suspiciously nice."

Starr looked at Gabe, hoping she was projecting a calm demeanor that belied the fast beating of her heart. "The company values their employees."

Only she hadn't been one of them. Layoffs had to happen, and someone had to go. Why not the hardworking PR associate who saved more butts than the others? She'd only worked for the company for two years, which meant she was the easiest to say good-bye to.

Story of her life.

Her ex, Ashton, had had no trouble saying good-bye after taking one long look at Angel.

"I see." Gabe met her gaze, raising an eyebrow in skepticism. "You know you can talk to your big brother, right? Tell me your worries. Your *secrets.*"

"I don't have any." She faced straight ahead, looking out the windshield, then gasped and leaned forward. "Is it snowing?"

"Just a few flakes. They didn't even salt the roads, so it's nothing."

"Or we'll get a bigger snowfall than expected and be trapped at home." She did *not* want to be trapped at home with all her siblings to poke their noses in her business.

"Works for me. I don't want to go to work tomorrow anyway."

Starr snorted. "Working for your parents is *so* difficult."

"Don't be jealous. You know Dad would give you a job if you wanted."

"I do *not* want to work in finance." She hated math. Had *always* hated math and had the grades to reflect that. Too bad everyone else in the family was a math genius.

Even Angel.

Lord, I pray that I hold up seeing Angel again. After all, she didn't intentionally steal my boyfriend. She's just . . . Angel.

A selfish, manipulative—

No, no. She really didn't think Angel was aware of how Starr truly felt. After all, Starr hadn't called her names or threatened bodily harm. After introducing her boyfriend to her sister, Starr had later listened incredulously as Angel described her meeting with Ashton as fate in some star-crossed-lover-type drama. Apparently, Ashton felt the same way. He dumped Starr so he could ask Angel out and live happily ever after.

Starr sighed.

"What's going on in that head of yours?"

"I was just wondering what the holidays will be like." She offered a stiff smile. "You know how Mom is."

Gabe grimaced. "Unfortunately. My prediction is full-on Christmas drama with an extra helping of wedding chaos thrown in."

Just what she feared. "Great."

"Hey, you wanted to come back. You didn't seem to mind missing the last couple of Christmases." Gabe glanced at her. "Why break the streak now?"

"Angel's getting married." As much as she had hurt Starr, Angel was still her sister.

"True, but you could've come down the day before and left after Christmas Day. No need to torture yourself the whole holiday season."

Except now Starr had nowhere else to go. Her severance package wouldn't have lasted long in New York. Staying with her parents would give her time to plan her next steps. Only, she couldn't let anyone know that.

She pushed aside her feelings and pasted on a smile. "I missed you guys."

Gabe snorted. "You mean your friends."

"What?" She gasped. "I love all of you guys."

"You never hung around us growing up."

"Well, it's not my fault Noel and Eve were so much older. They've always had their own friends." Sometimes being born last was the pits. Starr had been lonely until she took matters into her own hands.

"True. But you didn't hang with me and Angel either."

"That's because you had your twin superpowers activated and didn't let anyone else in the club."

Gabe took advantage of the red light to give Starr a long look, confusion written all over his face. "Is that really how you felt?"

"It's the truth."

"Starr . . ." He sighed and hit the gas. The car lurched forward. "We never meant to exclude you."

"I get it. I'm the fifth and last kid. Everyone had already paired off by the time I could talk and play. I had to make my own friends in order to have some, not because I didn't love my family."

"I'm sorry, Starr."

She shrugged and looked out the passenger window. The Lewis family liked to portray themselves as close-knit, but she'd always been on the outside looking in. She didn't expect the holidays to change that. And Angel's wedding definitely wouldn't.

Maybe she'd be able to reconnect with some of her friends who still lived in the area. Anything to occupy her days and keep the melancholy at bay.

"I'll make it up to you, 'kay?"

"How?" She peeked at Gabe.

"You can hang out with me and my friends."

"Really, Gabe? I'm a little too old for the *kid sister tagging along with the older brother* bit."

"You'll like them."

We'll see. "I'm sure."

He grinned, his straight teeth a testament to the years he'd worn braces. "Then it's settled."

"First, let's get through dinner."

Gabe turned down their street, and Starr's pulse picked up speed. The neighbors always joined forces to decorate for the Christmas season. She knew this week had been spent decorating the exteriors of the multimillion-dollar homes. Every house glowed with white lights. Starr sank into her seat as their white-washed brick home came into view. Navy shutters surrounded the candlelit windows, and a silver wreath decorated the matching front door.

"The inside is decked out, isn't it?"

"From top to bottom. Mom decorated all yesterday."

Starr chuckled. Their mom was a little too enthusiastic about Christmas. It's why they all had Christmas names, even though Gabe and Angel were the only ones born in December. Every year, the day before Thanksgiving, her mom would pull out the decorations and play her Christmas music for "atmospheric purposes."

Gabe pulled into the garage, and Starr was out of the car before the garage door could close again.

"I'll grab your bag."

"Thanks, Gabe."

"Mom's probably in the kitchen."

Starr entered the house and headed straight to the kitchen. Her jaw dropped. Gone were the black cabinets and red backsplash. The room seemed bigger with white cabinetry and black fixtures. The sapphire-blue backsplash went with the silver and blue Christmas decorations her mother was fond of.

"Baby girl!" Her mom threw open her arms as she came around the island and swept Starr into a hug. "Happy Thanksgiving."

"Happy Thanksgiving, Mom."

"I'm so glad you're home. Now all my babies are home." She grinned at Starr and folded Gabe into a group hug.

After a few seconds, she stepped back.

"Gabe said dinner was on hold. I didn't mean to make you guys wait," Starr said.

"Gabe." Her mother's black brows dipped in consternation. "Dinner won't be ready for another thirty minutes." She shook her head. "He's just making trouble."

"Me?" He pointed to his chest in mock horror. "I'm the angel, unlike your middle-born daughter."

"Ha. Go take your sister's suitcase to her room."

"Yes, ma'am." Gabe strolled out of the kitchen with a parting wink to Starr.

"You changed it." Starr gestured around the kitchen. "It looks good, by the way."

"Thank you. Angel brought my ideas to life."

Of course Angel redesigned it.

"But don't worry," her mom continued, "your room is the same as you left it."

Starr paused, her hand in midair with the meatball she'd swiped from the appetizer tray. "You mean, *exactly* the same?"

"Of course. The cleaning staff go in to dust once a month and don't touch anything else."

"But I haven't lived here since college." She'd graduated five years ago and moved to New York shortly after. This was really the first time she'd been back home apart from a visit here and there while staying at hotels—because she could afford to.

"You'll always have a room here, baby. You know that." Her mom dipped her head and shook it at the same time.

Now would be a good time to inform Mom about her unemployed state, but that news could wait. Maybe after the wedding, when everyone returned to their regular schedules. "Is everyone coming to dinner?"

"Of course. Noel will be here straight from work. He said he invited a friend."

"A *girlfriend*?"

Her mother rolled her eyes. "I wish. He's in his thirties, for goodness' sake. How much longer is he going to make me wait for grandchildren?"

"He's married to his work."

"Don't I know it. But ledgers don't produce living, breathing babies." Her mother turned a burner off as she checked on another pot. "Eve is already here. Her condo got flooded from an upstairs neighbor, so she's staying in her old room until the repairs are done."

"That's awful." *Guess I'm not the only one dealing with stuff.*

"It was just *terrible*. She lost everything."

Poor Eve. Starr straightened, then put on her calm façade. "And Angel?"

"Angel and Ashton will be joining us too."

Her stomach dropped. "He—they will?"

"Of course." Her mom gave her an odd look. "Wedding preparations are in full swing, and those two are never out of each other's sight."

Disgusting. What had she subjected herself to? Maybe she should've looked harder for a job in the city. Anything to avoid seeing her ex and sister fall all over each other.

Her mother stilled, her brow furrowing. "You aren't jealous . . . are you?"

"Of course not." Starr put her practiced *as if* expression on. She'd perfected the look in the Amtrak bathroom because she knew someone would ask at some point. "We're old history."

"Well, not that old. It was only two years ago you two were together."

Way to rub the salt in, Mom. "We weren't serious." Well, *he* hadn't been. She hadn't known how serious she'd been until he'd willingly parted ways to go after Angel.

"I didn't think so. You never introduced us to him."

"We lived in different states!" She stared at her mom, shock running through her.

"Oh, sweetie, that won't matter when you meet the right guy. You'll see."

If her mom was going to ignore how Angel and Ashton got together, Starr wouldn't be expecting any sympathy this holiday season.

Welcome home, Starr.

Sign Up for
Sarah's Newsletter

Keep up to date with Sarah's latest news on book releases and events by signing up for her email list at the link below.

FOLLOW SARAH ON SOCIAL MEDIA

Sarah Monzon, Author   @sarahmonzonwrites   @monzonwrites

SarahMonzonWrites.com